GLEN ROBINS

Off Course_Final w Off Guard preview

This novel is entirely a work of fiction. The names, characters and incidents portrayed in it are the work of the author's imagination. Any resemblance to actual persons, living or dead, events or localities is entirely coincidental.

Glen Robins asserts the moral right to be identified as the author of this work.

First edition

ISBN: 978-0-9863517-3-0

Cover art by Brady Anderson

This book was professionally typeset on Reedsy.
Find out more at reedsy.com

Contents

Prologue

The room was dark. A thick cloud of cigarette smoke hung over the makeshift conference table. Eerie, bluish light from seven laptop screens bounced off the haze. Small holes in the heavy brown curtains allowed shards of muted sunlight to pierce the gloom. No one spoke. No one dared to. Instead, each man stared intently at his computer screen, afraid to make eye contact with him. These men knew him as their fearsome leader, and he wanted to keep it that way. Fear was, after all, a powerful motivator. Fear and respect.

Pho Nam Penh stalked back and forth near the head of the table, trying to tamp down the rising anger. Maintaining control of one's emotions was absolutely paramount, especially in front of subordinates. The seven in the room squirmed under his scrutiny, unsure how to respond to his questions about their quarry. Some gazed intently at their screens, as if riveted by the data displayed there. The rest kept their eyes down to avoid drawing his ire.

He inhaled, with great satisfaction, the scent of fear. Power was an intoxicating drug and Penh relished the control he had over these men. He loved to watch them quiver in his presence. His next goal was to make the entire Western world tremble and quake. With the money he would soon recover from Collin Cook, Penh would increase the size of his team and expand his global reach. He and his Komodos would be feared by their enemies and hailed by their allies.

Penh gazed around the room, reading the body language of each man and surveying the conditions.

The table at which the men worked was really a door held up by two-by-fours. It was surrounded by his hand-picked cadre of computer hackers and technical whiz kids from around the region. They were sought because of their skills, yes, but also because of their allegiance to the cause: the fall of Western capitalism and the filthy, greedy, gluttonous pigs who gorged themselves at the expense of the rest of the world. Every man in the room wanted a front row seat to watch the chaos and clamor as the proud and mighty, the wealthy and shameless Americans and their smug British and European counterparts, sank into economic ruin.

This team seemed also to enjoy the prospect of spreading some of that ill-gotten Western wealth among themselves. Their promised reward had seemed imminent before Collin Cook escaped into the eye of Hurricane Abigail. Frustrated and harried, the team had worked tirelessly to track any sign of the man they sought and his hidden fortune.

An elaborate array of monitors, modems, servers, switches, wires, and power strips crowded nearly every inch of the painted wood surface. The only other items on the table were a handful of overflowing ashtrays, a smattering of white cube-shaped boxes of takeout food with chopsticks stuck in them, and dozens of water bottles, most of them empty.

Penh, clad in a tailored gray silk suit, patent leather Italian loafers, and a dark purple silk shirt, sucked in a lungful of smoke from the cigarette held between his thumb and forefinger. He wanted elegance and sophistication to ooze from his every movement, from his every fiber. Image was all about garnering respect and keeping an edge. He removed the sleek, narrow sunglasses that veiled his eyes, dropped the butt of the cigarette. As he ground the cigarette butt into the pocked concrete floor under his foot, he finally exhaled with an air of satisfaction. A thin vaporous trail of smoke wafted toward the low ceiling, being blown slowly and evenly from the tight crease of his mouth.

His men watched his every move, each of which was calculated to bolster his finely-honed image as a man of means and power.

For an Asian man his features were sharper, more distinct than most of his countrymen. Although only five foot seven inches in height and weighing one hundred forty pounds, Pho Nam Penh's presence was, he knew, enough to turn blood to ice. Study and practice, along with his natural gifts, had helped him craft the persona he projected. Maybe it was his eyes, dark and penetrating. Maybe it was the knowledge that he was a master martial artist or that he held two PhDs that made him so intimidating. In any case, the seven men huddled over their computers remained silent and fearful.

The stench was thick and ripe. A mixture of stale cigarette smoke; the aroma of the morning's grease-laden, assortment of fried fish, noodles, and spiced vegetables; and the body odor of seven sweaty and stressed men filled the cramped space. These men had been confined to the sixteen-foot-long, twelve-foot-wide room for days, trying to track down the missing Collin Cook and his money, looking for any hint or clue that would help them pinpoint his location. They already knew they couldn't drain his accounts. That had been tried repeatedly and had failed each time.

Collin Cook, the enigma, had grown to become an obsession with Penh. Never had any target been so mind-numbingly tricky. It was no longer just about the $30 million that Cook was hiding. It was more about regaining face.

Cook had been on the run with Penh's money for months, outmaneuvering Penh and this skilled team. Even the FBI, Interpol, and law enforcement agencies the world over, called into the hunt surreptitiously by Penh when he posted pictures of him sitting with Collin in a London pub and shaking his hand in the Bahamas, were baffled by Cook. Thanks to Penh's clever ruse, Collin was now a prime suspect in the string of cybercrimes perpetrated by this select team and others. The chase had spanned the globe from Europe to the Caribbean, to Central America, to South America, to Canada, the United States, and back to the Caribbean.

Meanwhile, the money had become invisible. There was only one way to get it back. They had to find Cook and his computer. Certainly, the information they needed was contained on its hard drive. If he was smart—and every indicator suggested he was, more so than Penh would have ever guessed at the onset—the data on that computer was ultra-secure. Killing Cook, therefore, was not an option—yet.

Despite their dedication, Penh's highly skilled cyber mercenaries cramped in this sweltering room were essentially being held captive until his, their master's, bidding was complete. Two old army cots in the corner were provided for short rest periods. Food was brought in twice a day. There was a squalid bathroom down the hall, which was really just a closet with a stained porcelain-lined hole in the floor and little more than a trickle of water to flush it. No one had showered since being brought here except for their illustrious leader, who appeared at random times of day with a bodyguard or two, hissed at them and threatened harm against their families if they failed, then would disappear again.

This time, however, he lingered on purpose, sensing a subtle shift in the atmosphere. It was his longest stay thus far and he hoped it would be productive. His most recent tirade had dissipated, but not his resolve. Without a word, he stopped in front of a grimy glass pane—maybe three feet square—that adorned the outermost wall, pulled back the dark curtain, and folded his arms across his chest. Silent and foreboding, Penh stared at the street vendors squatting and squabbling with customers over their plastic buckets full of produce, sea food, and various animal parts. The chaos of the open-air market below provided a stark contrast to the orderly, systematic way his brain sorted through the myriad options proposed, considered, then discarded. His moment of hot displeasure had given way to a smoldering caldron of wicked contingencies. There would be hell to pay for the misdeeds perpetrated against the cause and Pho Nam Penh vowed to deliver Collin Cook on Satan's doorstep personally to arrange the transaction.

But not yet. Cook still held valuable information.

At length, he spoke. His words projected an introspective calm born of supreme intelligence and imposed self-mastery. "Have you confirmed that it was Cook who withdrew that $500,000 cash from the Bank of George Town? Do we have photographic evidence yet?"

One of the men at the far end of the table stood, bowed in deference to him, the leader, and spoke clearly and assuredly. "We do, sir. It just arrived. I can show it to you if you wish."

"Yes, show me," demanded Penh.

The man turned his laptop to make it visible to Penh, who now hovered over his shoulder, and clicked the mouse. A twenty-three-second video stream rolled. An American dressed in a dark sport coat and a wide-brimmed mesh hat, lugging a knapsack on one shoulder and a computer bag on the other, walked across the marble floor of the Bank of George Town. His gait was brisk and business-like, but it had a familiarity to it. Pho Nam Penh ordered his face to be enhanced and magnified. A few clicks later, he was looking into the eyes of the man that had taken his $30 million and embarrassed him for nearly seven months now.

Penh clinched his jaw, the muscles tensing as he took in the image. "That's him. That's our target. Do we still have men on the island?"

"Yes, sir."

"How many?"

"Four of them, sir."

"Are they properly prepared?"

"They are ready, sir."

"Armed?"

"Yes, sir. They are positioned as instructed and are waiting for the target to appear."

"Good. Send them this video. The target is undoubtedly coming to their location. They are to report directly to me when they make contact. Cook must be kept alive. Is that understood?"

"Yes, sir."

Another man spoke up from across the table. "Sir, I am receiving a text message now from our men in Grand Cayman. It states they have a visual on a man wearing clothing that matches the target in the video. He just exited a taxi near the marina."

"Ah, he has returned, just as I suspected he would," said Penh.

"Wait," said the man, holding up one finger as he read something on his screen. "The target has disappeared again."

"Where did he go?"

"Our men have a limited view from their position, sir. It is very difficult for them to get a full view of the street."

Penh drew his mouth tight. "Nonetheless," he muttered. "Stay with the plan. We know he is heading for that boat."

"Yes, sir." There was a pause while the man at the computer typed a message. Everyone sat still and waited for the ding of an incoming text. "The team leader has acknowledged his understanding."

"Remind him to keep Cook alive until we are finished with him."

Another round of furious keyboard tapping before the man responded. "He acknowledges your request, sir."

"Good. I will check with him later."

Pho Nam Penh and his followers knew much about Collin's life, both before the tragedy and after, but they didn't know everything. They were continually perplexed by how an average guy like Collin Cook with average skills had hidden $30 Million in numbered accounts in some of the world's most secretive financial institutions within seconds of receiving the settlement money from Penh's front company, Tranquil Pacific Casualty Insurance, and without leaving a trace. That took skills that most equipment salespeople never needed, so never acquired. Beyond that, Cook had eluded Penh's men every time they got close, slipping into oblivion at just the right time. Even after Penh had lured law enforcement into the hunt, using their vast resources to track and chase his quarry, Cook remained at large and his money safely tucked away, inaccessible to Penh and his skilled team.

No one knew Penh's MIT classmate, Lukas Mueller, was involved. Lukas was supposed to be dead, killed by a roadside bomb in Afghanistan. Therefore, he was never given a second thought. No one knew Lukas was working as part of a deep-cover NSA cyber terrorism task force. Penh and his men only knew Cook had become an aggravating enigma. A cursed and resilient pest. A squirming, looming, irritating threat to his entire operation. No one knew why.

Penh's top priority was to bring Cook's run of good fortune to an end.

"What is the time stamp on this video?" Penh snapped his fingers as if a thought had just struck him.

"It's less than an hour old," the young man stated.

"He is moving very cautiously, as he should," said Penh.

"Yes, sir, but it seems our men have reestablished visual contact with the target, sir."

"What is he doing?"

"He stopped and is leaning on a rail, sir. It seems he is surveying the area, looking for something."

Penh inhaled sharply. "He is nervous. I can't blame him. Interpol has been combing the entire island searching for him. He must suspect them around every corner, especially near that boat."

"Some of our informants reported all but two undercover agents left the island this afternoon, returning to Europe and America," said another man on the other side of the table.

"The government has given up their search, have they? They must not want him as badly as I do," Penh paused, tapping his chin. "Where is Cook now?" he asked the man in front of him.

"Walking, sir, from his vantage point toward the boat."

After waiting for what seemed like an appropriate amount of time, Penh asked again.

"Still walking," answered the man. "It is a very long distance."

"Remember. They must be patient, and they mustn't kill him."

Chapter One

George Town, Grand Cayman Island
    June 13, 4:55 p.m. Caribbean Time

  Collin Cook had returned to the only place on Earth he felt at home anymore. Having spent nearly two weeks with the Captain and crew of the *Admiral Risty*—a for-hire sixty-foot fully appointed sailboat based in the Cayman Islands—and having escaped his pursuers on two different occasions with the help of the *Admiral*'s crew, it was a comfortable place for him to return. As he exited the taxi on the street overlooking the George Town Marina and surveyed the boat and its surroundings from a distance, scenes from recent experiences onboard the *Admiral* welled up. He stopped and leaned along the railing to watch the Captain and the crew, who had come to feel like a father and brothers to him, clean and polish the majestic sailboat and to check for any sign of a trap. It almost felt like returning home.

  Collin strode purposefully down the docks toward the *Admiral Risty*, keeping a keen eye for anything out of the ordinary. Everything he owned fit into a backpack and computer bag, both slung over his left shoulder. He leaned to the right as he walked to keep the bags from slipping off, reminiscing all the way. The reggae music blaring from the boat's speakers, which could be heard from a hundred yards away, and the banter between the crewmates as they worked, helped set Collin's worried mind at ease as he approached. He looked forward to reuniting with them, but he did not want them to recognize him yet.

  Collin turned from the main promenade to the narrower access walkway on the port side of the boat and tried to remain cool and calm as he asked to speak to the Captain. When Captain Sewell stepped forward and introduced himself, Collin handed him a thick envelope. His disguise was working so far. The Captain eyed the envelope warily before he opened it and found a handwritten note inside. The note asked if he could rejoin the crew and offered to return the dinghy. The Captain examined the note, then the man who handed it to him. He also examined the wad of cash that accompanied the note. It all clicked into place, causing his face to light up as he welcomed the man aboard the *Admiral Risty* as if he were the prodigal son, a smile stretching from ear to ear as he shook his hand and patted his shoulder, exclaiming, "We always have room for you, wanderer."

But the Captain's jovial smile quickly faded. Collin frowned and shook his head slightly, his index finger to his lips. Collin's demeanor and movements were unnatural and uncharacteristic. Collin could see from the expression on the Captain's face that he was curious about Collin's guarded approach. Collin wanted more than anything to exult in the warmth of their reunion, but he kept a serious countenance as he moved purposefully toward the cabin.

The Captain cocked his head at Collin and looked unsure of how to react. Without a word, Collin pointed down the steps toward the cabin, signaling for the Captain to follow him.

Collin, dressed as one of the elite businessmen of the islands, sporting a neatly trimmed dark brown goatee, insisted the Captain and crew shove off immediately. His voice matched his looks. Both were hardened, cool, and aloof. Even his accent carried an air of superiority and affluence. Collin's commands, grim countenance, and decisive tone were echoed by the Captain. The crew hesitated, as if unsure of the intentions of this stranger. The puzzled looks on their faces displayed the sudden atmospheric change. The Captain barked again, and the men began obeying his orders and preparing the *Admiral* for an immediate departure.

The crew scurried about the deck, attending to their assigned duties, sizing up this new customer. Theirs was not to question; only to follow their skipper's orders. His boat, his rules.

Captain Sewell followed Collin, who had become his best customer, into the cabin below deck. "Why so serious, man? You should be happy. I'm happy. You're not dead," he said with a forced chuckle.

"Yeah, I should be happy, right?" said Collin as he opened the secret compartment in the wall of the lower bunk and began to stuff his bags into it. "You don't mind if I stick this in here, do you?"

"Be my guest."

"I'm a bit leery these days," said Collin as he worked the computer bag into place. "I always feel like someone's watching me, ready to get me. Know what I mean? I guess these last few months have made me paranoid."

"I was worried about you, man," said the Captain, his voice growing serious. "That was a dangerous move, driving the dinghy into the storm like that. I thought that was it. You were gone forever."

When the Captain paused, Collin jumped in, trying to lighten the mood. The last thing he needed right now was high emotion. "You thought you wouldn't ever see the money I owe you." He forced a laugh, but the Captain only lifted an eyebrow and tilted his head.

"We have traveled many miles together. We have shared many stories, many meals, and much laughter. It is not about the money now. You know that. You are part of this family," said the Captain, opening his arms and gesturing toward the men above them on the deck. "You are one of us."

Collin stopped in his tracks, looked the Captain in the eye, and nodded his head as he spoke. "I know. That's why I came back. If I can't be home helping my sick mom, I want to be here, helping my friends. Plus, I never got the chance to thank you and the crew for risking your lives to help me get out of Florida. I'd be rotting in a jail somewhere if it weren't for you guys."

The Captain paused a moment, deep in thought. "Remember how you told me I could do dinner cruises any time, but I would be happier finding adventure?"

"Yeah, kind of." Collin was pulling items out of his bags as he spoke. They were too bulky to fit in the secret compartment. He dropped a worn T-shirt and his favorite cargo shorts on the bed next to his bag and removed the linen sport coat and the fancy button-up shirt. He finished changing while the Captain spoke.

"Well, you were right, man. Always sailing to the same places, serving the same meals, pandering to the rich American and European tourists gets to be very boring. Safe and profitable, but boring. With you, things are different. The men see it, too. Because you help them, cook for them, tell them stories, make them laugh. You listen to them. That is very different from other customers. You treat them with respect. That is why they are willing to do great things for you. You are their friend, their brother."

Collin smiled as he absorbed the sentiment of those words. "I know. I feel the same way. But this time, there will be no need to do great things for me. This time, we'll relax and enjoy the ride. A real sailing trip. You know, a leisure tour, like your other clients. Only much, much longer."

"Ah, yes," said the Captain with a smile. "That will be nice."

"Perfect. But I do want to get out of here as soon as possible. Is that all right?"

"Of course, man," said the Captain in his customary lilt. "We push off very soon. The question is, where are we going?"

"I don't have much of a preference. I'm fine if we just stay lost for a month or two. I need to stay below the radar for a while, you know, off the grid. I need time to let the dust settle and come up with a game plan. So, it doesn't matter much to me where we go. Let's see something new."

"Well, I suggest we head to the east side of the Caribbean. There are thousands of small islands there, full of pleasure cruisers. No one will notice you, my friend. You can remain safely anonymous."

"Sounds great. How much?"

The Captain laughed out loud, waved a dismissive hand at the air, then turned on his heels and climbed the steps up to the cockpit. He switched on his instrumentation as he sat in the padded Captain's chair behind the large steering wheel. "Rojas, Jaime. Are we ready?"

"Aye, Captain," the two said in unison as they hopped to the dock and moved toward the tie lines.

Captain Sewell fired up the boat's small engine so he could maneuver out of the harbor. It chugged and sputtered as it came to life, throwing out a blue cloud of fumes.

"Miguel, Tog. Man your stations," he bellowed in his hearty, baritone voice.

"Aye, sir," they called back one at a time. Each man scurried into position, one at the bow, one at the stern.

Jaime and Rojas untied the ropes from the dock cleats fore and aft and gently guided the *Admiral* out of its slip as Captain Sewell started up the little engine. Neither of them noticed the activity on the boat in the next slip.

After the Captain went topside, Collin pulled the contents out of the computer bag and backpack. He had placed a few items of clothing, the dozen false passports he owned, his laptop, and $500,000 worth of cash into the overstuffed bags before coming to the marina. They were too bulky to fit in the compartment, so he began to repack things into a large waterproof sea bag the Captain had loaned him on their last voyage. Moving quickly, he reloaded his computer, the money, and his passports into the long, cylindrical sea bag, then crammed it into the smuggler's hideaway, as the crew called it. With those items out of the way, he tossed the nearly empty computer bag in a closet.

One of the items Collin had removed from his backpack was a small waterproof pouch which contained his iPhone, a seaworthy GPS unit, and a few thousand dollars in several different currencies. He tugged at its sides and nodded to himself. Collin pulled a cheap cell phone he had purchased in Chicago from the pocket of his blazer and checked that it had a full charge. Its twin was in Emily's possession. The thought of her, his eye-popping high school sweetheart, made him smile. As he squeezed the little phone into the small sea pouch with his iPhone, a strange commotion erupted on the deck above. Loud footfalls on the fiberglass hull at the bow were rushing toward the stern. Commands were barked out by an unfamiliar voice in short, guttural bursts. Sensing danger, Collin grabbed the waterproof pouch and jumped down two steps to the galley. He swung open the door to the microwave oven, reached to the back, pushed on two soft buttons to release the latches, and shoved the pouch in the secret compartment behind the back wall of the microwave.

Captain Sewell had purchased this boat at auction and later learned it had been confiscated by the DEA during a drug bust. Unbeknownst to the Captain at the time of purchase, the original owner had designed features into this boat necessary for his trade. Jaime had shown Collin these secret compartments and he had used them to his advantage on previous occasions.

Both hands were inside the oven when an angry voice barked something he didn't understand. Collin whirled around, slamming the door shut with his elbow, to stare down the muzzle of a snub-nosed, semi-automatic Uzi pointed right at his face. The ill-tempered Asian man carrying it glared disapprovingly at him. Collin's hands shot straight up in the air. There was no other option but to surrender and trust that God would somehow deliver him again.

The gunman approached suspiciously, making as wide an arc as he could in the tight quarters below decks. He wore a flowered shirt and a straw hat, but the rippling biceps and the thick chest indicated he was something more than a tourist. Using the weapon as a pointer, the man motioned for Collin to move toward the stairs, using quick jabs in the air and short, unintelligible grunts. Checking his surroundings, he then maneuvered like a stalking panther in a slow semicircle opposite his prey. When Collin reached the steps, beyond arm's reach, he stopped, obeying the gunman's gesture. The man opened the microwave door and stole a glance inside. Collin's heart was in his throat, unsure if the back wall had snapped shut all the way. If his phones and laptop were discovered, it would be all over. Pho Nam Penh would win because every detail of Collin's finances was stored on those devices. Penh would crack his sophisticated firewall eventually and know the whereabouts of the nearly $30 million stashed in several banks around the world. The lion's share of the money, however, was held in a top-secret bank in Panama City, Panama, used primarily by the US clandestine community operating in the region. Lukas, with his knowledge of deep-cover operations, had helped Collin gain access to this hidden gem. Having the account numbers and pass codes from Collin's laptop, Penh would have much of what he needed to syphon away everything. Collin maintained safeguards, but Lukas had warned Collin at the beginning to guard that laptop and iPhone with his life. Information on those devices, including the instant messages between Collin and Lukas, could also expose Lukas's covert operational involvement in the war on terrorism, thus blowing his carefully guarded existence.

It took only seconds for Collin's already unbalanced existence to shift once again. In that instant, he realized he had placed the life of every man on board the *Admiral Risty* in jeopardy. The feeling of being in total free fall caused him to stagger backward, before catching himself on the bulkhead by the steps. This drew an angry look from the gunman. Collin knew if he didn't play his cards right, they would all die, Penh's terror group would receive a healthy round of funding and enough classified information to help them stay under the radar indefinitely. None of these outcomes boded well for Collin, his friends, or his country.

The stocky gunman peered again into the microwave, pulled out a coffee mug, and sniffed its contents. He dumped it into the sink and checked inside the oven again. As he did, Collin forced himself to remain composed and keep a poker face. Disgusted, the man grunted and slammed the door shut. Startled, Collin let out a nervous cough. The gunman's focus returned to Collin as he climbed the two steps up from the galley.

The attack was swift and sudden. The gunman pounced, closing the distance between them in milliseconds, and smashed the butt of the gun into the side of Collin's head before he could adequately shield himself. The force of the blow snapped his head sideways into the wall on his right, causing his world to go dark.

Three more gunmen stood on deck with Uzis aimed at the other four crew members and the Captain. The *Admiral Risty* had not yet cleared the harbor, but these men boldly displayed their hardware, apparently unafraid of anyone. The gunman closest to the Captain directed him to move out of the way. The green-shirted man fiddled with the instruments in the cockpit for a moment, then pointed to a spot on the Captain's GPS map. "We go there. Now," he demanded.

"Panama? You want to go to Panama?" asked the Captain.

"Yes. We go now."

"OK, you're the one with the gun. But you know it will take a week or more, don't you?"

The lean, long-haired one standing to the Captain's right cocked his head slightly. "You go faster. This boat very fast. You go faster. Three days." His face was like stone and his eyes were hidden behind dark sunglasses. Every movement was calculated and efficient. Every word carried meaning and consequences.

The Captain looked from one armed man to the other, studying their expressionless faces. He had no idea what they might do, but he had to set the right expectations from the start. He knew mean men and he knew they had to be handled with the right balance of firmness and cooperation. It was important to set the boundaries early in these situations, so the Captain held silent for a long moment, showing no fear and no desire to acquiesce to their demands. "That depends on the wind, you know?" he said, waving a hand in the air and looking at the sky around them. "No wind, no going faster."

It was a rather surreal scene. In a matter of seconds these four highly trained, heavily armed Asian mercenaries took control of the *Admiral Risty* and altered its course and the lives of everyone onboard.

Chapter Two

L a Jolla, California
June 14, 6:08 a.m. Pacific Time

Dr. Emily Burns stood in front of the large plate-glass window in her dining room, staring out over the fog covered Pacific Ocean, which stretched to the horizon like an endless, gray Berber carpet eighteen floors down and across the road. She dabbed her face with a towel after her morning run. As she drank from her sport bottle and pulled her sandy hair from its ponytail holder, she once again found her mind reeling over the tumultuous orbit of her dear friend Collin Cook.

Her life had not been the same since he reentered it. All too often, absentminded day-dreaming interrupted her problem-solving thought trains. Collin was indeed a problem that needed fixing, but there seemed to be no obvious or scientific solution, unlike the problems she worked on professionally.

A mix of hope and mourning occupied the space in her brain that used to try to unravel the mystery surrounding him and his disappearance. Since he had been reported missing and presumed dead by the Coast Guard over a week ago, Emily's heart had been troubled. The account on the FBI's website detailed the circumstances surrounding his disappearance at sea, but she hadn't yet fully accepted it as truth. Perhaps part of her doubt came from Collin's mother, Sarah Cook, who was certain Collin was as alive as she was. Sarah had almost convinced Emily to believe. But Emily, the scientist, was trapped in the void between theory and proof. Sarah had a theory and the government lacked evidence to prove otherwise. What was she to believe?

Her machinations and her breakfast were interrupted by a call from an unfamiliar number originating from San Francisco. Despite her initial hesitation, she answered it.

"Dr. Burns, this is Special Agent Reggie Crabtree from the FBI. I would like to ask you a few questions about your friend, Collin Cook. Is now a good time to talk?" said a deep, sincere voice.

Astonished, she balked at the intrusion. It was 6:08 a.m., hardly a good time for anyone to be calling, let alone a government agent who, for all she knew, played a part in Collin's death and may be calling to gloat about it. "At six o'clock in the morning? I'm sorry, Agent Crabtree, but isn't it a bit early to be calling to harass me about a friend I recently lost?"

"I realize it's early, Dr. Burns. And, yes, this is highly unusual. I'm not in the habit of questioning people this early. But, trust me, nothing about this Collin Cook case can be termed "usual." And if it weren't very urgent, I would wait until you had a little more time to cool down after your morning run."

"How did you—"

"I'm a detective, Dr. Burns. A very good one, at that."

Emily felt like she'd been knocked off balance. Her mind raced, trying to connect dots she couldn't see and certainly couldn't make sense of at this early hour. She wasn't used to interacting with people before work. This was her quiet time, her alone time, and he was infringing—no, imposing—upon it. Why? There had to be a compelling reason. She had to come back strong. And quickly.

Feeling suddenly lightheaded, she sat at her dining room table. A single sunflower stood in a tall beaker of water half filled with glass marbles. It, too, pointed toward the window, searching for light. "I don't know why you're calling me, Special Agent Crabtree. Collin Cook is dead. Says so right on your agency's website." Not quite the strong comeback she was looking for.

"That may be true, Dr. Burns, but we are still investigating the circumstances leading up to his disappearance," said Crabtree. "We need to know everything you know about him."

Emily vacillated, not sure what to tell him but feeling like she had to say something. "I know nothing. We broke up years ago."

"Don't play dumb with me, Dr. Burns. I know more about your relationship with him than you think I know."

Still trying to recover, she blurted out the first thing that came to mind. "There's nothing to know, Agent Crabtree, because there's been no relationship since high school." As soon as she said it, she regretted it, sensing she could get trapped in her lie.

"Now you're assuming I haven't done my homework. I see," said Agent Crabtree, who sounded like he was moving and breathing quickly. "Well, we know you saw him in Chicago two weeks ago and spent some time with him there. I can only suppose you know something more than we know based on that time together." Reggie paused. When Emily didn't respond, he continued. "We also know you were at the funeral for Amy Cook and the children and at Petaluma Hospital with Mr. Cook after he injured himself at the time of his wife's accident. Shall I go on?"

Her hand went to her forehead as her stomach did a back flip. She stared through the glass tabletop at her well-worn neon-pink running shoes as they tapped the floor anxiously. Breathing became a chore and forming coherent sentences a laborious effort. "It sounds like you know quite a bit. Why do you need me?"

"Isn't it obvious, Dr. Burns?" asked Reggie. "You've spent more time with him in the past year than any other human being we're aware of."

"I don't think I know anything that can help you, Agent Crabtree." Emily's voice was flat and unconvincing. She knew it and figured Crabtree was smart enough to pick up on it.

During the pause that followed, she heard something like the ding of a bell—no, an elevator door—in the background above the sound of his breathing.

"We need to know what he told you while you were together in Chicago. Certainly, the two of you talked in that little café. You remember the time you spent sipping coffee at the Bio Med Conference?"

This guy knew everything. These revelations stunned her, and she struggled to keep up with the conversation. It was as if she was treading water in a sea of questions on a test that she had failed to study for. "What he told me? You want to know what he told me? Do you mean the part about how he liked my presentation? Or that he thought I looked nice?" Now that felt a little more like the spunky girl she knew she had to be.

"Dr. Burns, we can handle this one of two ways: either you cooperate with us on your own, over the phone, or you keep this up and we'll continue this conversation at our LA field office with you in handcuffs, seated on a metal chair in front of a two-way mirror with a video camera and microphone. You choose."

There was a forceful knock on her front door. She heard it in stereo, although the left ear heard it through her phone just a fraction of a second after the right ear heard it from across the room. She approached the door cautiously. "You're outside my front door, aren't you, Agent Crabtree?"

"I am, Dr. Burns. Trust me. This is for your protection."

Emily peered through the peephole in her front door and saw a tall black man in a suit and tie holding up a badge with one hand and a cell phone to his ear with the other. He was flanked by a blond-haired man wearing a dark blazer and knit tie. "Would you like me to call out my badge number so you can verify my identity, Dr. Burns? I've got time to wait."

"No, no. I'm not that skeptical," she said, swinging the door open as if revealing a grand prize. "This is for my protection? At six o'clock in the morning?"

"We believe it prudent to proceed with an abundance of caution based on the folks we're dealing with."

"I see," said Emily. "But I assure you I don't have any significant details, probably not the ones you want." She spoke to his face, although the phone was still connected to her ear.

"Let's start with the most important items first," said Agent Crabtree, holding the phone in front of him as he ended the call. Emily followed suit. "Did he tell you where he was going or who he was planning to meet?"

Emily grimaced and gestured for him to enter. Not unexpectedly, his partner entered right behind him, a muscled blond standing roughly six foot four. Crabtree introduced him as Agent McCoy as he crossed the threshold of the room. She walked the door to its nearly closed position, but stuck her head out into the hallway before she shut it, as if anticipating more agents streaming in. She pulled her head inside, closed the door, and leaned her back against it.

"No."

"Did he indicate who was helping him? We know he's not working alone."

Emily paused while she studied the faces of the two agents. Crabtree, the more experienced of the two, had a few creases around his dark eyes and in the otherwise smooth skin near his mouth. The white at his temples and in his mostly black mustache indicated he was probably in his early fifties. McCoy, she guessed, was in his thirties and from Texas.

She answered hesitantly. "I, of course, had a million questions for him. But he said that the less I know the better. He said it was for my own safety. He also told me I should go to the FBI and tell them my story."

"Why would he say that? What about your story is so important?"

"He said that I could be in danger now since he and I met. He thinks the bad guys that are chasing him will follow me or use me to get to him."

"So why didn't you come to us? Why did I have to initiate this conversation?"

"I checked the FBI website shortly after I returned from Chicago and saw the reports that said he's dead. I didn't think you needed to know anything about a man you thought was dead. And if he's dead, why would I be of any significance to the FBI?"

Reggie paused for a moment. "As it turns out, we believe he has some connections to crimes that are ongoing. We believe someone helped him survive that storm and that he is out there potentially committing more crimes."

"Interesting . . ."

"We also believe you may be in grave danger."

* * *

La Jolla, California
  June 14, 6:22 a.m. Pacific Time

A white Sprinter van pulled up behind the dark blue Taurus, the one with the government-issued white license plate and blue lettering. The cargo van had no side windows other than for the driver and front passenger. Magnetic decals read: "Mission Bay Home Stereo: Wiring your home for the full HD experience." The driver was an Asian man wearing a black coat. A menacing tattoo climbed up his neck from below the coat's upturned collar toward his scowling face. A chic pair of sunglasses hid his eyes. His partner, a fellow Asian with manicured black hair that lay at a sharp angle across his forehead with spiked tufts on top of his head, sat in the passenger's seat. He was at least ten years the junior of the driver. His hands were gloved and his wrists adorned with spiky leather bands. He pointed an impressive camera with a long telescopic lens at the Taurus and rattled off a barrage of photos, careful not to snag the eyepiece on the long stud poking through his eyebrow. Next, he aimed at the condo complex's front door, then toward the penthouse eighteen floors up, clicking more photos as he did.

The driver dug a cell phone out of a pocket, tapped a previously dialed number, and waited for the connection to be made while the passenger surveyed his work on the camera's display screen. He zoomed and adjusted settings to ensure the pictures were clear and that the important details could be easily discerned. He then connected the camera to his phone in order to transmit the photos to the boss.

In his native tongue, the driver explained the situation to the boss on the other end of the connection. "Feds are here . . . Because it's the same car, government plates . . . They must have driven from San Francisco . . . Probably because the first nonstop from SFO doesn't land here until 7:45 . . . Must be in a big hurry . . . I don't know how, no one has followed us or traced us . . . No, nothing out of the ordinary."

The driver stepped out of the van and surveyed the area. Satisfied, he walked to the front of the Taurus and put his hand in front of the grill. "The engine's still hot. They haven't been here long . . . Will do, boss . . . Yes, I will. Right away."

As he climbed back in the van, the passenger grunted as an impious smile spread across his face. "They can see what we see. Now we just gotta get inside."

"That is not the plan. We watch and wait until the opportunity presents itself," the driver said with a sneer.

"I could get in there easily and get some really good footage," said the passenger with a raunchy cackle. He reached into a black duffle bag behind his seat and pulled out a device no larger than his thumb and a handful of zip ties. "We also have cameras on the drone."

"Not now. Not in daylight. Later, if we need it." The driver shot his passenger a sideways glance, threw the van's transmission into drive, then pulled away from the curb. The streets were coming alive with activity. A few cars were emerging from underground garages along the street and filing onto the wide avenue that separated the high-rise luxury condos from the vast fog-enshrouded Pacific. A handful of joggers trotted along a path at the edge of the bluff in the distance. No one paid any attention to the van or its occupants, so the driver and the passenger continued their work.

There was a lone signpost directly across from the subject's condo building. It wasn't ideal, but it would have to do for now.

The driver worked his way around the block and came back to the front of Emily's building from the north, so the ocean was on the right side of the van, thus giving the passenger the shortest distance possible to the sign post. The van would provide some cover. The passenger hopped out, checked his surroundings, then moved swiftly to the metal pole. He wrapped two zip ties around the pole and fastened the tiny camera to them. A few adjustments were necessary. He checked the image on his phone. The front entrance was visible, as was the Taurus. Step one, accomplished. The driver texted the boss to report their progress.

The driver grunted as he held his phone up to read the message that buzzed in. The passenger looked to him in anticipation, so the driver shared. "I told the boss about the FBI being here. I told him we put the camera in place. Listen to his response: 'We cannot allow the unexpected arrival of the FBI to hinder our efforts. We must find a way to succeed in our mission and stick to the schedule. There is no giving up. There is no settling for less.'"

The passenger clinched his jaw, cracked his knuckles, and nodded.

Chapter Three

estern Caribbean Sea, 75 miles south of Grand Cayman Island June 14, 10:25 a.m. Caribbean Time

W Waves of pain radiated through his skull, inward and outward from both sides. He tried but could not open his eyes. He slipped back into darkness, where he saw his beautiful wife, Amy, tied to a chair, arms behind her back. The chair slid toward him, then slid back across a smooth, polished floor. The room was dark, but her figure was illuminated no matter where she was. As she approached the second time, Collin struggled to reach out to her, but his arms wouldn't move. They were pinned to his sides. Then she began to slide away from him again.

After several repetitions of this frustrating scenario, Collin was awakened by a sudden pain on his cheek and the loud slapping sound that accompanied it. With his return to consciousness came the frightful realization that he was still alive, and Amy and his children were not. Her image and the sense of helplessness that accompanied such visions continued to shroud his fragile mind, even eleven months after the accident.

Collin had been awakened and slapped several times throughout the night. He had lost count and had lost track of time. It was as if he was trudging through a haze, searching for Amy and every time he found her, he got hit in the face and jarred back to reality. Only, it didn't seem real. Was it all a dream? He was confronted repeatedly by the same Asian man who spoke harsh words he could not comprehend.

Light filtered into his half-open eyes. The pain in his head kept rising and falling, rising and falling; intensifying, then dissipating. Someone was squeezing his face—hard. It really hurt. Then cold water hit him, and he sputtered and struggled for air. *I must be drowning. No, it's gone. I can breathe.*

A few blinks later he remembered everything—where he was, how he got there, and the sudden assault. Collin started putting together the pieces. The same Asian man with the flowery button up shirt, the one who had attacked him, stood over him and slapped him again and barked something he could not understand. Perhaps it was English; he couldn't be certain. He realized he was on the lower bunk. Behind its wall, his most valuable belongings were hidden in a smuggler's compartment. His hands were tied behind his back with something sharp and stiff. Must be plastic bands of some sort. His wrists burned and bled from his mid-sleep thrashing. The boat was rocking side to side and waves slapped against the hull in a familiar and comforting rhythm which lulled him back toward the hazy dream state.

When his body was jerked into a sitting position and a fist connected with his lips, the haze disappeared. Hot salty blood and a coppery taste filled his mouth and more guttural barking filled his ears. It was apparent now that another man had joined them below deck so that one could prop him up while the other one punched. Collin knew the man wanted something because he kept shouting and staring at him and hitting him. He was demanding something, but what? What did he want? And why wouldn't he stop punching and shouting?

The boat continued to sway and the pain in his head multiplied and spread to his gut. A chill ran the length of his body, turning his skin cold and clammy. Everything was spinning, so he closed his eyes. That didn't help. Everything went white and his stomach revolted. Without warning, he lurched. A warm stream of vomit shot out and landed on the flowery shirt as a fist approached.

Though he could not understand the man's words, Collin was sure it was profanity, unleashed in a torrent of anger. Collin coughed and gagged, bent over at the waist. He continued to heave, but his handler pulled on his hair and shoulder to straighten him up. Then several one-two combinations landed on his cheeks, eye sockets, mouth, and head before everything went dark again.

* * *

Huntington Beach, California
  June 14, 8:27 a.m. Pacific Time

Sarah Cook braced herself against the light marble countertop in her bathroom's vanity area to avoid collapsing. Her legs shook. Her whole body quivered. There was so little strength left in her she wondered how she could manage the stairs alone. The aggressive experimental treatments Emily and the Scripps team had given her had leached every ounce of energy out of her. This was a targeted cancer-fighting therapy that was supposed to reduce the symptoms typically associated with chemotherapy, which made Sarah wonder how anyone ever survived chemo.

She thought briefly about the alternative and decided life, even with the queasiness and pain, was still worth living. Her family made it so. Besides, Collin was still out there somewhere and still needed his mother. She couldn't give up until he was home.

The familiar sound of the door downstairs slamming shut echoed through the house. Henry had re-entered the house from the garage and its spring-loaded hinge created the unmistakable "phht" sound that signaled her husband's return. Before he reached the top of the stairs, Sarah tried to stand on her own so as not to worry him. She pushed back from the counter and mustered all of her strength to straighten up and hold her head high. The image staring back at her was a much older woman than just a few months ago. Her reflection startled her.

It had been nearly a year since she lost her beloved daughter-in-law, Amy, and the three precious grandchildren she and Collin had provided. But she had lost even more than that, including Collin—not permanently, she hoped—and several pounds. Without her son, his family, and her health, her life had become akin to a roller coaster ride.

She would be no use to anyone if she wallowed in self-pity, so she stopped and counted her blessings, which included Henry, her other two children, and her two grandchildren, her home, her rekindled friendship with Emily, and her admittance into the trial program which promised to extend her life. Yes, she convinced herself, it was a blessing to be alive still.

Ever since that catastrophic day last July, her youngest child's life seemed to be careening out of control. Losing his family had changed everything—and not just for him. She knew he needed his mother. His problems were foreign to her, but a mother's love is a powerful thing and she knew he needed it more now, after the tragedy, than ever before.

Sarah primped her hair one last time as Henry entered the room. "How do I look?" she said into the mirror.

"Gorgeous as ever and ready to conquer." Henry always knew what to say to make her feel like a million bucks.

Sarah smiled and opened her arms to embrace her knight. Henry held her tight and kissed her forehead. She knew he could feel her trembling but wouldn't say anything for fear of deflating her.

"Your chariot awaits you downstairs, my lady. Your purse, water bottle, and a sweater are all in the car, too. Shall we?" He held her around the waist and stayed by her side down the sweeping stairway, across the marble foyer, past the den in the hallway that connected the family room and kitchen to the garage. Henry escorted her through the garage to the car in the driveway. He didn't let go until she was comfortably seated in the soft leather passenger's seat of his Cadillac STS. As usual, Henry had everything prepared ahead of time, including having punched the address of the treatment center into the GPS. The screen said the estimated time of arrival was 9:41. Her appointment was at ten o'clock. Henry was always punctual and anticipated potential delays. She was blessed to have such a diligent, caring man to share her life. He managed the details so well and provided so much strength and comfort. It seemed he never wearied, never tired from the additional strain. No, Henry was as steady as ever, the rock of the family. A tear formed as she contemplated her situation and the extra burden it had placed on Henry.

Henry grinned at her as he slid into the driver's seat, then leaned across and reached for her seatbelt—a trick he'd started years earlier. It put his face directly in front of hers. She smiled as he kissed her softly.

20

As he backed out of the driveway, Henry asked, "Have you heard from Emily today? Will she be there?"

"She texted me and said that she would try to make it, but that there was something she had to do first."

"Didn't say what it was?"

"No and I didn't ask. Why?"

Henry paused as if he was contemplating some deep mystery. "Because I got a call from Agent Crabtree this morning. It came in around 5:45. Sounded like he was in the car. He asked me if we had had any contact with Emily since the storm."

"5:45? That's awfully early. What's the urgency, I wonder?" said Sarah, concern spreading across her face. "That was over a week ago, why is he asking about it now?"

"He didn't explain that part. Just said he needed to gather as much information as he could about Collin's last hours. He wondered if the two of them had talked before he headed out to sea, and if so, when," said Henry.

"What did you tell him?"

"I told him you and she had talked on the phone several times as she arranged for you to participate in this clinical trial. I told him that she seemed emotionally distant now, but still involved in a medical sense."

"That's an honest answer now, isn't it dear?" said Sarah. "She has not broached the subject of Collin with me since those first few days and I haven't pushed it. I figure she'll talk when she's ready. We all have our own ways of handling these things, don't we?"

"That's good to hear. I don't want him to find out otherwise, then think I was lying to him," said Henry.

"Do you think something's wrong, Henry?"

"I don't know what to think. It's just unusual, isn't it, for him to bring her into the conversation when we never mentioned anything about her to him or anyone at the FBI as far as I can remember."

Sarah thought for a moment. "No, I think you're right. I don't remember ever saying anything to him or McCoy about Emily."

They rode in silence for several long minutes until they reached the onramp to the 405 Freeway and began heading south. "How would they know about her?" asked Sarah.

Henry shrugged. "It's the government. They get paid to know all about us and when there's an investigation, especially with suspicions of terrorism, there's no end to their justifications for invading our privacy." Though spoken softly and evenly, this was an unusual editorial comment for Henry. He rarely spoke ill of anyone, let alone his own government. To Sarah, it signaled Henry's deepening concern for their son's perilous predicament and for her health, especially for him to bring up a sensitive subject when she was so frail.

"What are you saying, Henry?"

The creases in his forehead tightened. One of his large hands rubbed across his mouth and chin as he let out a long breath. "They know Collin is alive and they're still after him. That's the only reason he would call and fish for information like that. If they really believed he had drowned in the Caribbean during the storm, they wouldn't care about Emily and they would leave us alone to grieve."

"And they think Emily can help them somehow," Sarah interjected. "I wonder if she's had contact with Collin since the storm. I hope so. It would be so nice to hear some news from him."

"They're still after him, hunting him like an animal. I wish there was something I could do." Henry's voice had grown indignant, but it trailed off. He stopped short, then turned to her and smiled a tight-lipped smile. There were more thoughts in that wonderfully brilliant mind of his than he would share. She knew he didn't want to worry her, so the rest of his concerns he would mute for her sake. "I trust Collin will find his way through this mess, eventually. He's a bright kid and has proven to be very resourceful. I just wish I could help."

Henry thumped the steering wheel with his thumb, then gripped it tightly. He turned to Sarah with a forced smile and added, "Everything's going to work out, dear. Don't you worry about it. Everything's going to be alright." He reached over and squeezed her hand. Sarah squeezed back and tried a smile of her own.

A normal conversation was out of the question now. Plus, her strength was fading, so Sarah leaned her seat back and closed her eyes for the rest of the hour-long trip.

Chapter Four

estern Caribbean Sea, 76 miles south of Grand Cayman Island
June 14, 10:31 a.m. Caribbean Time

W The humor of fresh vomit dripping down a $400 silk Tommy Bahama shirt worn by an angry assailant cursing Collin in his native Asian language was mostly lost in the situation, but Collin couldn't help himself. As irate shouts echoed like drums inside his throbbing head, a smile turned his swollen and bloodied mouth upward, even in his semi-conscious state. The smile disappeared and his cognizance clicked into gear when something sharp nicked the soft tissue under his chin. A warm trickle ran its course down his neck to his chest. The draft swirling through the cabin became especially noticeable on the torn flesh.

"Ah, you think this is funny? A game, perhaps?" the angry man growled.

Through his puffed-up and tender eyelids, Collin could make out a face, an Asian face, directly in front of him. So, close, all he could see were the eyes—enraged to the point where he thought they might catch fire—and the nose, flattened but flaring erratically. Collin became aware that his handler, sitting at his left, simultaneously gripped his throat and pulled a wad of the hair atop his head so tightly he thought it might detach from his scalp. So many synapses were firing he couldn't possibly process all of the pain at once. Each new stimulus took a protracted length of time to register. Even then, there was a distance between his body and the pain.

"This is no game, Mr. Cook. This is serious business. You have our money. Lots of it. We want it back. It's ours, not yours. Do you understand me?"

Collin surveyed the cramped quarters below deck. While he was out cold, the place had been ransacked. Nothing was in its rightful place. Everything had been overturned, ripped apart, slashed, or broken. The few articles of clothing he carried, two sets of false teeth, three boxes of assorted hair dye, contact lens cases, and sundry toiletries had been pulled out from his backpack and spread across the wooden floor. Even the door to the microwave lay cracked near his feet. These were angry men, he concluded. His eyes closed involuntarily, and he felt himself slumping down until a stiff whack to his back and a tug of his hair straightened him up again.

Collin wished he could disappear. In that moment, more than at any time before, he wanted his boring old life back. He wanted to be home with Amy and his kids, destitute but happy. He wanted to go to work each morning and labor at the job he used to hate until it was time to come home and play with his kids and watch Amy's favorite sitcoms while snuggling on the couch. He'd give anything at this point to have that dull but fulfilling life again.

All this violence and terror and pain—he just wanted it to go away. He thrashed with his elbows; twisting fiercely he connected once with his captor. His captor's reaction reminded him of the desperate reality he faced: his destiny was no longer his own. The man wrenched him backward by the hair while the one with the vomit on his shirt slapped his face viciously as he cursed at Collin.

Collin sat teetering on the edge of the bed as the boat pitched up and down through the rolling sea. His mind attempted to carry him somewhere else to escape, but these angry men continued to batter his aching body. With his eyes still closed, he sensed someone drawing near, very near, but try as he might, Collin could not force his eyelids open.

The pungent smell of puke wafted to his nose, carried the short distance from the flowered shirt by a breeze entering through the stairwell a few paces to his right. A fresh wave of nausea gurgled from his belly. This time, the man heeded the warning signs and deftly backed away as Collin heaved the last of his stomach's contents onto his own lap. The stench itself caused him to gag and choke repeatedly.

Before he could recover, a new assault began. A backhand across the cheek followed by a kick in the chest followed by spit hurled in his face. The ribs he had cracked last week when he fell asleep at the wheel and crashed during his escape from Chicago hadn't yet healed. He groaned as a fresh wave of searing pain spread through his torso and doubled him over. Without warning, the man at his side pulled him up, wrenching all the air out of his lungs. Collin couldn't breathe, but neither of these men seemed too concerned about that.

"Tell me now where it is and this will all stop." The words were spoken slowly as the stinky man with the vomit shirt tried to pronounce the words properly.

Collin was slow to process the question and utter a reply. While he waited for the pain to subside enough to inhale, another backhand slapped his bruised cheek and mouth. More blood ran down his chin, meeting up with the previous streamlet. "I don't know. What are you talking about?" Another slap.

"Where are the codes, the account numbers?"

Collin stared blankly. "For what?"

"For your secret bank accounts. Remember? Where you hid our money? You have $30 million of our money. You give it back, or your friends will die."

Collin, still slow on the uptake, struggled to formulate an appropriate reply. His mind went first to Rob Howell, his best friend and next-door neighbor since first grade. Next, the image of Emily, his former high school sweetheart, flashed behind his eyes. Then he thought of Lukas, the one who was dead as far as the rest of the world knew. Things started to click, somewhat. "What friends?" he mumbled. "My friends think I'm dead."

"These friends," said Stinky, waving a hand toward the deck above.

It took him a moment to comprehend and formulate a response while the man glared at him. "The Captain and crew?"

"Yes, of course. These are your friends, no?"

Collin remained silent for another long moment while his mind began to churn and come to life, despite the urgency of his inquisitor. He guessed these soldiers of Penh's knew nothing about sailing and needed the crew to get anywhere. "You want to hurt them?" asked Collin. He paused as he stitched more thoughts together. "*You* going to pilot this boat while your buddies, Larry, Moe, and Curly here, run the lines and riggings, hoist the sails, and tack at *your* expert command? You know how to navigate? Read the instruments? Set a bearing? When and how to jib or gybe? Do your guys even know the difference between the bow and the stern? Starboard and port?"

Another slap across his face, harder than before. The blood flowed faster from the corner of his mouth and down his neck.

"Silence!" Stinky, in all his flowered-shirt glory, smelling like barf, panted like a tiger ready to pounce. He used the long-bladed knife, the one with Collin's blood dripping off it, like a pointer aimed first at Collin's right eyeball, just inches away. This was especially unnerving due to the rocking of the boat and the man's lack of "sea legs." Then he waved the knife and directed the man holding Collin's hair toward the hatch and up to the deck. Collin's body slumped, but he forced himself to remain upright. A moment later, a new man, one he hadn't seen before, returned with Tog and Miguel at gunpoint, their hands behind their heads.

Tog and Miguel wore steely, defiant looks on their faces as the Asian man with the gun pushed them forward into the cabin.

As the procession rolled in, Collin sized up his captors. If he was right, these guys were nothing more than hired help Penh had thus proved the length of his reach and the depth of his resolve. These goons were mercenaries, not sailors. Thugs with guns, not masterminds with plans. They had one mission and one mission only. Until he could think his way out of this predicament, Collin knew he had to play along and wait for his opportunity. It would come, but he had to be patient.

Stinky leaned in close again. "I ask you one last time. Where are the codes?" The man with the gun lifted the muzzle and aimed it at Tog's temple. Tog, a short, but wiry man, was quiet but proud; tough, uncompromising, and unafraid. He made eye contact with Collin and gave an almost imperceptible headshake. Collin understood him. Tog didn't want to budge an inch. Not for this guy; not for anyone.

"What? You think I'm smart enough to memorize them? Sorry, but I'm not that smart. They're on my laptop, but I'm not stupid enough to keep that with me." Collin spat the words out as convincingly as he could. He moved his head and eyes in a circular fashion toward the littered floor of the cabin. "Looks like you already tried to find my computer but couldn't. That's because I don't have it."

Stinky glared at him, jowls quivering, nostrils flaring like a bull. Two more punches, a right-left combo that sent Collin backward against the bulkhead. The hollow bulkhead into which he had crammed his five foot ten-inch body to hide from the Coast Guard a month ago. The same bulkhead where his laptop was now hidden. He wished he, too, was hiding in there now, even with his claustrophobia, where this brute couldn't touch him.

Stinky sprang forward, grabbed the front of Collin's faded T-shirt, tearing it as he yanked him forward to an upright position.

Everything was spinning, but he had to answer. Forcing back another wave of sickness, Collin came up with a plausible tale. "I left the computer in Chicago. In a safe deposit box downtown. It has all the codes."

"You lie!"

Collin straightened himself as best he could, forced his bruised eyes open as far as they would go, set his jaw, and angrily protested. "Why would I lie to you? What have I got to gain? These are my friends. The only friends I have left in the world. Why would I put them in danger?" His emotions were true, even if the part about the location of the computer was not. He pushed aside the thought that the computer was stowed in the hidden compartment two feet behind him.

Stinky, still glaring, held up a hand and mumbled something to the other guard. The man with the green shirt lowered the muzzle of the Uzi and pulled a handgun from his waistband. Taking a step back, the man pointed at Tog's head. Stinky looked at Collin and said, "This man's life depends on you."

But there was something else going on. Collin noticed it before, but it hadn't dawned on him until now. His abuser was beginning to look pale. He staggered slightly with the constant movement of the boat as it bounced through the waves. His eyes were swimming and less focused. Stinky was getting seasick.

The boat continued to rock and sway. Stinky's balance continued to diminish. Collin hoped to prolong the standoff long enough to formulate some sort of rescue plan.

"What will it be, Mr. Cook? The codes or your friend's life?"

Collin assessed Stinky's resolve and said, "We need him. We *all* need him to sail this ship."

"Do you want him to live, Mr. Cook?"

"Yes. We all need him to live. He's an important part of the ship's crew," said Collin, his voice straining under the pressure of the escalating situation.

"Then give me the codes."

"I told you, I can't. I don't have them."

"Very well, Mr. Cook. You leave me no other choice."

Stinky's seasickness did not reduce his meanness. The hand he held up dropped to the outstretched position and his fingers formed the shape of a gun. When his thumb came to rest atop his forefinger, a loud bang shattered the air inside the cabin.

* * *

La Jolla, California
June 14, 7:33 a.m. Pacific Time

Emily checked her watch again. She was behind schedule, but this did not seem to bother Agents Crabtree and McCoy. They sat on her ultra-modern stainless-steel-legged black leather couch, taking notes. She sat across from them, an odd-shaped glass coffee table between them. The interrogation seemed to spin in circles and Emily was growing agitated.

"Dr. Burns," Crabtree said, tapping his pen on his notepad. "Tell us again how you knew this Genevieve person would meet you in Chicago and escort you here to San Diego."

"I told you. He called me," she replied, checking her watch again. "He told me exactly what to do and how he had planned for my escape. He said he would do his best to protect me from the people that were after him, even if he couldn't be there to do it himself."

"Dr. Burns, don't you think we checked your phone records before we came here? Do you think we would drive through the night from San Francisco to ask you questions that we knew the answers to?"

"I'm still trying to figure out why any of this matters, Agent Crabtree, when no one has officially admitted Collin's alive, nor provided any proof to confirm it. It seems we're wasting our time talking about someone who is presumed dead."

"It matters to our national security, that's why," said Crabtree. "Whether Collin is alive or dead is beside the point. We need to establish a trail, a timeline. We have to establish his connection to this Asian syndicate and map out where he went and who he might have met with. It seems he had some sort of meeting with these guys either in Chicago or after he left there. It's important to piece together all of the clues in order to complete the puzzle and locate the bad guys so we can bring them to justice before they bring the whole US economy to a grinding halt."

Spinner McCoy took up the questioning. "Ms. Burns, we've researched every number on your call log while you were in Chicago. We've identified every caller and the origin of every text you received in that time period."

"Now that's just creepy," huffed Emily. "That's an invasion of my privacy."

"It's a necessary intrusion, as deemed by the Patriot Act authorized by Congress, being as how it involves the security of the United State of America, Ms. Burns," said McCoy matter-of-factly. "Now explain to us how you knew about this Genevieve person."

"I've already told you, Collin texted me."

"We don't see a record of an incoming text that mentions anything about Genevieve, Ms. Burns."

"I deleted all his texts." She knew this wouldn't stand up to scrutiny, but she had to stick to her story.

Reggie Crabtree gestured to his partner and resumed control of the conversation. "Dr. Burns, don't make us talk to Mike Zimmerman. We will if we have to, but we realize what an uncomfortable situation that could present for both of you."

Emily shifted in her seat and squeezed the fingers of her left hand. She spoke quickly, which she often did when she was nervous. She thought about Mike Zimmerman, her boss, and wondered how the socially awkward, mildly autistic genius would perform under the pressure of an interrogation about something completely new and foreign to him. Surely he would then ask her to divulge the entire story. It would most certainly rattle him. Being put in such an uncomfortable situation, Mike would undoubtedly come to her for an explanation. No matter the outcome, she feared the whole thing had the potential to shatter his confidence in her and create an awkward distance between them. It could harm her career, and possibly his. He didn't need this kind of stress and she couldn't work out all of the negative ramifications of the FBI interrogating Mike Zimmerman.

Emily decided it was best to protect Mike and her working relationship with him. "Collin slipped a cheap little phone in my purse at some point during the few minutes we had together in Chicago without me knowing. My guess is that he did it while we were walking through the convention center. He texted me later and told me it was so we could communicate. He said it was to be our little secret."

"What sorts of secrets have you two been sharing, Ms. Burns?" asked Crabtree.

"You want to see these secret texts? Fine. I'll show them to you. Excuse me one minute while I get the phone out of my purse." Emily disappeared around the corner and returned with the cheap little flip phone in her hand. "Here. Take a look. You'll see that he is quite concerned about his parents, especially his mother. Nothing too exciting."

Spinner McCoy held out a hand and took the secret phone. He opened it and began pushing buttons and reading what was on the screen. Crabtree leaned over as McCoy pointed to something.

"Like I said, he wanted to be able to talk to me. We only sent a few texts," Emily said as if that would clear things right up.

"Ms. Burns, we're going to need to clone this phone. You can keep the original, but we're going to need to use the data from this phone in our investigation," said Reggie. "We're also going to need to know more about the conversations you had using this phone."

"Oh, no. I don't want it used to incriminate Collin."

"Our goal is first to find him and bring him back to the United States safely. We'll figure out from there whether or not he's guilty of the crimes he's suspected of committing," said Crabtree. "Besides, this way we don't have to arrest you for obstruction of justice and withholding material evidence in a federal terrorism investigation. I would think that could do more damage to your career than our interviewing Mike Zimmerman."

McCoy added, "Cloning this phone will also allow us to track his movements and yours so we can keep you both safe."

McCoy pulled a device out of his briefcase and plugged the secret phone into it while Emily watched. He then pulled a laptop out of his shoulder bag and began punching keys and tapping the mouse pad.

The procedure lasted about three minutes in total. McCoy handed the phone back to Agent Crabtree, who handed it across the table to Emily. He asked several follow-up questions and reviewed a list of things she should and should not do. It all passed by her. A thick mental fog enveloped her, and she hardly heard a thing being uttered. Her mind was caught up in the revelation that the government was seeking information regarding a man, her friend, whom they had declared dead just a few days prior because maybe he wasn't as dead as they wanted everyone else to believe. They had also just admitted that they were going to invade her privacy and track her and Collin. They would use the phone she held in her hand to do it. What they would do with Collin once they found him remained a mystery. Their intentions were, and would likely remain, concealed. All these thoughts made the ground upon which her trust had been placed shake and it was unnerving.

"Dr. Burns, are you following me?" Agent Crabtree interrupted her thoughts.

"Yeah, you mean the part about being wary of any and all strangers? I didn't hear you mention, however, the part about needing to be wary of you. Or the other FBI agents who may be monitoring my every move."

"We are taking precautions for your safety—" he started to say.

But Emily wasn't done yet. "I'm sure *my* safety is far more important to you than, say, capturing Collin Cook, if he's even alive, and extracting any and all useful information out of him before you dump him on the side of the road, so to speak."

"We're concerned about his safety, too," Crabtree said, more defensively than before.

"I'm still unclear about why you're concerned about his safety when your agency considers him dead. What sort of horrible things will that permit you to do to him?"

"Dr. Burns, you've got it all wrong—" Crabtree started.

Emily didn't miss a beat. "And, if you guys were interested in helping him and keeping him safe, you could've done so by now. You could've rescued him and given him safe shelter somewhere before he drove a little rubber boat into a hurricane. You could have protected him long before that. Instead, you hunt him like some sort of animal to hang on your wall or a dangerous criminal or a thug and expect him to just fall into your trap."

"I don't understand the reason for your mistrust, Dr. Burns," said Crabtree. "Your friend has proven to be very elusive. We are simply using the resources available to us to locate him so we can first ascertain any useful information from him to protect the citizens of the United States from potential harm."

"I understand that. It's the methods you will use to extract that information that I question. May I ask how you will go about getting the answers you seek?"

"I can assure you, Dr. Burns, that there is no need to be concerned."

"Then I can safely assume that Collin will have legal representation present during such questioning, can I not? I've heard about how suspected terrorists are treated."

"Dr. Burns, your friend Collin is a US citizen and will be afforded every protection granted by the Constitution."

"That includes, does it not, the right to have a lawyer present during questioning to protect his rights?" said Emily, finally gaining a sense of balance in the conversation.

Crabtree maintained eye contact as he drew in a long breath. "Yes, it does,

Dr. Burns. You have my word."

"None of that matters, though, if Collin is dead. You have no reason to extend Constitutional rights to someone who is not even alive."

"We have good reason to believe that he is alive and may be contacting you soon, Dr. Burns. We would not be here if that were not the case."

"Your website says he's missing and presumed dead, so how is it you know he exists and will be contacting me soon?"

Reggie Crabtree paused for a moment, but his gaze never left Emily's quizzical face. She was smart and quick on her feet and unafraid to speak her mind. When he spoke, he spoke slowly, as one does when he's choosing his words wisely. "Dr. Burns, we don't know positively if Collin is alive or if he's dead. We hope he's alive. We want him alive. We want him to help us bring down an enigmatic terrorist organization that has disrupted the financial dealings of the US and our allies and threatens to bring international commerce to a grinding halt. That would have a very negative impact on the livelihoods of millions of people in the free world for a very long time, I'm afraid. If we don't figure out a way to stop this Pho Nam Penh and his group, life in America will not resemble the life we are used to for very long. Some of our cyber-crime experts believe this group is poised to launch an all-out assault on the computing systems of all of the major banks in the Western Hemisphere."

"How do you know this and what makes you think Collin has anything to do with it?"

"We don't know that he does, but we know he has visited several of those banks in the past several months and has withdrawn large sums of money from them. We also have pictures of him meeting with Penh and a man we suspect is one of his top lieutenants," explained Crabtree.

"That doesn't prove he's involved in these crimes," said Emily.

"Collin is the only person we know for sure who has spent time with Pho Nam Penh. We have photographic evidence. We have every reason to believe, based on his behavior, that he is mixed up in this thing deeper than you would ever like to suspect."

Emily didn't back down. Her face was a mask. Her words were like arrows.

"Then why would he risk meeting me in Chicago? Why wouldn't he just stay hidden? You admitted it yourself: this Pho Nam Penh has been so far below the radar that you guys haven't been able to track him. Why wouldn't Collin just join up with him and hide? Why has he been visible enough for you guys to almost catch him so many times, unlike Penh? Your explanation doesn't add up, Agent Crabtree."

Agent McCoy, growing agitated in the background, sat forward and cleared his throat as if to speak. Crabtree, the lead investigator and senior partner, held up an arm to both stop and silence his partner. "I understand your skepticism, Dr. Burns," he said calmly. "I don't have time to lay out our whole case, but I assure you that we are acting not only in his best interest, but yours as well. I promised Mr. and Mrs. Cook that I would do everything I could to bring their son home safely. I also took an oath to uphold, protect, and defend my country against all enemies, both foreign and domestic. If Collin can help us defend against an enemy, I'll have the privilege of keeping two promises at the same time."

"You seem to believe, Agent Crabtree, that Collin is an enemy, one you are sworn to protect our country against."

"I never said he was an enemy, only that he has had contact with Penh and his group. We will treat him as an informant. If we're able to apprehend him, he will be in protective custody until we arrest Pho Nam Penh."

Her bravado was beginning to crumble as she practically glared at Reggie for a long moment. When she finally spoke, her demeanor was less forceful, more analytical. "Up until now, you and your agency seemed hell-bent on eliminating this threat and disposing of it." Her voice was cool and her tone even. This was not an emotional accusation. This was a scientific evaluation.

"Like I said, I promised the Cooks that I would bring their son home safely. I am not trying to eliminate him, as you say. I am convinced that he can help us solve a crime—multiple crimes, actually—and eliminate the threat posed by the real enemy, this Pho Nam Penh. I need you to trust me, like the Cooks trust me."

Emily's eyes bored into Reggie's. Her expression didn't change, but she nodded her head slowly. "Proof is in the doing, not in the saying, Agent

Crabtree. You've cloned the phone that Collin gave me. Use it to bring him home safely. I will hold you to your promise."

"I will do just that, Dr. Burns. I just want to get to him before Penh and his men do. Trust me, he will be much safer with us." Looking at McCoy, who nodded, he added, "A protective detail will be put in place for your safety. They should arrive here shortly and will escort you to work, then remain outside your building."

"And how long do I have to endure this breach of privacy?"

"As long as it takes to neutralize Penh and the threat he poses to your safety, Dr. Burns."

Long after this conversation, Emily would replay it in her mind and wonder if she had done the right thing. Collin had told her to talk to the FBI and now she had done that. They knew everything that had happened between her and Collin since they reconnected two years earlier. She knew Collin was smart enough to have a purpose behind the suggestion. Despite having done as he asked, something gnawed at her insides.

Chapter Five

*Western Caribbean Sea, 77 miles south of Grand Cayman Island
June 14, 10:35 a.m. Caribbean Time*

The acrid smell of gun smoke, mixed with blood, stained the air. All other sounds were drowned out by the reverberations from the gun shot. Nobody moved. It was as if the scene was freeze framed. If not for the constant pitching of the boat, Collin would have thought time had stopped. Horror ruled the moment.

Stinky barked a command to the man with the gun, who wore a green island-print button-up shirt with palm trees and hammocks on it. His Nikes were black with fluorescent green trim. These men's apparel belied their true natures and dark intentions. The man wearing green's arms had tattoos near the wrists, some sort of insignia that must have meant something. Collin had noticed this before the man pulled the trigger.

Now, he sat stone still, trying to comprehend what had transpired.

Upon hearing Stinky's command, the scene came unpaused and Mr. Green began to move about as ordered. Blood had splattered on Mr. Green's face, which he wiped on the shoulder of his shirt as he stepped forward toward Miguel, who had dropped to his knees at the side of Tog's lifeless body. He, too, was covered in his friend's blood. Mr. Green pushed the muzzle of the gun against the base of Miguel's head and looked to Stinky, waiting for him to say something.

All the blood had drained from Collin's head and a new, heavier kind of sickness gripped him. He could hardly breathe, let alone think. His ears were ringing, and his eyes were forever tainted by what they had witnessed. In shock, Collin sat motionless, staring at Tog and the blood pooling around him, hoping somehow he would sit up and shrug it off; hoping somehow to rewind the scene and follow a different script, one with a brighter outcome.

Miguel, paralyzed with a gun at his head, stared wide-eyed at Collin. Collin felt hollow inside and numb outside. He dropped his head until his chin met his chest, unable to withstand the pleading look from his friend. Collin pinched his eyes closed. His mind blank, he couldn't begin to fathom what Stinky might do next.

Another unintelligible command and more movement to his right grabbed Collin's attention. Fearing another horrific murder, Collin winced as he stole a glance toward Miguel.

"You will change your mind, Mr. Cook. If you do not wish this friend," he said, waving his knife toward Miguel, "to experience the same fate, I suggest you deliver the codes."

Miguel's jaw tightened and his eyes narrowed as Mr. Green pulled him to his feet and pushed him toward the stairway. His pleading gaze took on new meaning as he shot a glance at Collin.

The smug look of supreme authority and absolute impunity on Stinky's face brought an irrepressible surge of hatred, contempt, and rage bubbling to the surface. The numbness and hollowness Collin had felt moments before were swept away, replaced by a boiling cauldron of ill wishes. Miguel was safe for the moment as the tattooed gunman shoved him through the cabin door and up the steps, but Collin was left alone with Stinky and a host of conflicting alternatives to ponder.

* * *

Scripps Cancer Research Clinic, La Jolla, California
  June 14, 10:09 a.m.

Emily rushed into the waiting room of the clinic, but it was empty. An attendant slid the frosted glass window open and peered at her. Seeing the white lab coat and ID tag hanging from Emily's neck, she asked, "Are you looking for a patient, Doctor?"

"Yes, has Mrs. Cook already been taken in for her treatment?"

The young Hispanic gal behind the glass smiled and said, "You must be Emily. She asked about you and seemed anxious to see you. Mr. and Mrs. Cook are in the treatment room, but Dr. Navarro has not yet arrived to begin the procedure. Come on back. I'll show you where they are."

Sarah smiled wanly as Emily entered the room. "I'm so glad you came, Emily," she said softly.

Emily forced a smile of her own as she moved to the bedside and grasped Sarah's outstretched hand.

Just then the door swung open and a forty-something-year-old Hispanic man with a white smock and a stethoscope rushed in. Two nurses, one in blue scrubs, one in green, flanked him and moved quickly to either side of the bed and began checking things. Dr. Navarro was polite but reserved. Kind, but quiet. And, apparently, in a hurry. He nodded toward Emily and Henry as he entered and thanked them both for coming, then turned his full focus toward his patient.

"Hello again, Mrs. Cook. How are you feeling today?" After listening to her assessment of her condition, Dr. Navarro looked at Emily and Henry and thanked them again for being there to support Sarah. "Beating cancer, we find, is as much an emotional response to the treatment as it is physical. Having loved ones rally around our patients, we've noticed over time, can be as much a determining factor as catching the cancer in its earliest stages. Thank you for coming." He and the nurses exchanged data and reviewed the procedures.

Dr. Navarro consulted his tablet computer, tapping and swiping at the screen a few times until he came to the page he wanted. "I'm pleased to tell you your blood work looks good. Just what we had hoped for. The T-cell levels are not growing, or at least not like they were. It appears the first two treatments have radically reduced their growth rate, which is exactly what we want." He issued instructions to the nurses. They began pinching tubes and opening color-coded syringes and laying them on a metal tray next to Sarah's bed. The doctor checked the labels, then read something on his tablet and made some notes by tapping on the screen with dancing fingers. Satisfied, he set his tablet down and took up a syringe, flicked it twice, squirted a couple of drops out, then pulled back the layers of blankets and asked Sarah if he could untie one of the strings on her gown. Emily turned away. She could inject rats but couldn't watch a needle go into a human.

"You're going to feel a sharp prick here, just under your left breast. There may be a slight burning sensation that accompanies the injection, but it won't last long."

Sarah gasped, held her breath a moment, then exhaled unsteadily. The nurses began injecting the other syringes into the tubes below the IV bag that led to a vein in her arm.

"There. That does it. Now, just relax and rest for a while. We'll let this IV bag and the medicines in it empty. There's also a sedative and pain killer in the IV lines now. They should help you rest comfortably. We'll come back and check on you in about two hours." Dr. Navarro made a few additional notes in his tablet. "Mrs. Cook, this will be much the same as last time. I would expect your reaction, symptoms-wise, to be very similar. There is a good chance, however, that the effects of the treatments will produce a cumulative effect, meaning you may experience an increased amount of lethargy and bloating. This is normal and to be expected. Get plenty of rest and drink lots of clear liquids in the days to come. I'll bring a prescription for the pain and nausea when I return." He nodded politely and excused himself from the room. The nurses followed.

Henry moved to the side of the bed and held his wife's hand. Within minutes, she drifted off to sleep, a peaceful smile on her face. "Have you got a minute to talk, Emily?" he asked softly.

"Of course. What's on your mind, Mr. Cook."

"Call me Henry, please." He stood and moved to the far corner of the room. Emily followed. "I got a very disturbing phone call this morning from Agent Crabtree of the FBI. He and his partner have been our primary contacts at the

FBI since Collin disappeared. We've met with them twice and had multiple phone conversations. It appears they are still very interested in Collin's case. Strange, the whole thing. He called at 5:45 this morning, spoke quickly, and sounded like he was in his car."

"What did he say, exactly?"

"He asked if I had spoken with you since Collin was lost in the storm."

Emily arched an eyebrow and paused momentarily. "Why would he mention me?"

"My thoughts exactly. Neither Sarah nor I remember telling the FBI anything about you or your involvement. It's strange. It's also strange that he didn't confirm the FBI's stance on Collin's status. I have to believe that they think he's still alive. They must have evidence that they are not sharing with us. Certainly, they wouldn't contact me otherwise," Henry said, motioning toward his sleeping wife. "Not at a time like this."

Emily covered her mouth with her hand and cast her eyes to the floor as she mulled over her options. She knew the Cook's didn't need any distractions while Sarah fought cancer. On the other hand, Emily knew they were fully engaged in Collin's saga and no amount of illness or medical treatment would replace the gnawing emptiness created by their son's prolonged absence. It felt right, so she dived straight in. "Agent Crabtree and his partner showed up at my door shortly after six o'clock this morning and asked me all sorts of questions about Collin's whereabouts, his plans, his money, our relationship, my involvement in his escape from Chicago. It was mind-numbing. In the end, I told them what little I know and gave them the cell phone Collin gave to me in Chicago."

"Did you feel coerced into doing that?" Henry asked.

"Not exactly. I felt compelled, yet conflicted. Part of their story made sense. They need to try to find him, if he is alive—something they have not yet admitted out loud to me, either—and want whatever information I can provide since I was the last known friend or family member to have seen him. They said it was for his safety and mine. If Pho Nam Penh were to find him before they did, it could be disastrous for him and for the country. So, I told them what little I know since Collin didn't tell me anything and handed over the cell phone. They cloned it while we talked. They think it will help them find him. I don't know how. I had assumed his phone got ruined at sea because I haven't heard anything from him since that day. I figured I would not be compromising him in any way to give them the phone."

"They'll track his movements and determine his last known location using the signal from the phone if it's still working," muttered Henry, almost to himself. "What good that will do them, I don't know, but at least it shows them that you are willing to cooperate. I suppose that should work in your favor. And, who knows, maybe it will help them find Collin and bring him home."

"That was my thinking, too. It can't hurt. Oh, and by the way, they sent a pair of agents as protection for me. I guess they fear this Asian mobster will come after me next as leverage against Collin."

Henry's brow furrowed and the deep creases in his forehead reemerged. "Leverage," he mumbled as he gazed at his sleeping wife.

* * *

Kuala Lumpur, Malaysia
  June 15, 1:17 a.m. Kuala Lumpur time

"We must call him," said one of the computer geniuses in the smoke-filled room as he clicked his mouse. He was one of only three men still awake. Two slept on cots in the corners of the room. Two more slept in their seats, heads resting on folded arms on the table. One of them stirred, repositioned, and went back to sleep.

"Are you absolutely certain? 100 percent?" asked the foreman.

"Yes, sir. 100 percent. The description of the car and the license plate matches. The CHP and local traffic cameras show a man and a woman in the car. Both faces match the photos we have. They are both there, inside the building. We need to call right now."

"Let me see what you have first," said the foreman, as he shuffled around the table to look over his teammates' shoulder. After a thorough examination of the evidence, he picked up his phone and punched the number. "Yes, boss, I have some news for you . . . Yes, it's very important . . . Yes, sir, we have confirmed that the mother and the father are in the San Diego area . . . Yes, sir, the Scripps Clinic . . . No, it's a different building, but we believe she is there, too . . . Yes, sir, we will monitor the situation and report any changes . . . Yes, they are still in the area . . .Yes, sir, I will, sir. Thank you."

He ended the call and ordered the other conscious man in the room to call the two operatives in La Jolla.

* * *

Scripps Cancer Research Center, La Jolla, California
   June 14, 10:38 a.m. Pacific Time

Emily said her good-byes to Henry and Sarah in the darkened and sterile room, although Sarah slept peacefully through it, and made her way out the building to her shining white BMW. The sun overhead was doing its best to maintain Southern California's image, bouncing its brilliant rays off the bright white paint and windshield, nearly blinding her as she drew near. She averted her eyes to the left to avoid the glare. That's when she saw it. At first, nothing seemed unusual about a Sprinter van pulling into the parking lot, but as she watched it, she felt something peculiar. The two Asian men inside seemed to pay her close attention, as if they recognized her. Men often stared at her, but she felt greater discomfort than usual as the van moved closer.

As she chirped her car unlocked, Emily glanced around and noticed the van maneuver into a tight parking space next to what she later learned was Henry's Cadillac. There were dozens of open spots nearby, but she shrugged it off and settled into the driver's seat, parked a row behind and a dozen parking stalls to the left of the van. She couldn't help but watch for a moment before she started the engine. She sent a quick text message to a co-worker giving instructions for the next step in the experiment he was working on.

Emily looked up and saw that the two Asian men remained in the van. Since there were no windows, it was unlikely that there were passenger seats inside. That meant they probably weren't there to pick up a patient. The decals on the van's side indicated that they were in the business of home entertainment, so it was equally as unlikely they were at the Scripps patient clinic to install the latest in theater quality surround sound equipment. She cocked her head, took a mental note, and fired up her 328i. She was in a hurry and had to get back to her lab, but the thought crossed her mind that she ought to call security.

The driver of the van watched her from behind dark sunglasses through his side mirror. Her unease grew but was soon quelled by the realization that the FBI detail starting up the Ford Taurus behind her was on the job. It was time to get away from the creepers in the van and get back to work. Her phone rang as she backed out of the parking spot. Soon she was involved in a discussion about her current experiment's control group at the lab and forgot all about calling security.

* * *

After the white BMW and the gray Ford sped away and exited the parking lot, the tattooed driver squeezed out of the van into the narrow gap between his vehicle and Mr. Cook's. The driver's door banged into Henry's passenger door, leaving a mark. His cell phone dropped, as if by accident, hit his foot, and skittered under the back bumper of the Cadillac. He strode to the back of the car and glanced in all directions before leaning down to pick up the phone. As he bent over, his hand slid deftly out of his coat's pocket to a spot beneath the bumper. He tapped the spot, collected the phone, stood up, checked his surroundings, and climbed back in the van. His visit to the clinic's parking lot, according to the security camera footage reviewed two days later, lasted approximately two and a half minutes.

Chapter Six

L os Angeles, California
June 14, 1:05 p.m. Pacific Time

Reggie let out a long, exasperated sigh as he leaned forward in his government-issued vinyl-covered swivel chair, and placed both elbows on the imitation wood grain-topped metal desk. He had just read aloud for his partner an email from Nic Lancaster, the Interpol agent in London they had been working with on the Cook case.

Spinner McCoy sat across from him and smiled that Texas smile of his. "Come on, Reg. You know you were just like that kid when you were starting out," he said with a mile-wide smirk.

Head still shaking, Reggie looked up at his partner. The gray hairs at his temples and the wrinkles around his eyes seemed more pronounced after the all-night drive from San Francisco to San Diego the night before and the growing angst at all levels concerning the whereabouts of their quarry, Collin Cook. "I know. That's what bothers me. He's too impetuous, too heavy-handed, and too damn eager."

"Rumor has it you were much the same as our friend across the pond, this Junior Agent Lancaster," McCoy said as he stood and stretched. He turned to survey the view of L.A.'s West Side from the sixth-floor window of their borrowed office at the FBI's Los Angeles Bureau. "Question is, Mr. All-Knowing Expert, how do we utilize his strengths without letting his bull-in-the-china-closet tendencies screw up another opportunity."

"Exactly. He can be useful, you know. He's bright. He's familiar with the case. Lord knows he's hard-working—it's what, nine o'clock over there and he's still grinding away. The kid is just dying to show someone what he can do," Reggie said with a check of his watch.

"And don't forget, he's got those bankers in the Caribbean scared. Whatever he's said or done, he's got them working for him," added McCoy.

"It's just a matter of harnessing all that energy he's got. We need to keep him in the loop and share information, but somehow prevent him from rushing in too early and too heavy again. You know, kind of like having him prepare the patient so we can perform the surgery." Reggie was now smiling, too. "Everyone wins, right?"

"That's what I'm saying, boss. Now, let's look at that map again and see where that boat is headed."

"My guess is Panama," said Reggie before Spinner had time to pull up a map.

"Why do you think that?"

"I'd bet Penh knows Cook was there. Probably suspects he hid a bunch of money in one of the many underground banks in the city, one of those that is supposed to be unknown and unknowable except to a select few—the real movers and shakers of the financial underworld. Either he's the one that directed Collin there in the first place, or he is directing him there now. Collin may be trying to get away from him or on an errand for him. We have no way of knowing, do we?" Reggie stopped and rubbed his face as he thought. "There's one more possibility: If Penh and Cook were working together, it's feasible that Collin got caught trying to double-cross Penh. If Cook hid the money so well that we can't trace it, then maybe Penh can't either. All outward signs indicate that Penh must not be able to hack into the bank to get the money. He's going to force Collin to get the money for him, since he undoubtedly knows where it is and how to get to it."

"Which means he's going to double-cross Cook," interjected McCoy.

Reggie nodded. "However you look at it, Collin loses. He's in a heap of trouble with little chance of surviving, I'm afraid, unless we can get to him first."

Spinner scratched the stubble on his chin. Neither man had shaved since

47

early the previous morning. "What are you saying, Reggie, send in the Navy SEALs?" he said, turning again to the window.

"I don't know, Spinner," Reggie said. His voice dry and growing hoarse. Exhaustion seeped from every word as he spoke. "This whole scenario makes me nervous. It might already be too late for the SEALs. And even if it's not, the whole thing could backfire on us."

"How so?" asked Spinner.

Reggie balled his fists and leaned into them. "One hint of intervention, and Penh could put a bullet in every man on that boat. That wouldn't bode well for us."

"It wouldn't help him, either."

"Yeah, but I think he'd rather win the game, to show us how serious he is. The money is less important than maintaining control over his syndicate and trying to keep the upper hand against us and Interpol by proving to be merciless. Penh ain't playing around."

* * *

Scripps Cancer Research Center, La Jolla, California
   June 14, 2:13 p.m. Pacific Time

It was after two o'clock before Dr. Navarro returned to Sarah's room. The fact that Sarah had not yet awakened concerned him. His apprehension caused Henry a fair amount of consternation. The good doctor checked the read-outs on the machines and looked at the tubes running from the IV bag. He tapped his tablet's screen and swiped and read and swiped some more. His facial expression changed only slightly as he let out a succession of "hmmphs" after each page was read. He turned to Henry and said, "I expected her to come around some time ago. Everyone reacts differently to these treatments and, being experimental, we don't have a baseline established yet for patient reactions. Maybe we just need to alter our expectations. Either that, or we need to alter our approach to your wife's treatment plan."

"Is there something wrong, Doctor? You seem much more concerned this time around," said Henry.

"My concern is that we find the proper balance between aggressively attacking the cancer, managing pain, and maintaining quality of life. Her body may not be ready for such a potent dosage," said Dr. Navarro.

"But if we don't treat the cancer aggressively, it could spread, right? We don't want that. She very much wants to live, even if it means she has some setbacks in the short term," said Henry.

"Very well. We will continue to monitor her condition very closely. Please page the nurse when she wakes up." Dr. Navarro left with a promise to check back in another hour or two.

* * *

London, England
June 14, 10:55 p.m. London time

Nic Lancaster's jaw dropped open in surprise. Things in the Caribbean rarely moved at the same speed as things in London. The people there were friendly and relaxed, and the island culture catered to vacationers looking for that very change of pace. So when the president of the Bank of George Town returned his phone call near the end of their business day, Nic was pleasantly surprised. When the head of the bank's security promised to send him a clip from the previous day's video footage, he was stunned. Now that a link to the footage showed up in his email just an hour later, he was nothing short of shocked. He pumped his fist and let out a triumphant, "YESSS!" when he opened the link. He jumped up from his seat and did a dance after reviewing the footage. "It's him! It's him! The little bugger's alive!" he shouted into the darkened and empty cube farm.

Cutting his celebration short, Nic sat down at his computer, not wanting to waste any time, and forwarded the email with the link to Reggie Crabtree, then dialed his cell phone. "I found him," he said when Reggie answered. "You were right. He went back to Grand Cayman and withdrew another half-million dollars. The link I just emailed to you shows him in the bank. Sure, he's in disguise, but I know it's him."

"Have you run it through FRS yet?" asked Reggie, referring to facial recognition software.

"I haven't yet, but I will," said Nic, trying to maintain an air of professionalism. Overly enthusiastic rookies got mocked and he didn't want that.

"Well, it may be a moot issue anyway. The cell phone he's been using to communicate with the girlfriend places him nearly two hundred miles south by southwest of Grand Cayman as of one hour ago. We've also picked up reports of armed men boarding a sailboat in the harbor and heading out to sea."

"Any description of these gunmen?" asked Nic, feeling somewhat deflated that his news was not the most earth-shattering of the day, but trying to assert himself.

"Nothing conclusive, just that they appeared to be Asians, dressed as tourists, and in a big hurry," said Reggie.

"Is there video available? Or photos?"

"Nope. Neither. Only eyewitness accounts. The best thing we have is that cell phone, which will be very useful until the battery dies," said Reggie.

"I'd imagine, though, that we'll get a pretty good sense of where they're heading before that happens."

"We think they're heading to Panama. We must try to intercept that boat before anyone gets killed." Reggie's voice was grim and urgent and Nic could hear the tapping of a keyboard in the background as he spoke. "We're working to get help from the US Navy on our end. See what you can do on your end. Once these guys have what they want, no one onboard stands a chance."

Chapter Seven

L a Jolla, California
June 14, 3:08 p.m. Pacific Time

The driver with all the ink on his neck checked his watch and nodded to his passenger. Speaking in his native Malaysian dialect, he rattled off the list of items to report to the boss. The young passenger stared at him and curled his lip.

"You want *me* to talk to the boss?" he asked, a thinly veiled tremor in his voice.

"I drive. You talk. If I drive and talk on a phone here, the police will pull us over. That would be a very bad thing. You talk. Tell the boss we are ready for either scenario."

The passenger hesitated. He looked at the driver, then at the phone in his hand, then back to the driver, who nodded calmly, providing the assurance he needed.

The call lasted ninety seconds. The passenger sighed as he turned to the inked driver and said, "The boss says to go to Plan B."

The driver nodded, his countenance ice cold as he continued to drive through the streets of La Jolla. "First, let's make sure Plan A is still operational in case he changes his mind."

"But what if we miss our chance to initiate Plan B?"

"We will have many opportunities to initiate Plan B, but we will have only one chance to set up the original plan. We will go there now," the driver mumbled. He first checked the GPS on his phone, then dropped the shifter into Drive and pulled away from the curb.

The passenger shrugged and pulled the duffle bag onto his lap and began raking his hand through the bottom of it. He pulled out four similar packages, each containing a video camera no larger than the eraser at the top of a pencil. Next he searched for the right wires and the super-extended life batteries that would supply power for up to sixteen hours. He tore open the packaging and began connecting wires to batteries and transmitters.

By the time they reached their destination, the passenger had also connected all four cameras to his smart phone using a special app. Now they would be able to monitor their subject and act when the opportunity presented itself.

* * *

Western Caribbean Sea, 200 miles south of Grand Cayman Island
June 14, 5:35 p.m. Caribbean Time

Slowly, Collin became aware of his surroundings. Time had melted away along with the initial shock of watching his friend and shipmate murdered. As his eyes opened and focused, he saw that Mr. Green had stationed himself across the salon from the lower bunk bed where Collin lay with his hands zip tied behind his back. He was maybe twelve feet away, wiping his weapon with a cloth. The galley was to Collin's left. The steps leading up to the deck were a few paces to his right, along the center line of the hull. Immediately to his right was the second set of bunks that lined the port side. Mr. Green sat on the end of a U-shaped bench that wrapped around a teakwood table capable of seating four men for dinner. Down a small passage to his right was the crew's head, situated beneath the cockpit where the Captain piloted the boat, complete with toilet and shower. Beyond the galley to Collin's left, tucked under the bow, was the Captain's quarters with his own bathroom and closet.

Things had changed while he was unconscious. Stinky was nowhere to be seen and Mr. Green, the trigger man, was now guarding him. Collin pushed down the rising anger that pushed him to take hasty vengeance. Everything was shiny—the walls, the floors, the table. Tog was gone. And there was a strange scent, like lemon cleaning solution had been poured over hot copper. That scent mixed with the gun oil Mr. Green was applying to his weapon.

Collin tried to move into a more comfortable position, but every movement jostled his brain, which caused a pulsing sensation inside his skull, as if a steam piston was knocking one side of his head, then the other. The constant wave action, limited amount of fresh air, and lack of food and water combined to increase his misery. Every attempt to think and string concepts together so he could make some sort of plan ended in shear frustration. He allowed his swollen eyes to shut again and his bruised body to remain prone on his left shoulder.

Mr. Green didn't notice Collin's eyes had opened. His snub-nosed Uzi lay across his lap, while he tumbled the slide-action handgun over and over, inspecting every inch of it as he wiped it clean.

Collin lay still, trying to push away the images of what he had witnessed, but his efforts were fruitless. And his guilt over it would not be assuaged. *If only I had just turned over the laptop to them*, he thought.

The farther south the *Admiral Risty* plowed, the more the sea roiled. Collin needed rest. The short catnaps these hijackers allowed him thus far were not enough to aid in his recovery. He tried once again to close his eyes and his mind, but the constant battering of the swells against the ship's hull, accompanied by the violent rocking side to side, thwarted any chance of sleep. A call from above deck caused Mr. Green's head to swivel and lock in anticipation. He stood and moved to the stairwell. He called out in his native tongue, then listened for a reply. Moments later, an unfamiliar face appeared, gun at the ready, to trade places with Mr. Green. Collin watched through the slits of his barely opened eyelids.

This man walked immediately to the bunk, grunted as he hovered over Collin, poking his ribs with the muzzle of his machine gun. Collin raised his head. Another grunt, but nothing else. As Collin lay motionless, trying to sleep, this new guard roused him every ten to fifteen minutes. Each time Collin grew comfortable, slipping into a fanciful dream about breathing fresh air or having the use of his hands or standing on solid ground, Grunter would repeat the same sequence of actions: Grunt, mumble, poke, grunt.

Collin had now met all four hijackers. So far, Grunter appeared to be the least violent of them. But he remained vigilant at his post, not allowing Collin to rest and regain his strength.

Time passed, although it was hard to measure in his semi-conscious state. All Collin knew was that the rays of the sun were at a much shallower angle now, coming in the small, shaded window above the dining table on the starboard side. Dusk approached. And with it, a calming of the wind and the waters. The sounds outside now were less boisterous. The sails flapped with less intensity. The slap of the waves against the hull less potent and less frequent. All seemed more languid and peaceful. Collin's prospects for rest were increasing.

The illusion was shattered when Stinky's raucous voice breached the still in a virulent stream of high-pitched inquiries. It was obvious he was questioning the Captain; his voice climbed an octave at the end of each word string. Collin could not make out the words, but he could imagine what was being asked. *Why are we slowing down? Did I say to slow down? What are you doing, trying to cause trouble?*

As he strained to listen, Collin could hear the Captain's deep voice as it projected from his perch at the helm into the open hatch, calm and assuring, explaining the situation and attempting to educate the armed novice before him of the ways of the sea. It seemed to Collin the Captain's efforts fell short of their desired effect. Stinky kept shouting, his tone brooding and suspicious.

"I told you," the Captain said, "I cannot control the wind. If there is no wind, we cannot go faster."

Stinky screamed some more and the Captain responded with, "Yes, we do, but if we run the engines we will run out of fuel and will be helpless in an emergency."

As expected, Stinky stomped his way down the steps and entered Collin's immediate space. He yanked Collin by the collar into a sitting position and demanded his cooperation. "We go too slow now. Your friends making trouble. You want more trouble?" Stinky's face was just inches from Collin's. His breath was sour, and his beady eyes shot daggers.

It took Collin a moment to reply. He tried to lick his parched lips and form words. At last, with his eyes closed in concentration, he slowly muttered, "This happens sometimes when sailing. It's called the doldrums. The wind just stops, and the water gets calm." Collin braced for the onslaught. It didn't come.

Stinky barked at Grunter and a short conversation ensued. Collin under-stood nothing.

Before marching back up the steps, Stinky approached Collin and shook him by the shoulders. "You better hope no funny business," he commanded. "Or you lose another friend."

Collin slumped back down and tried to sleep, knowing it was not an idle threat.

Chapter Eight

L ondon, England
    June 15, 12:20 a.m. London Time

For Nic Lancaster, the Collin Cook case would go down in his personal file as either a brilliant rookie triumph or an embarrassing start to his investigative career. Either way, his pride was involved, and his emotions poured into it. Yes, this case had become personal and he knew that was unprofessional, but he also knew it could define his trajectory.

Because he felt his career track was in jeopardy, Nic was more nervous than he had been on his first date. Collin Cook, the crafty little bugger, had finally made the mistake that Nic had been waiting for. The cheap cell phones he bought for himself and his lady friend would prove his undoing. Now that he had the ability to track Cook's location, it was time to coerce some cooperation from the higher-ups, starting with his section chief, Alastair Montgomery.

The sometimes-helpful Alastair didn't often see things Nic's way. Knowing this and having spotted a pattern of irregular behavior, Nic had done some sleuthing into his boss's out-of-the-office activities.

Nic reviewed the video recording he had of Alastair getting out of the taxi in Kensington during the middle of the day, having claimed to be off to a meeting with Scotland Yard. Nic had checked the validity of the meeting and learned that it was bogus, so he had followed him in a cab and used his phone to video the whole incriminating scene.

On the video, Alastair checked in all directions as he exited his taxi and strode blithely across the street. The footage became jumbled as Nic jumped out of his taxi, paid the cabbie, and darted behind a parked car to continue filming. He captured Alastair heading into a flat, the door held ajar by a very young and very beautiful lady, who he later learned was the daughter of a member of Parliament. He stitched the end of that video to the beginning of the next one, careful to show the time stamps on each. Approximately forty-five minutes elapsed before Alastair stepped out from the flat and into a waiting taxi.

With the potentially career-ending scandal for Alastair caught on his phone, Nic had the goods he needed to persuade his boss to bend to his will. The trap was set.

The next step was to convince Alastair that Collin Cook was alive and could still lead them to Pho Nam Penh. He had video footage from the bank in George Town and eyewitness accounts from boat owners at the marina. With some more arm twisting, Nic hoped to get surveillance video from the dockside cameras as well, to corroborate his findings and prove Cook was still breathing and moving and, more importantly, in real danger. The reports of hijackers increased the urgency of the mission to capture Cook before Penh and the Kamados put an end to him. Once they had what they needed from him, he would no longer be useful. Without Cook, Nic feared he might never find a way to take down Penh. Collin Cook, he knew, was the bait he needed to catch the big fish and the bait had provided a way for Nic to track him. That, the crowning piece of evidence, being the cheap burner phone Cook had hoped no one would find out about. *Thank you, Collin Cook.*

Quick and decisive action was necessary, but Crabtree's attempts to get the Navy SEALs involved seemed a long shot at best. Nic would be the one with a plan in place, knowing the Americans would not be able to move in time. He would be the one to save the day and all previous embarrassments stemming from this case would be swept away.

Nic knew that Alastair, like the rest of the world, viewed Collin's demise at the hands of Hurricane Abigail as certain and hadn't given him another thought since he had disappeared over a week ago. It would take more than mere words and pleading to get Alastair to assist in finding a man he believed to be dead. Nic had his body of evidence concerning Cook's state of undeadness compiled and ready to present.

One more call to the chief of security at the George Town Marina, then he would call it a day.

* * *

Scripps Cancer Research Patient Clinic, La Jolla, California
June 14, 5:44 p.m. Pacific Time

Sarah Cook woke as Henry's large, but gentle hand caressed her cheek. "Dear," he said. "The doctor is here to check on you. Can you wake up and talk to him?"

Dr. Navarro moved closer and studied her face. "Mrs. Cook, I'm so glad you're awake now. I've been a bit concerned." A scowl receded and gave way to a contrived smile.

Sarah cleared her throat and attempted to sit more upright. "Oh? What time is it?"

"It's almost six o'clock, Mrs. Cook. You've been out much longer than I would have anticipated. How are you feeling?"

"I feel like I've been drugged," said Sarah with a wry grin.

Dr. Navarro first hesitated, then allowed himself to chuckle. "I see you still have your sense of humor. That's good. Your blood pressure, breathing, and heart rate are all back to normal now, so that makes me feel better about letting you return to your home tonight. We ran some additional tests, but they were all well within normal limits. You are free to go and rest comfortably at home after you eat and walk a little way for us. We just need to make sure everything is working. How's your appetite?"

"I feel like I could eat a horse," Sarah said.

Another slight hesitation. "Very well, Mrs. Cook. I'll have the nurses bring you a horse for dinner," Dr. Navarro dead-panned without looking up from his tablet. This brought laughter from both Sarah and Henry, easing the tension. The humor disappeared and Dr. Navarro's brow bunched together. "In all seriousness, Mrs. Cook, I must remind you that your diet during this clinical trial must be highly regulated." He turned to Henry, who nodded his acknowledgment and consent. "We'll make sure your dinner conforms to that meal plan. The nurses will provide you another copy of the detailed meal planning guide. It shows not only what you should eat, but the schedule you should keep, including a suggested exercise routine."

"Thank you, Doctor," said Henry. "That will be very helpful."

"We've now set up an online profile for you to report your daily activities. It's quite detailed, but it will allow us to monitor the effectiveness of the prescribed diet. The nurses will provide you with the login information. You can even do it from your phone, which I think is extremely convenient and really cool," he said with the grin of a schoolboy who had just learned a new trick. "Hopefully, by monitoring your diet and accounting for it, we can make the dietary adjustments needed to restore your strength and energy."

Henry and Sarah both stared wide-eyed at the doctor, who looked back at his tablet and continued.

"It's very important to keep your strength up so your body can utilize the enzymes we've injected and fight the cancer," added Dr. Navarro. "Without proper nutrition, the enzymes die, and the cancer thrives."

"How do we do that when she hasn't had much of an appetite, Doctor?" asked Henry.

"She'll need to eat smaller meals more frequently. I know that doesn't sound like much, but it has proven to be a significant factor. Remember, this is a clinical trial, so we need to regulate and monitor everything—food intake, caloric burn, even waste evacuation. Not only is it important to follow the meal plan and exercise routine, you'll also need to keep a journal of all these activities. I assume this was explained to you when you volunteered for the program."

"It was, thank you," said Henry. "I have adjusted my work schedule so I can be there and take care of her."

"That's good. I can't stress enough the role diet, especially, plays in this treatment. We believe there is a strong interplay between the enzymes we've injected, and the foods patients eat in fighting the cancer cells and reversing the tumor growth. So, if it seems strict or restrictive, keep that in mind."

"Will do, Doctor. Thank you again."

"No problem. We'll bring her dinner, then have the physical therapist come and walk her through the halls. After that, we can send her home." Dr. Navarro turned to Sarah and continued, "I suspect we can have you out of here in a couple of hours. How does that sound?"

"The thought of sleeping in my own bed sounds too good to be true. I'll take it, though."

* * *

Scripps Cancer Research Center, La Jolla, California
  June 14, 6:05 p.m. Pacific Time

Mike Zimmerman stood and clumsily attempted to retreat between the chair he had been sitting on and the empty chair holding his briefcase during this pow-wow. As Emily's boss, it was his custom to debrief at the end of each day. These meetings were informal and friendly—a chance to review and plan—and part of a well-established routine. Like most people with Asperger's, Mike thrived on routine. Emily needed little in terms of guidance and Mike did little in terms of micro-management but sticking to the pattern was important. Theirs was a productive partnership based on mutual respect and a shared love of science and research.

Despite his position on the high-functioning end of the autism spectrum, Mike's contributions to the laboratory research community were now legend. He was one of the most published researchers at Scripps and a pioneer in enzyme enhancement. His compliments, therefore, carried significant weight.

After Mike shuffled out of her office, Emily sat down and pondered her recent run of good fortune and the high praise Mike had just heaped upon her. He thought this current set of experiments using an obscure protein chain—an idea conceived during one of her early morning runs while preparing for her presentation at the Bio Med Conference—would be her third breakthrough in two years. Of course, it would take another two years of development and perfecting before it would be ready for clinical trials on humans, but the thought that her work could benefit cancer patients, gave her a warm sense of accomplishment.

She didn't spend long luxuriating in Mike's accolades. Her success only mattered if it resulted in helping real people and their families to live longer, more productive lives—something ingrained in her brain during graduate school. That thought led her back to Sarah, so she picked up the phone and dialed Dr. Navarro to check on her.

During her conversation with Dr. Navarro, Emily learned of Sarah's difficulties recovering from the anesthesia and Dr. Navarro's concerns about her general weakness. "As you know, Dr. Burns," he told her, "Sarah's cancer is the most advanced of any patient in the study and while her cancer type makes her a good match, her condition makes her less than ideal for total success. Having said that, this treatment is her best option to prolong her life. I'll also tell you what I told her and that's how imperative it is for her to strictly adhere to the diet."

* * *

Scripps Cancer Research Patient Clinic, La Jolla, California
   June 14, 7:42 p.m. Pacific Time

A white van sat parked along the street, under a tree, several hundred feet from the Cook's Cadillac and out of range of the institute's cameras. Inside, the driver with the ink up his neck nudged the passenger with the spikes, who had nodded off after hours of watching and waiting. "Look. There. It's them. They're getting in the car," he said as he held out the binoculars.

The passenger put the binoculars to his eyes and adjusted the focus through the dim twilight. Sarah Cook sat in a wheelchair pushed by the tall white-haired Henry Cook. The parking lights of the Cadillac blinked on, then off as Henry pushed the button on his key fob and slipped it back into his pocket. "You're right. Let's roll," said the spike-wearing passenger. He placed the binoculars in their case and returned it to the duffle bag on the floor between the driver's and passenger's seats. His hand dove into the hip pocket of his coveralls and pulled out a sleek smart phone. He tapped the face of it a few times until a map opened up. Two dots blinked on the screen—one blue and one red. As Henry Cook's Cadillac began to cross the parking lot across the street, the red dot blinked faster.

"It's working," said the passenger.

The driver nodded his head as he watched the red blip on the screen.

"Remember, the transmitter has a range of less than one mile. Don't follow too close, but don't let them get too far ahead," said the passenger.

Annoyed by the patronizing tone, the driver grunted, "I know, I know," and started the engine.

Chapter Nine

Western Caribbean Sea, 225 miles south of Grand Cayman
June 14, 8:45 p.m. Caribbean Time

Captain Sewell, his crew, and their hijackers were treated to a phenomenal sunset that night, though it went largely unnoticed. The Western horizon off the starboard side glowed purple, pink, and orange, the colors streaking across the glassy surface of the water. Ordinarily, a setting such as this would elicit a philosophical discussion among the Captain and his select crew. Conversations about life, death, God, nature, hopes, dreams, failures, and worries often occurred on nights like this. Collin had joined several during his time on the boat. Not tonight. Not after what had transpired. Everything had changed in the blink of an eye.

No one spoke. The beauty of the sunset stood in sharp contrast to the brooding, dark emotions fermenting inside the Captain's heart. A heavy silence enveloped his three remaining crew members, still in shock from the suddenness and brutality that had claimed their friend and shipmate. The Captain had no words of comfort or solace to offer, not after watching the hijackers toss Tog's body overboard like refuse, against Sewell's angry protests. This turn of events violated everything the Captain held sacred. Life deserved more respect than these monsters gave it and death deserved more solemnity than they had allowed.

Captain Sewell remained silent, trying to control himself and prevent further violence. Thoughts of Tog and concern for Rojas, Jaime, Miguel, and Collin wrestled within him, stealing all joy from what should have been a glorious scene. He shook his head, cast his eyes toward his instruments, and fought back the boiling rage inside, knowing if he acted on it the outcome would be disastrous. Powerless to console and lost in his own angst-riddled mourning, he steered the ship toward the mounting storm to the south.

Then Stinky appeared from below and the stillness shattered.

The *Admiral* had been languishing for hours in the doldrums, chugging along at a mere eight miles per hour under power from the seventy-five-horsepower engine. The sails were at full flap, but that hardly helped. Every few minutes a lazy breeze would come along and provide a little push, but their southward progress was slow and tedious and Stinky had had enough.

"Go faster," he commanded the Captain. "We move too slow.

"This is a sailing boat. It has large sails, but not a large engine. It's going as fast as it can without wind," the Captain explained for the umpteenth time. His patience was wearing thin and he had given up masking that fact.

Stinky's impatience was less anger-driven, it seemed, and more motivated by a sub-surface urgency that was perhaps part of his Type-A personality. He never stopped moving. When he spoke, his words were clipped, sharp, and hurried. There was nothing about him that indicated he could tolerate the doldrums or anything that did not move at his command.

The shirt Collin had decorated for Stinky had since been rinsed out using seawater. When it dried, the silky fabric had stiffened, causing him to constantly adjust, itch, and tug at the salt-laden fabric.

"No good. We must go faster," he insisted without conviction.

The Captain pointed to the western sky and said, "Enjoy this while you can. By tomorrow afternoon, we'll have plenty of wind. And clouds. We'll go much faster then." His eyes smoldered as they narrowed; his tone radiated spite.

Darkness approached. The Captain ordered his men to top off the fuel tank while there was still enough light, so Jaime and Rojas set to work untying two of the red, five-gallon containers and moving them into position near the stern. As they worked, the Captain addressed Stinky. His voice barely under control.

"Our men need to rest. Tomorrow will be a difficult day. They will need all of their strength. We all will."

Stinky thought about that. Clearly, he had not anticipated this scenario. "This is a trick—" he began to say.

The Captain cut him off. "No tricks," he said sharply, pointing to the screen in front of him. "Look right here. Tomorrow, a storm will come. I need my men to be ready. If they don't sleep now, they won't be ready."

Stinky glared at him, unused to being interrupted. Captain Sewell returned the stare, then added, "You can do what you want with your men. Mine are going to get some rest." He signaled for Jaime and Rojas to head below decks. The Captain instructed Miguel to stay topside to help. They would rotate in four hours, he said.

Stinky huffed again and signaled Mr. Green to accompany them down the steps.

That's when Stinky's phone rang, a muffled and unfamiliar melody. He fumbled as he dug it out of his hip pocket. As he put the phone to his ear, a frown contorted his mouth.

Captain Sewell stood at the wheel, listening but not understanding the words Stinky uttered except when he said, "OK."

* * *

Collin had been sleeping off and on for the past several hours. There had been no new attacks and the pain was starting to subside everywhere except his head. It pounded and throbbed. His mouth and throat were so dry it made him cough and choke. He realized that he must be dehydrated, but he dared not ask for anything, fearing another assault, so he lay still and listened to the rustling of the three men who had just entered the room.

Rojas and Jaime conversed softly in Spanish. At first, they seemed to be testing the waters to see if either of the two gunmen in their company would tell them to stop. "Where's my pillow?" "Do you want a blanket?" "I need my toothbrush." Their words were spoken more clearly than usual. Their

65

tone was still familiar and casual, but the conversation lacked the normal amount of slang incomprehensible to Collin, who spoke fluent Spanish but could rarely follow the exchanges between these two. It was a running joke.

When the guards said nothing to halt their chatter, they continued, still speaking softly and in the same tone. Rojas said, "Did you hear about Abigail's little sister?"

Jaime replied, "Abigail has a sister?"

"Yeah, she's coming to visit tomorrow."

"Really? What're you going to do?"

"Introduce her to our guests. Maybe she can take them out."

"I hope she does."

Both men grumbled and snorted, a sinister chortle shared between them. That's when Mr. Green stepped closer, gun in hand, and ordered them to stop talking.

Collin replayed the short conversation in his head, interpreting the code. He tried to suppress a smile. Abigail, the hurricane that nearly killed him over a week ago, had a little sister who was coming tomorrow. Jaime caught Collin's eye and gave Rojas a shove with his elbow.

* * *

Huntington Beach, California

June 14, 9:53 p.m. Pacific Time

With the push of a button mounted on the overhead console, the Cooks' garage door began to open as the dark blue Cadillac approached the end of the cul-de-sac. The handsome two-story, Mediterranean-style home was mostly dark, save a few lights, which were controlled by timers, glowing in the front windows and in the bonus room above the garage. The decorative landscape lighting illuminated the willows and the Japanese maple in the front yard. The garage door was fully opened by the time the Cadillac reached the driveway. Henry inched the car carefully forward until the dangling tennis ball touched the windshield. He smiled at Sarah as she roused from slumber.

"Oh, are we home already?" Sarah said as she checked her surroundings.

"Already? You must have been in a deep sleep, my dear. Traffic was horrendous coming into Orange County."

"I'm sorry, Henry. I should have stayed awake to keep you company."

"No, no. I'm fine. Did you enjoy your nap?"

"I just can't seem to keep my eyes open. I'm sorry to be so out of it."

"Don't you worry your pretty little head. Rest is good for you. Now, let's get you upstairs where you can sleep comfortably in your own bed," said Henry as he turned to open his door.

Sarah watched as he swung his legs out, stood, and stretched his tall frame. Once he closed the door, she began to gather her purse and sweater while she waited for him to open her door, as was his custom. She leaned her head back and closed her eyes, summoning her strength for the journey up the stairs.

It seemed to take Henry longer than usual to make his way around the back of the car. And it seemed strange to hear the garage door closing already. He didn't usually do that until they reached the door to the inside of the house. That's where the button was, the one mounted on the wall right by the door frame. Why had he closed it already, she wondered? When her door opened, she reached out for his hand without opening her eyes. A hand, a much smaller and gloved hand, grabbed it and yanked her up with such force, she lost her breath. She was hurled into the arms of another man, short and wiry. One of his hands covered her mouth while the other wrapped around her waist and lifted her off her feet. She kicked and tried to scream, but it was to no avail.

A strange smelling cloth was placed over her nose. That was the last thing she remembered from that day.

* * *

Western Caribbean Sea, 285 miles south of Grand Cayman
  June 14, 11:45 p.m. Caribbean Time

Collin tossed and turned all night. His captors had offered him a small drink of water and some bread shortly after Rojas and Jaime settled into their bunks. It was not enough. A splitting headache, an empty stomach, and hands cuffed behind his back by plastic zip ties kept sleep at bay although his body was beaten, bruised, and exhausted. His wrists were raw, swollen, and painful. Everything hurt. And now, his mind ached with a yearning for freedom so powerful he could taste it. Thoughts swirled in his brain like leaves in the wind with no aim, constantly changing direction.

During the few short bouts of sleep he managed to get, Amy would appear to him. One time, she sat next to him and stroked his hair. It was comforting and soothing but ended too quickly. Another time, she brought the kids to him, but he could not reach them, nor hug them, nor wipe away their tears despite his desperate attempts. Each attempt brought more pain to his wrists and to his heart as he struggled against the bands and against reality. The last time, he saw her driving her minivan down the mountain with the kids buckled into their seats, engrossed in a movie. She talked on the phone with him using the van's hands-free Bluetooth connection. Then his mind replayed the sounds he had heard over the phone nearly a year earlier: screeching tires, the faltering brakes of a loaded big rig, metal scraping against metal. Amy's gasp followed by her high-pitched scream. Crunching. Breaking glass. Absolute silence.

This agonizing replay startled him awake. His body jolted upright in the bunk, and he let out a scream, which he stopped short as he realized where he was and recalled the events of the day. As he struggled to normalize his breathing, he surveyed his darkened surroundings, including the lemony disinfectant smell, the sploshing sounds of the waves against the hull, and the gentle bobbing action of the boat. His insides tightened and his breathing constricted as it often did when he counted his losses. His situation at the moment was hopeless, his outlook bleak. Tog was dead. Collin had every reason to believe that the rest of the crew would be expendable once they reached Panama, if not sooner. Knowing he had brought this danger and the accompanying pain to his newest friends and protectors, felt like a white-hot branding iron had seared a mark inside his heart. He could never undo it. There would always be loss and heartache and emptiness. No amount of money could change what he had brought to the men who considered each other family and called the *Admiral Risty* their home.

Mr. Green approached; gun drawn. He eyed Collin suspiciously, then yanked him forward by his shirt collar until their faces were inches apart. "What are you doing? You keep quiet."

Collin nodded and said, "But I need water."

Mr. Green opened a bottle and poured it on his face. Collin caught as much of it in his mouth as he could and gulped it down hurriedly, not wanting to waste a drop.

"No more noise," Green demanded, shoving Collin back down.

Collin felt himself spiraling into a round of self-pity, once again at a critical crossroads, endangering his safety and the safety of his friends. Scenes played on the screen in his mind like an accelerated slideshow: Stinky's initial attack, Tog's murder, Stinky punching him in the face, the dreams of Amy and the kids at his side, driving the dinghy through Hurricane Abigail, Amy beckoning for him to come to her. Collin's thoughts were rising up like a tsunami ready to sweep him up and drown him. *Don't let this happen*, he thought as he tried to push them out of his head. He knew he could not afford another disastrous meltdown. He had to pull himself together. It was time to will his way back into usefulness. But how? When every possible factor was stacked against him, and the odds of success so frightfully low, how could he hope to escape this time?

Collin forced his mind to start thinking about solutions instead of problems. *Focus on the outcome you want*, he remembered hearing in a sales training session years ago. *Forget the negatives you don't want. Train yourself to think past the crisis of the present and into the future you design for yourself.*

Collin closed his eyes and started unraveling the problem by first reviewing the conversation he had just heard between Jaime and Rojas. They were sending him a message so he could prepare as much as possible. A storm was coming, and the crew planned to use it to their advantage. This both buoyed his spirit and filled him with dread, not knowing how severe the storm would be or what he would be able to do to help. And in his impaired condition, he wondered how he'd survive if things got too dodgy.

Next, he thought about Lukas. Surely Lukas was monitoring his movements by pinging his iPhone. Remembering he had the phone attached to an external battery charger eased Collin's concerns, knowing it could send a signal, even out at sea, for up to forty-eight hours.

The memory of Stinky as he appeared to be getting seasick flashed across his mind, bringing a small measure of hope.

Another bright spot was that Captain Sewell and the remaining crew members were veterans of the sea. They could handle the weather much better than the hijackers could and turn it to their advantage.

The storm could prove to be a blessing, but Collin had no idea how far away it was or how large. Knowing the Captain and crew anticipated it, added to his tentative but rising level of comfort. The hardest thing to do was waiting for it to arrive. Freedom beckoned and pulled at him, like a dog owner tugging on a leash. Collin was not unwilling to follow the call; he was unable. He wanted to end his captivity now and avoid suffering the excruciating angst of being held inside in a cramped space for days on end.

With his mind spinning on the potentially positive outcomes, Collin's painful memories receded into the background. Time slipped away and Collin was lost in dreams of seeing the sun again and moving about freely and not worrying about being struck repeatedly. As the moonlight streamed into the cabin of the boat, he drifted deeper into a dream-like state where he saw his family and friends standing on a shore at the edge of his vision. He could just barely make out the faces on the figures in the distance. But they kept changing. At first, he saw his wife. Then the face changed to his mother. Standing next to her was his father, who then became Lukas. In his dream, he looked away, then looked back. When he did, the faces were Stinky, Mr. Green, and Pho Nam Penh, laughing and jeering while a fire burned in the background. Then it was Tog lying in a pool of blood just a few feet from him.

Collin woke with a start, breathing hard and sweating. The cabin was dark, except for the streams of gray light filtering through the round, tinted portholes in the wall next to the upper bunks and above the dining table. Half of Mr. Green's face was illuminated. His eyes were shut, and his body swayed with the gently rocking waves.

With his guard at rest, temptation skittered through Collin's mind. How easy it would be to knock out Mr. Green. A swift kick to the side of the head ought to do the trick. Collin sat up and eased himself to the edge of the bed, calculating the movements required to execute his scheme.

The second phase of his plan was still murky and required cooperation from the other hijackers. If they came down to the cabin one at a time, he would simply ambush them as they came down the stairs. He felt he could handle any of them one-on-one as long as he had the element of surprise working for him, as well as his hands. That was a problem. Surely Rojas and Jaime would jump in and defend themselves. If they could cut his hands loose, it could be a fair fight—three on three—except for the weapons.

Collin summoned courage from his vast reservoir that had only grown deeper over the past few weeks. It was now or, perhaps, never. A sleeping guard presented an opportunity he could not pass up. He reviewed his plan of attack in his head one last time as he adjusted his body into a perfectly balanced position, then rose to his feet. As he stood for the first time since early in the morning, another wave of nausea overtook him. He closed his eyes to fight it back, his body reeling with the swaying of the boat. Instead of making panther-like treads toward his unsuspecting victim before he pounced on him, he lost his balance and knocked into the wall next to the bunk bed. His feet slapped the floor as he struggled to regain his equilibrium.

It took only a few milliseconds for Mr. Green to launch his counterattack. Collin didn't see it coming. A powerful kick to his abdomen knocked him backward and forced the air out of his lungs. It was followed by a blunt object striking the side of his face. He didn't remember anything else and didn't wake up until the cabin was full of sunlight late the next morning.

Chapter Ten

Washington, DC
June 14, 11:55 p.m. Eastern Time

"C'mon, Rob, pick up your phone," Lukas muttered to himself. The phone continued to ring until Rob's cheery, pre-recorded voice answered saying, "This is Rob Howell. I'm unable to answer the phone at the moment, but if you'd kindly leave me a message, I'll get back to you as soon as I can."

Lukas did not leave a message. He was on a secured, untraceable line deep within the NSA's main office complex. There was no way Rob's incoming call would be routed to him. He dared not use his cell phone with civilians, even lifelong friends like Rob, despite the fact that he was one of only two people outside of the clandestine government agency network who knew Lukas was alive. Collin was the other. They were the only two people on the outside he trusted and the only two people still living that he loved or cared for enough to contact. Rob, Lukas, and Collin were practically inseparable in middle school and high school. After graduation, each had chosen a different path, but no amount of time apart, no amount of distance between them, nor tragedy, nor intrigue could break their bond.

After two minutes of rapping his knuckles on the table and reliving memories of his youth with his buddies, Lukas dialed again. This time, Rob answered on the first ring. A groggy voice came on the line. "Lukas, is that you?"

"About time you picked up. Did I wake you? Awfully early for a mover and shaker of your caliber to be sleeping. Shouldn't you be working on the next deal?" Lukas said in his gentle Austrian accent.

"At what, 4:55 in the morning? I'm in London, you know. Just got here a few hours ago. Supposed to meet a client tomorrow. Why? What's up?" Rob tried to sound upbeat and ready to help, but it was a hard sell after only four hours of sleep.

"I'm worried about Collin. Have you heard from him lately?"

This got Rob's blood moving. "Not directly, no." He sat up and kicked his legs out from under the covers. "You were the one who passed along the last bit of info I got. Why? What's wrong?"

"He hasn't responded to any of my texts or voice messages. When I ping his phone, it shows me that he's in the middle of the Western Caribbean," Lukas said.

"Is that bad?" asked Rob, clearing his throat.

"Well, it's not what he and I discussed last time we spoke. He was going to hide out in the islands, avoid sailing and roaming around, and just doing nothing for a while."

"Maybe he's still planning to do that, but is taking a different route," said Rob.

"If I'm not totally wrong, it looks to me like he's heading back to Panama," Lukas said with a tone of exasperation.

"Panama? Why would he go there again so soon? I take it you didn't instruct him to go there." Rob's voice was beginning to sound clearer and his thoughts more coherent.

"No, I didn't," said Lukas with a sigh. He stood at his computer and ran one hand through his thick, blond hair.

"Who did?"

"I don't know. I told him stay hidden in the islands somewhere, but to stay on the lookout because the FBI and Interpol were still leery and still keeping a watch to see if he would return to the same boat. Looks like he did that and is now on the move, going the wrong way."

"That's bad news, then, isn't it?"

"Yeah, and that's not the worst of it. There are reports out of George Town that four Asian men carrying guns stormed a sailboat in the harbor this morning."

"Penh?"

"His men, at least."

"That *is* bad," Rob groaned. He was now standing at the coffee machine in his hotel room, rubbing his eyes. "Is it the same boat he was on before? The *Admiral* something-or-other?"

"The *Admiral Risty*. It appears that way, yes. Last time Collin and I spoke, he was aware that the Interpol agents had not left the island yet. We knew when the FBI guys left, but I was waiting for a contact to confirm on the Interpol guys. I also had people on the lookout for Penh's men."

"I thought no one knew what they looked like," said Rob.

"That's true, but we knew what to look for in terms of their activities and demeanor. We had built a profile, and it wasn't just based on race, but never got a match."

"What's your theory, then? You wouldn't call me if you didn't have a theory," said Rob, trying to lighten the mood.

"You're right, I do have a theory," Lukas said slowly, as if putting the pieces together as he spoke. "If the reports are true, the gunmen jumped out of the boat parked in the slip next to the *Admiral Risty* in the George Town Marina. None of the witnesses—that includes other boat owners, security guards, maintenance crew, the whole bit—ever saw anyone board or leave that boat in the last week or longer." Lukas snapped his fingers.

"So?"

"So that means Penh guessed first that Collin survived Hurricane Abigail and, second, that he would return to the same boat. Makes sense, right? Collin had spent a couple weeks on that boat in May, then used it again to get away from the FBI earlier this month. Typical of Penh. Probably had guys waiting in Panama, Huntington Beach, San Diego, and a bunch of other places he knew Collin had been or might go."

"And you think these guys played invisible all that time just waiting for Collin to show up?"

"Makes sense, doesn't it? Penh knows by now that Collin is pretty smart.

74

He would assume that if Collin were to come back, he would be suspicious, right?"

"Yeah, that makes sense. Collin's managed to avoid capture all these months. That's a logical assumption," said Rob.

"It's therefore logical for him to assume that Collin would suspect law enforcement to be on the lookout for him, right?"

"I'm with you. So Penh tells his guys to hide out until the cops are gone—probably has a way to know that, too—and alerts them to that fact knowing that Collin is more likely to come out of hiding when the coast is clear," said Rob, putting the last piece into the puzzle.

"You got it."

"That's great, Lukas. Glad we got that figured out. The big question now is: What's next and how can I help?"

"Do me a favor, OK?" said Lukas.

"Sure, Lukas. What do you need?"

"First, I need you to not use my name."

"But you're on a secure line . . ."

"I know, but I don't want it to become a habit. It's just better that way. Remember, people think I'm dead."

"OK, what else?" asked Rob.

"The second thing is I need to gather as much information as I can as quickly as I can. I'm getting limited bits and pieces from the intelligence community. The FBI seems to know where he is, too, but I can't see that they've done anything about it as yet."

"OK, what do you need me to do?" Rob offered. "Shall I talk to Henry and Sarah and find out what they know?"

"Maybe you should start with Emily. Remember, Sarah's in treatment for cancer. I don't want to do anything to upset her."

"Good point. You're always one step ahead of the rest of us."

"That's not all," said Lukas.

"Uh-oh, sounds like something really bad is coming."

"I'm afraid so. Putting two and two together, I think you need to get back to Huntington Beach. The phone lines are tapped at Emily's and the Cooks', so you can't call them to get this info. And, I think it would be a good idea to keep an eye on Henry and Sarah."

"What do you mean keep an eye on them, Lukas?"

"I mean protect them."

"Why?"

"The FBI has a two-man protective team following Emily, so apparently they're worried about her being in harm's way. But they haven't done the same for the Cook's, perhaps because they think Sarah's too fragile or because they know Collin risked it all to see Emily in Chicago and they figure there's some sort of link there that will help them."

"OK, I'll get back there as quickly as I can."

"Thatta boy. But, Rob, whatever you do, don't tell her or anyone about me or this conversation. It's extremely important that my cover not be blown."

"I'm with you, buddy. If there's anything I'm really good at, it's gathering important information and keeping secrets."

"I know. That's why I called you. But remember to stay off the phones and away from their homes. It would be best if you were not seen."

"Oh, yeah. Good point," said Rob, stirring some sugar into his coffee. "I'll charter a flight out of here as soon as I can. I'll have to cancel my golf game at Carnoustie, too. You know how long I've been waiting to play there? We're talking a PGA Tour course here. I wouldn't do that for just anyone."

Lukas tried to muster a chuckle. "I know. That's a big sacrifice on your part, my friend, but I'm afraid it's urgently necessary."

"You'll call me back, I assume?"

"In twenty-four hours, yes."

"I'm all over it. All for one and one for all, right?"

"That's the spirit," said Lukas, trying his best not to let his exhaustion show through the phone line. "Thanks, Rob. You're the best."

"Collin would do it for either of us if the tables were turned. He needs us right now," said Rob, a sudden seriousness drawing at his tone.

"We're all he's got," added Lukas.

Ninety minutes later, at London's Gatwick Airport, Rob climbed aboard a Gulfstream 6 headed to JFK in New York, joining an acquaintance and business associate he had worked with a few years ago. The Internet, with its myriad useful websites, provided wonderful tools for connecting people who needed something with people who had something to offer. In this case, a plane ride across the Atlantic. The modern-day, high-tech equivalent of the college ride board.

By 11:45 a.m. the next morning California time, Rob had landed at Lindbergh Airfield in San Diego in a corporate Learjet coming in from JFK owned by a young, high-tech millionaire whom Rob had helped during his company's start-up phase.

* * *

London, England
  June 15, 8:30 a.m. London Time

Junior Detective Nic Lancaster rushed into Alastair Montgomery's office precisely on time. He knew his boss was not a morning person, so he refrained from showing up early. Nic's enthusiasm was hard to tame on a normal day. Today, it reached epic proportions as he contemplated the ramifications of this meeting. He could hardly contain himself.

Nic Lancaster loved the game and loved the idea of getting promoted. His ambitions produced a jittery energy that drove him to excel. Failure was a bad word never to be spoken or considered anything but completely unacceptable. This drive, he knew, irritated the hard-drinking, ready-for-this-career-to-be-over Section Chief Montgomery. Today, however, his energy percolated from the knowledge that he alone held regarding their quarry, Collin Cook. The unsuspecting Alastair would be forced to take Nic seriously or face the shame of a scandal unleashed on YouTube for all the British press and public to consume.

Alastair's office door was partly open, so Nic knocked once as he pushed his way into Alastair's cluttered workspace. Alastair, coffee mug in hand, eyed Nic from behind a stack of file folders on his desk as he sauntered into the room. "You look ready for war there, Lancaster. What have you got?" His voice was husky, like it often was first thing in the morning. The eyelids were swollen, too. Another common occurrence.

"Me? Nothing. Nothing at all. I'm just ready to start my day, sir." Nic remained standing, his notepad and pen at the ready. Alastair despised many of the high-tech gadgets that had become common tools in law enforcement, most notably the tablet computer. Anyone who attempted to take notes on one in his presence received a thorough lecture for carrying his brain around in his hands instead of using the one in his head.

"You can't pull that on me. I'm a detective and have been since you were a tot. Don't you go forgetting that now." Alastair tried to clear the rasp from his throat.

"Right. It's just that I've gotten some very good news lately."

There was a pause while Alastair studied his brightest, most ambitious Cyber Crime Task Force rookie. "Well, out with it now. I haven't got all day."

"It's nothing, really, sir."

"Can't be nothing. Not with that look on your face. Let me guess: You're having a baby?" Alastair cackled out loud at his own joke. The cackling soon turned into a bronchial cough, followed by a round of throat clearing.

Nic clinched his teeth and shook his head. "No, sir. I'm not married. Not even dating anyone at the moment."

"Married to the job, I know. Problem is, I haven't seen you this excited since you told me you had that Cook character pinned down in Florida."

Nic's head shot up, his face stone still.

"No, you're not still working on that one, are you? Not after he died out there in the ocean?"

"That's just it, sir. He's not dead. He's quite alive and pulling half a million dollars out of a bank in the Caymans. Just yesterday morning, he did."

Alastair dropped into his chair and looked up at the ceiling, trying to digest this morsel of intelligence. "I assume you have some sort of proof, do you?"

"I do, sir. Shall I show you?"

"No, no. That's not necessary. You're sure it's him?"

"I am and so is Crabtree."

"You're saying the FBI admits he's alive?"

"Maybe not the whole FBI, but Crabtree for sure."

"What're they doing about it?"

"He's working on arranging an intercept as we speak." Checking his watch, Nic corrected himself. "Well, as of yesterday afternoon his time, I suppose."

"No word on that yet, eh?"

"No, sir. But I presume I'll have confirmation from him by day's end."

Alastair sat quietly, staring at nothing. "Why are you working on this? That case was closed when the FBI declared the man a goner and now you tell me you're dedicating your valuable time to a closed file on a dead man?" Alastair's face was reddening as he spoke, working to control his emotions. "I could run you back to a beat cop for this, you know."

"I doubt that, sir. With all due respect," said Nic, the sarcasm in his voice not well hidden. "I've got a lovely video of you exiting the flat of a certain young lady—the daughter of a member of Parliament—at lunchtime. Certainly you remember that, sir. I believe you were calendared for a non-existent meeting with Scotland Yard."

"What are you on about Lancaster?"

"Would you like to see the video, sir?"

"Video?" Alastair's face went bright red.

"Not that sort of video. That's plain creepy. The one I've got shows you giving your girl, the MP's daughter, quite a long good-bye kiss at her front door before you shuttle off in a taxi. Right in the middle of the working day. Has all the makings of a fine tabloid scandal, if I do say so myself."

Alastair had to back down gracefully. The last thing he wanted was to flush his pension down the toilet while the newspapers mocked him to scorn. He remained silent as Nic wagged his cell phone in front of him. "Knock that off, Lancaster. OK, you've got my attention. But let me remind you, neither of us can afford to be chasing ghosts at this point. Not after all the mishaps before."

"Right, sir. I'm well aware of the embarrassments we've suffered but imagine the triumph of nailing this guy. Or, better yet, bringing down Penh and his syndicate."

Alastair perked up. "That would be a coup, would it not? But my point is that you were to be working on your assigned case-load, which no longer includes Collin Cook."

"If it's any consolation, I've only been working on this case after hours. I've stayed until midnight or later nearly every night this past week. I work on the assignments from you during the day, and I'm all caught up on them," Nic said, his jowls quivering with pent-up frustration.

"Right. Brief me on the Cook case before I leave tonight, in any case. I expect you won't commit any Interpol assets to another one of your red herrings."

"No, sir. The FBI is handling it. I'm just working my contacts in the islands."

"So long as we're clear, then. They'd have my hide if they knew you were spending your time chasing a ghost. Imagine what would happen . . ." Alastair's words trailed off as he shook the thought from his head and began combing through a stack of papers on his desk.

"I assume, however, that the hunt for Pho Nam Penh is still active and still a priority, is it not?" asked Nic, trying to sound all-business.

Alastair answered without looking up, still intent on finding the right file. "Of course it is. He's still Prime Suspect Number One for the RBS hack job, as well as half a dozen smaller ones. Now that Cook is out of the picture, we need to find him somehow."

"Right. I presume since he's still one of our top priorities, that committing ourselves and our resources in pursuit of him or his accomplices still has patent approval, does it not?"

"Yeah, that's right, Nic. You see the big picture now," Alastair muttered through his distraction.

Nic smiled to himself and waited for Alastair to find what he was looking for. He casually reached into his pocket and turned off the voice recording app running on his phone. Mission accomplished. He had his angle.

Chapter Eleven

L os Angeles, California
June 15, 6:45 a.m. Pacific Time

McCoy found Crabtree in the hallway, stirring cream into a cup of coffee fresh out of the vending machine. 1100 Wilshire Boulevard's finest. Without so much as a glance, Crabtree greeted him with a hearty "Good morning, Spinner" long before he had entered the customary range for such a greeting, the distinctive clacking of his cowboy boots on the linoleum having given him away.

"I wish it was good," replied McCoy. "Have you seen what's going on in the Caribbean?"

"What? You mean that tropical depression off the coast of Cuba that turned east and is heading toward our man?"

"Yeah, that one," said Spinner.

"It doesn't look good, does it?" said Crabtree, shaking his head.

"No. A small boat advisory has been sent out. All small craft have been warned to leave and avoid the area, but Collin seems to be heading straight toward it—again," said McCoy.

"I know. I saw that, too. Can't say it surprises me. Maybe by now he considers himself invincible."

"Well, either that or the fact that there are four armed men onboard . . ."

"Maybe. Unless it's part of a hoax intended to throw us off."

"That's a long way to go for a hoax, don't you think?"

"Who knows? Got any brilliant ideas on how we're going to bring him home safely?" asked McCoy.

"I just got off the phone with the Coast Guard. They've got their hands full already trying to prepare for potential rescues and/or evacuations. They don't have the resources to go that far out of their jurisdiction to chase a guy we claimed was dead." Reggie grimaced as he spoke these last words.

"Can't say I blame them. Cook's not their priority. He's ours. Maybe we can get some help from the navy," said McCoy.

Crabtree took another long swig of his coffee, stared at the contents of the cup, and winced.

"The US Navy?" said Crabtree.

"Yeah, the navy."

"You think we should ask the navy again? Remember how the navy searched the same boat last month and found nothing?" said Reggie.

"We need the SEALs to go in and do a rescue," Spinner said. "That's Collin's only chance."

"Then his chances just went from slim to zero," Reggie said with a sigh. "They couldn't get there in time if they tried. Plus, there's no way we'd get that requisition through the ranks. Come on, be serious."

"Maybe Lancaster's got some magic up those British sleeves of his."

Crabtree nodded his head slowly as he thought about the overly ambitious Nic Lancaster in London. "Let's see if he does."

* * *

Western Caribbean Sea, 310 miles south of Grand Cayman; 100 miles north of Providencia Island

June 15 10:07 a.m. Caribbean Time

The *Admiral Risty* sliced swiftly through the gentle swells on its southerly course under full sail, having left the doldrums behind in the early hours of the morning. With a gentle breeze blowing, she was able to maintain a speed of fifteen knots without the use of her engine.

Even though they were moving, and the hijackers had been placated, Captain Sewell's face sagged. With no sleep and the constant strain of being threatened by men armed with semi-automatic weapons and short tempers, his mood was foul. He remained silent and distant, working through the loss of Tog and figuring out the best plan to get rid of these criminals.

The ascending musical scale of a phone's ring tone rose above the flapping of the sails and the rush of the wind. Stinky retrieved the phone from his hip pocket, pulled its antennae to its full length, and cupped his hand over it as he spoke his greeting. He listened for a moment. "OK," he said, and held the phone toward the Captain. "My boss wants to speak to you."

The Captain eyed the thick satellite phone and took it from Stinky's outstretched hand. "Gordon Sewell here," he said.

"Captain Sewell. It is a pleasure to speak with you. I will be brief as I am sure you are presently occupied with the demands of piloting your craft."

"What is it you want?" said the Captain, not bothering to hide his disdain.

"Captain, the safety of my men is of utmost importance to me, as I'm sure the safety of your men is to you." The boss spoke with a high-brow, proper tone and precise pronunciation, showing his British university education. It bothered Sewell from the get-go.

"What's your point?" asked the Captain, cutting off what he supposed would be a long-winded soliloquy.

"My point is, sir: you are heading toward very dangerous conditions. I'm sure you are aware of the storm mounting in the Caribbean, to your south and east."

"I am aware of it, yes."

"Good. Then I would like to know your plans to keep my men and yours safe."

"We are heading to the Island of Providencia. The island is mountainous, especially on the north end. Along the northwest side of the island is a harbor that should provide a safe place to anchor and wait out the storm. I am heading there."

"Why not turn west toward Nicaragua?"

"The Nicaraguans have been notoriously unfriendly toward sailors. I'd rather not end up in one of their prisons. Providencia is roughly the same distance and with the prevailing winds and currents, we will arrive there faster and with fewer worries," explained the Captain.

"That's very good, Captain," said Penh in a condescending tone. "I hope for your sake and the sake of your men you know what you're doing."

"I don't need a coward like you to tell me over the phone how to run my own ship," barked the Captain.

There was a pause on the other end. When Penh spoke, his tone was even and controlled. "You are angry with me, though we have never spoken to each other before."

"You send your monsters here to my boat with their guns. They intimidate and kill innocent people. I suppose they did so at your command, as if this is some sort of play and we are merely characters on your stage. Why don't you come here and do it yourself? I tell you: it's because you're not man enough. You are a coward."

Again, Penh waited before answering. "You think shooting of one of your men was unwarranted? If that is the case, I suggest you bring it up with your passenger, Mr. Cook. He could have avoided such violence had he made different choices."

This time Captain Sewell was silent, so Penh continued. "Yes, that's right. Your friend, Mr. Cook, has possession of a large quantity of my money. I gave him a choice to hand it over peacefully, but he chose not to cooperate with me. He chose to allow your crew member to be shot while he refused to speak the truth."

"That's rubbish. He is an honest man."

"Maybe in some circumstances he is honest, but when it comes to money, he's certainly not. You see, Captain Sewell, Collin Cook stole millions of dollars from me. I simply asked him to return it. That's all. When he refused, my men showed him the consequences of his poor decisions. Now that he knows just how serious we are, I expect that when we get to Panama, he will give me back my money so that you and your crew can continue living. Any deviation from that course will bring about more severe penalties."

"You're threatening me? On the phone? First your boys murder one of my men. Then they dump his body in the sea—no proper funeral or last rites, no last words or memorial service. Complete disrespect. That is an insult. It is unacceptable to me and to my men. Now you call to threaten me?" The Captain's icy demeanor sparked to a flame of indignation.

"Captain Sewell, let me remind you that you are in no position to raise your voice to me or to lecture me about what is acceptable and what is not. My men have boarded your ship and have taken necessary actions to secure your cooperation because you have been harboring a known criminal, a man wanted by the FBI and Interpol for crimes against the United States and Great Britain. He has stolen millions of dollars from me and you have protected him. Did you expect to do so with impunity?"

"I don't know who you are. I don't know anything about the money or the crimes you say Collin has committed. And I don't care. He is my client. He pays me to take him sailing. That's how I make my living. I don't judge," the Captain said, clipping his phrases to keep his emotions in check and to ensure he didn't say too much.

"I'm sure that is not how the authorities will see it, Captain. You are aiding and abetting a known international fugitive. There are laws against that."

"I know nothing about his background. I only know that he is a good client and he pays well," the Captain said, trying to force calm.

"He pays you well because he is using my money," Penh replied through clinched teeth. After an audible intake of air, he continued. "Very well. We'll let the authorities deal with that portion of your involvement, if they so choose. I will deal with my own immediate needs by making this a business transaction. I will pay you $250,000 to take my men safely to Panama. Once my business with Mr. Cook is complete, you and your crew will be paid handsomely for your trouble and you will be allowed to carry on as you see fit."

"What about Mr. Cook? What will become of him?" asked the Captain.

"Mr. Cook is none of your concern. I am now your client. I will be paying you for your services, not Mr. Cook." The man's tone was firm and commanding, as if the decision had already been made.

Before the Captain could argue or reject the offer, the line went dead. The Captain pulled the phone away from his ear and studied the screen. He shook his head and frowned. "Damn him!" The Captain continued to hold the phone while he steered until Stinky put out his hand and motioned for him to return it.

* * *

London, England
June 15, 7:45 p.m. London Time

It had proven to be a day filled with futility and frustration for the ever-hopeful rising star on Interpol London's Cyber Crime Task Force. Nic Lancaster, working on his fifth cup of coffee since mid-afternoon, leaned back in his chair and stretched his arms and torso. He hadn't left his cube since lunch other than short bathroom breaks, a couple of trips to the vending machine for coffee and junk food, and a jaunt to the lobby downstairs to pick up delivery food. An open bag of Walker's Worcester Sauce Crisps—smoky bacon flavor—and a can of Dr. Pepper sat on one side of his computer monitor, a Styrofoam box of cold, half-eaten fish and chips on the other.

Despite his focused efforts, he had no progress to report. A text message on his phone from Alastair stared at him mockingly. He typed and backspaced repeatedly, trying to devise a clever response that would be truthful, yet optimistic. In short, he had contacted every branch of every military he could think of, as well as every American and British law enforcement agency listed. None would agree to hunt the ghost of Collin Cook. He was dead, remember. The only positive note he could sound was that the Colombians had a naval vessel in the area ready to assist distressed craft in the vicinity surrounding the Caribbean Islands they controlled, including Providencia, the closest habitable land to Nic's last ping of Collin's secret phone. The Colombians indicated that if there was an emergency, they would do what they could to help, but would not promise anything specifically. That was something, at least.

After a dozen attempts at crafting just the right message, Nic was finally satisfied with what he had typed: "Cook nearing Providencia Island. Colombian naval cutter in the vicinity. Could intercept our man within hours if an emergency were to arise." He pressed "Send" and drew a deep breath. *A whole day's work and that's all you've got to show for yourself. Pathetic.*

He emailed Crabtree and McCoy a similar message. Crabtree's reply was quick and to the point. "We're not getting any cooperation on this side, either. With a storm on its way, seems likely they are heading toward safe harbor at Providencia, don't you think?"

"Yes, that seems likely. I'm not having much luck either, but it's more than we had at the start of the day. Besides, Providencia is not that large an island. Shouldn't be that difficult to find a sailboat with four gunmen aboard," Nic typed.

"Depends on getting some assistance finding them," Crabtree replied.

"That is a bit of an inconvenient truth at the moment. I'm trying to sort something out. Good news is the storm is not yet getting any stronger as it moves westward."

"Saw that, too. Let's hope for the best, but some predict the warmer waters to the west will give it more strength. Something to watch, for sure. Keep me apprised, will you?"

"Roger that," Nic's email read. He sent this last message, then stood and surveyed the vast, open office. Only a handful of other cubicles had lights on in them. Working late didn't bother him so long as it moved him toward his goal. He couldn't help but wonder if this Collin Cook case was going to help him rise or bring him down. "Follow your instincts," he had been told so many times in his training. "A good detective has good instincts. Develop them. Trust them. Follow them."

Six weeks after receiving the assignment to bring in Collin Cook, Nic's confidence in his instincts was at an all-time low. He was out on a limb, as they say, all by himself. Words from another lesson he had heard so many times from his father echoed in his mind: "The path to the top is going to be lonely."

Chapter Twelve

L a Jolla, California; Scripps Cancer Research Center
June 15, 12:20 p.m. Pacific Time

Lost in thought, Emily's heels beat a steady rhythm on the short pile carpet as she marched down the hallway from the lunchroom. She carried her tablet in one hand and a Tupperware container she had retrieved from the refrigerator in the other. Lunch would be a quick salad from home eaten alone at her desk while she analyzed data. The usual.

In the lunchroom, she had realized she had nothing to drink. One of those all-natural juices from the machine sounded good, but she had no money with her. She strode back to her office, then realized she had left her purse in her car, so she tramped out to the parking lot. Crabtree and McCoy's early morning interrogation yesterday had thrown her out of her morning ritual, not only yesterday, but today as well. Their insistence on providing her protection had proven to be a distraction this morning as she watched the two young agents in the gray Taurus park right behind her car. She had felt their eyes on her as she got out of the car, which apparently made her leave her purse behind.

She shuddered at the thought of her privacy being invaded as she crossed the asphalt toward her white BMW. The two agents were still there, still watching steadfastly and dutifully.

As Emily retrieved her purse, she couldn't help but notice how the sun shone and a pleasant breeze blew in from the ocean. The morning's fog had dissipated, replaced by a lazy, inviting warmth. The weather was too perfect not to enjoy. On days like this, Emily often took her work outside during lunchtime. The problem was the two FBI guys.

The younger one in the passenger's seat sat up as she approached and elbowed his partner, whose seat was partially reclined. Leaning forward, the young agent kept a hawk-like watch over her as she gathered her purse from her back seat. She smiled and waved at him as she turned back toward the building, pointing at the purse and shrugging. He blushed and waved awkwardly in return. His half-asleep partner slugged him in the arm and chided him. "Don't do that. You're a professional, for Pete's sake."

Emily stopped by her office to retrieve her Tupperware and tablet, then to the vending machine in the break room, then out the back door toward the tree-lined walking path across the street from the Scripps facility. The weather was just too inviting; she had to get out and enjoy it without the company of the two armed agents. Several hundred yards down that walking path were a handful of benches that bordered a grassy field that she frequented on days like this. She needed some fresh air and right now a good stroll in the warm sunshine away from watchful eyes sounded like the perfect solution.

* * *

The two thugs in the white Sprinter van circled the Scripps campus in search of an inconspicuous place from which to watch Emily's car. The gray Taurus with the two FBI agents was hard to miss. The thugs knew they had to avoid catching the attention of its occupants. The passenger was absorbed with the images being streamed to his phone from the tiny cameras he had set up near Emily's office. "She just walked out to her car," he said. "But then walked back in the building."

As the driver approached the Scripps campus along North Torrey Pines Road, the passenger told him to slow down. "You won't believe this," said the younger man. He pointed the phone's screen toward the driver, who ignored it.

The driver's eyes were fixed, studying something through the window. "I believe what I see," he said, as he pointed straight ahead. A sandy-haired woman, wearing a beige silk blouse and maroon pants that shimmered in the sunlight and flowed as she hurried along, was exiting the building through a side door halfway down the block.

The driver waited at the stop sign and watched as their quarry stalked away from the campus, glancing anxiously behind and all around before stepping into the crosswalk not more than a hundred yards ahead of them. The tattooed driver stepped on the gas. As the van moved closer and she approached the halfway point of the intersection, a look of panicked recognition overtook her countenance. She stopped in her tracks, mouth agape, as she recognized the speeding van and its occupants.

The driver looked at his passenger as he stomped on the gas. His young partner was already preparing himself to jump out of the van. He had a cloth in his hand and was pouring the solution onto it. Emily began to run from them, but the driver crossed the lane toward the opposite curb, cutting off her route to the walking path and the relative safety of the small clusters of midday walkers. She burst into a sprint as best she could in her dress shoes, but she didn't get far. Shock and terror had stolen most of her breath, making it impossible for her to scream loud enough for anyone to hear.

The spiked one jumped out as the driver slammed on the brakes. Within seconds, the passenger had caught her. She tried again to scream, but the sound didn't travel far. She tried to fight, but the young man was agile, quick, and experienced. He deftly avoided her jabs and kicks and moved in to overpower her. As he did, he wrapped an arm around her neck, applied the cloth to her nose, and dragged her back toward the van. The inked driver hopped over the duffle bag between the two front seats to open the side cargo door. The younger partner turned to sit on the deck with his prey in his arms. The driver grabbed an arm and helped drag her limp body into the van. The passenger slammed the side door shut as the driver leapt back into his seat. He pulled the shifter down into Drive and sped away before anyone in the area was able to react to the commotion.

As the driver weaved his way through the winding suburban streets of La Jolla toward the freeway, the passenger rolled Emily over, pulled her arms behind her back, wrapped her wrists and ankles in duct tape and plastered a strip of it across her mouth, as well. His eyes ventured over her contours.

"Don't do anything to her. Not yet," called the driver as he watched from the rearview mirror.

The passenger sat back on his haunches, licked his lips, and responded. "There has to be some reward for our work."

"Not now. Wait."

The younger thug shook his head at the older driver who watched him through the rearview mirror. He dragged his prisoner to the back and fastened a thick nylon strap around her torso and locked it to a metal brace on the sidewall, just as he had done with Mrs. Cook, who sat strapped to the opposite side of the van, slumped over and unconscious.

The passenger took another long look at Emily, licking his lips as his eyes danced. The driver barked again, which got him moving back into the passenger's seat. The young passenger beamed with pride as he took his seat and buckled in as the van sped up the southbound Interstate 5 onramp. "Instead of one, we deliver both. Surely the boss will be pleased with our next report," he said with a hiss of satisfaction.

The driver grinned. "Yes, and we will have something a bit more pleasant to look at."

The two men cackled as they celebrated their great fortune.

* * *

Mike Zimmerman paced the hallway outside his office. He walked down to Emily's door, peered inside, and walked back to report his findings to the stranger waiting patiently in one of his chairs.

"She's still not there," he repeated for the third time in the ten minutes since the man arrived.

"Maybe she had lunch plans," said the stranger.

"Oh, I don't know. That doesn't happen often. And when it does, at least one of us in the group knows about it."

"Maybe she's running late from another appointment," offered the man, who sat back with one foot resting on the other knee. He was much less anxious than Mike. "Don't worry about it."

"But it's past one o'clock. She never stays out to lunch this long. I'm going to text her."

Rob Howell, seated comfortably in Mike Zimmerman's office, watched with amusement as his host fussed about in an agitated, obsessive-compulsive fit to satisfy Rob's simple request to take Emily out to lunch. Rob was an accomplished man, although barely thirty-one years old. He had been very successful at many of his endeavors. Developing relationships with people of all types and from all backgrounds was his specialty. Today, however, he had failed to do so, finding himself unable to calm Mike Zimmerman down or assure him that everything would be fine. Even his attempts to make small talk fell woefully short of the mark. Instead, the short man with the neatly trimmed beard paced the hallway nervously.

As time ticked on, Mike only grew antsier. Dr. Burns, he said, was not answering her cell phone nor responding to texts. This, Mike noted, was highly unusual. His pacing became more frenetic and his reports more worry-laden. Rob, however, leaned back and just smiled at his inability to make inroads with Emily's boss. The Asperger's kids, no matter their age, always gave him trouble.

* * *

Western Caribbean Sea, 50 miles north of Providencia Island
  June 15, 3:46 p.m. Caribbean Time

The four gunmen aboard the *Admiral Risty* kept watch over their captives, rotating positions periodically. The one Collin had dubbed "Grunter" now sat in the cockpit and kept a keen eye on the Captain and his instruments. The Captain had apprised them all of his intentions to seek safe harbor along the western shore of Providencia Island, one of several small islands clustered due south of the Caymans and due east of Nicaragua. It was the closest land mass that afforded the best protection from the storm.

Captain Sewell pointed out the mounting storm to the east and its projected course. Grunter, his gun trained on the Captain, leaned forward and followed the trace of the Captain's finger. A plume of swirling white lay at the far-left edge of the navigation screen, it being oriented to their southerly course. The *Admiral* was a blinking speck on the far right. Grunter grunted and nodded his head.

The crew was now battling increasing head winds, so they remained busy on the deck gybing as the *Admiral* tacked at high speed through the blustery conditions. The mighty vessel was racing against time, the Captain and his crew aware of the perils that lay ahead.

Sensing Grunter's uneasiness, the Captain pointed at the screen and shouted above the noise of the wind and the sails, "That storm is sixty miles to our east, moving this way at ten to fifteen miles per hour." His finger traced a line going east to west across the screen. "The Island of Providencia is fifty miles southwest." The Captain pointed to a spot beyond the screen. "We are traveling at nineteen knots per hour," he explained, pointing at the speed indicator on the GPS. "We'll be okay." He caught Jaime's eye as he said this, arching his eyebrow slightly as he did. Jaime's nearly imperceptible acknowledgment was a longer-than-normal blink and nod of the head. What Grunter didn't realize and what the Captain wanted only his crew to know was that they were not going to make it. The storm would be on top of them an hour before they reached the island. The GPS showed their speed, but with the zigzagging they were doing, their course was not a straight line. Therefore, they were not making nineteen knots per hour toward their goal. No, maybe eleven or twelve.

Jaime called over to Rojas in their colloquial, dialectic Spanish to make sure he heard. Rojas signaled with a thumbs-up and relayed the message to Miguel, who also signaled his understanding. Everyone except Collin, who hadn't seen the sun since he came on board, understood the peril they faced.

* * *

Below decks, Collin's body was slowly recovering from the excessive abuse heaped upon it during the previous day and Mr. Green's assault during his failed uprising in the night. His head was clearing, the swelling around his eyes had gone down, and the lacerations in his mouth were mending. However, his hands were still zip-tied behind his back. The skin around his wrists was shredded, raw, and puffy. The muscles of his arms and shoulders were stiff and ached from lack of movement and from trying to hold as still as possible to avoid more damage to his wrists. A fresh bruise had formed on his cheek from the blow Mr. Green had inflicted and his ribs still ached from the initial kick that he never saw coming.

Lack of food had made him weak, but the lack of water was placing him in dire straits. Stinky and his gang only allowed him a few sips at a time and only when they fed him a crust of bread, a bite of fruit, or a slice of cheese. His mouth was parched, and his skin was clammy. Collin had stopped sweating, despite the stuffy, ninety-five-degree temperatures inside the cabin. Stinky had made sure all windows remained closed. He wanted Collin to suffer. The lack of perspiration was a bad sign, and Collin knew it. Plus, his head was pounding—another bad sign—making it difficult to think.

Collin lay on the same lower bunk he had been on since this ordeal began, straining to hear what was going on above him. He heard the Captain yelling about the coming storm, but the details were literally lost in the wind. There was too much noise from the slapping of water against the hull, the pounding of feet on the deck, and the clanking of lines and riggings against the masts for him to make out all of the words. But he had heard "storm now moving toward us," "safe harbor," and "islands to our south" and felt comforted that the Captain, who knew the Caribbean like a well-used diary, had everything in hand. Nonetheless, sleep was not forthcoming. Thoughts of water made it impossible and blocked out everything else from his mind. His craving for moisture was now all-consuming.

Through half-shut eyes, Collin watched his new guard across the cabin. This was the long-haired one he'd only seen once before. Long Hair paid Collin little attention since Tog's death. The constant jostling of the ship kept him looking pensive and uneasy. With one hand, Long Hair held his semi-automatic Uzi. The other hand braced the bulkhead. As the sea grew rougher, Long Hair's attention to Collin grew lighter. The man looked out the small windows above the galley or behind him, shaking his head periodically.

Collin knew there was an opportunity opening up. He just didn't know how to take advantage of it in his weakened and battered state. The failure of his previous attempt and its repercussions lingered but didn't deter him from trying again. Forcing himself to concentrate, he closed his eyes and tried to reformulate his earlier plan, then add to it. Putting thoughts together and keeping them from straying toward his need for water proved even more difficult than he had expected. His ability to move was restricted. His coordination, balance, and strength were impaired even more so than before. Everything that could be used as a tool or a weapon was out of reach because his hands were tied behind him.

The planning effort was exhausting. There were so many ifs and contingencies to consider. Plus, the potential for additional violence against him loomed in his mind. Within minutes, Collin's strength gave out and he closed his eyes in defeat. There were four gunmen. He could only see one, but he felt another one was somewhere below-decks, either asleep or standing guard. Collin realized that even if he could close the distance between himself and Long Hair fast enough to catch him off-guard while keeping his balance, the only thing he would be able to do is kick him. Could he kick him hard enough and in the right place to incapacitate him? Even if he could, chances are the other guard would once again beat him senseless. What then? In his current state, this was the best plan he could come up with and it was doomed to fail.

Collin's eyes closed and his head sank into the mattress. The boat was being buffeted by wind and waves, rocking him vigorously from side to side as he tried to lay still and think. The movement caused the tight plastic band around his wrists to cut deeper into the worn skin, drawing fresh blood. He tried to steady himself by pushing his legs into the bulkhead at the end of the bed, but that did little to prevent his upper body from rolling back and forth.

The storm he had heard referenced by the Captain had arrived. Looking around, Collin realized he and Long Hair were alone. Everyone else had escaped topside for fresh air. Collin's legs shook and his head rolled from side to side with nervous energy. This restlessness came from the claustrophobia. He had been trapped below deck for more than thirty-six hours and the confinement was killing him, making him crazy and willing to do anything to get out.

Across the cabin, Long Hair struggled to endure the increasing tidal action and constant movement of the boat. Each tumble over a swell and each sideways turn through the surf as the boat tacked against the headwind drained more and more color from his face. His muted, involuntary moans gave away his physical suffering. Collin sat himself up and double checked his surroundings. He weighed his options and reviewed his plan of attack, realizing he was willing to risk the threat of physical pain in order to escape the dreads of confinement.

Now seemed like a perfect time to launch into Long Hair if he could just keep his balance.

Chapter Thirteen

L a Jolla, California, Scripps Cancer Research Center
   June 15 1:22 p.m. Pacific Time

In the midst of amusedly watching Mike Zimmerman pace and shuffle, Rob's cell phone buzzed. He checked the screen; not sure he should allow the distraction. Seeing that it was Lukas and knowing it hadn't yet been twenty-four hours since they spoke last, he answered. "Lukas? What's up?"

"Didn't I tell you not to use my name?"

"Sorry, I forgot."

"Are you alone?" asked Lukas.

"No, I'm here with Emily's boss, Mike. We're waiting for her to show up so I can take her to lunch."

"You need to politely excuse yourself. Your lunch date is not going to happen."

"What are you talking about?" said Rob, as he rose from the chair, dread spreading through his gut and across his face.

"I'll tell you in a minute. Just get out to your car," said Lukas.

Holding the phone to his chest and gesturing that it was important, Rob shook Mike's hand, thanked him for his hospitality, excused himself, and told him not to worry about Emily. He would catch up with her another time.

"Rob," Lukas called.

"Yeah, I'm here, just exiting the building," Rob said as he returned the phone to his ear.

"Listen, there are a couple of FBI guys on protective duty for Emily. I don't want them to see you, you hear?"

"I hear you. Where are they?"

"In a gray Taurus, parked near Emily's white BMW. Do you see them?"

"Should've guessed." Rob stopped short at the large glass doors leading to the parking lot, searching for both the BMW and the Taurus. "I don't see either car, but the parking lot is pretty full. I parked around the side, near the street, so I should be able to get out quickly and without being seen."

"Good. Keep your eye out for them. They're supposed to be on protective detail, but apparently Emily objected to them following her around all day—felt they would interfere—so they agreed to stay outside the building during the workday. I'm afraid that was a bad decision, though I can understand the reasoning."

"What do you mean a bad decision?"

"Are you in your car yet?" asked Lukas.

"I'm just about there," said Rob, as the car chirped. Once inside, he continued. "Tell me what's going on, Lukas."

"Don't use my name," Lukas chided again. "I have two bits of bad news to share with you."

"Sounds like one of them might have something to do with Emily and will explain why she's not here to have lunch with me."

"Very perceptive, my friend. The local police have taken witness statements from two people who watched a young woman matching Emily's description get hauled away in a large white van not far from where you're parked right now," Lukas said solemnly.

"You've got to be kidding. Must've happened right before I got here. I can't believe it," Rob barked as he punched the seat next to him. His breathing resembled that of an angry bull.

"Look, Rob, it's not your fault. Don't blame yourself."

"I knew I should have called first to let her know I was coming."

"But I told you not to, remember? I didn't want her worried and I certainly didn't want the FBI listening to your conversation with her. You need to stay disentangled."

"Are you sure it was her that was abducted?" asked Rob, trying to keep a hopeful tone.

"To confirm, I pinged her phone. If the GPS coordinates are accurate and if she has her phone with her, she's sitting on the median of the 5 Freeway about three miles south of your location. So, I decided to try the cell phone Collin gave her and found that she is heading south on Interstate 805 and my FBI liaison assures me that their guys and her BMW are still in the parking lot at Scripps. I'll keep a watch on that and figure something out."

"This is just great. I come out here to help keep her safe and this happens before I even have a chance," Rob said, still snorting angrily.

"Actually, you're supposed to get information from her and protect Sarah and Henry, but things are happening way too fast for any of that to matter now," said Lukas.

"What do you mean? Is that the other piece of bad news?"

"You're going to like this even less," Lukas said grimly. "They've taken Sarah Cook, as well."

"Those sick bastards," Rob yelled as he once again punched the passenger's seat.

"Yeah, they roughed up Henry, too. He called it in around eleven this morning after the nurse he'd hired to help Sarah found him tied up and gagged on the floor of his garage."

"Is he all right?"

"You know Henry. He's a tough old guy. But he's worried sick about his wife," said Lukas. "Apparently, the cancer treatments are really wiping her out, so she's weak and frail to begin with."

Rob sucked in a breath between his teeth and held it for several seconds. "First, what do you know about Henry's condition?"

"I haven't got the details yet. I'm hoping you can get over to the hospital to find out and be with him."

"Yes, I'll head up there right away, but I have to tell you this makes me sick. No, it makes me mad, real mad. If I find these guys—"

"Look, Rob. I understand your anger. It's natural in situations like these, but you have to put it aside for the time being. Anger causes one to make mistakes and act rashly. We can't afford that right now. We have to stay sharp and focused."

"I'm with you," said Rob, forcing calmness upon himself. "Just tell me where to go and what to do to help. I want to get to these guys before they do anything to hurt either one of those ladies."

"I know, me too. I'm making arrangements as we speak," said Lukas. Rob could hear the clicking of a keyboard in the background.

"The thought of Sarah being kidnapped or hurt or mistreated really burns me up. She's like another mom to me—I can't let anything happen to her."

"I know, Rob," said Lukas, sounding distracted. "Time is of the essence. Sarah is in no condition to withstand this sort of thing. And poor Henry is probably beside himself with worry."

"Where do I go? What can I do to help?" asked Rob.

"Go to Huntington Beach Hospital and take care of Henry. Let him know the FBI are working on finding Sarah, OK?"

"Can I go with them? With a gun so I can shoot these guys?"

"Tempting, isn't it?" said Lukas. "You'd have my OK as long as you promised to plug them once for me, too."

"That's the spirit," said Rob, a hint of a smile returning to his countenance.

"Seriously, I think it would be better for you to go see Henry," said Lukas.

"Not nearly as much fun as shooting the bad guys now, is it?" said Rob.

"I know, I know. Don't tell him too much, and don't make any promises, but let him know there are people working hard to find Sarah and bring her and Emily home safely."

"I understand. I'll play it safe—give him something to hope for without making any promises. Makes sense."

"Maybe you should contact Collin's brother and sister," Lukas suggested. "They should know what's going on with their parents."

* * *

Western Caribbean Sea, 45 miles north of Providencia Island
  June 15 4:04 p.m. Caribbean Time

Captain Sewell stood at the helm of the *Admiral Risty*, clutching the grips of the boat's wheel. The winds from the southeast were maintaining speeds of twenty miles per hour with gusts upward of thirty-five. With the intention of reaching the Island of Providencia ahead of the worst part of the storm, the Captain ordered "full sails" in order to maximize speed. It was a risky move with potentially heavier winds on their way.

His crew members prepared for stormy conditions. The wind rushed at them like a mountain stream in the spring, feral and erratic. Steady rain began to fall, so foul weather gear was passed out to everyone topside, even the three gunmen.

The winds had created a swell coming from the southeast, causing the *Admiral* to list and rock as it mounted the waves at roughly a thirty-degree angle. Every man clung to something solid as the boat tipped and swayed in the mounting surf.

The crew positioned themselves along the railing on the port side. They were tethered by lines that would keep them from falling overboard but would allow them to lean outward and use their weight to keep the boat from being pushed over as it sliced southward through the west-blowing wind. Before manning their posts, the Captain had instructed them to don life vests.

"Give us those, too," Stinky demanded, aiming his gun at the Captain.

"Very well, but you will have to open that locker on the bow," the Captain shouted above the noise, pointing to a rectangular holding compartment near the nose of the boat. "My men cannot help you right now. They must hike out like that or we will tip over. I must steer. You get the life jackets in that locker."

Stinky glared at the Captain as he held tight to the railing near the cockpit, watching as the bow repeatedly dove into the waves, sending a torrent of water across the deck. He raised his voice in his native tongue and pointed at the locker. After Stinky repeated himself, Grunter reluctantly shuffled toward the locker, keeping both hands on the railing as he picked his way forward. He lost his footing several times as the waves washed past him, and he finally resorted to crawling his way there. While carefully holding the railing with one hand, Grunter lifted the locker's lid and retrieved the vests, his knuckles white from clinging to the rail so tightly as he crawled back to the cockpit. Stinky, Grunter, and Long Hair struggled in the turbulent weather to get their vests on, which they did one at a time while the other two maintained a watchful eye on the Captain and crew.

But the Captain and crew were far too preoccupied with their battle to keep the *Admiral* upright and on course for the Island of Providencia to pay Stinky or his fellow hijackers any attention.

With each mighty gust, the sails would fill and begin to push the *Admiral* over to its starboard side. The Captain would turn to the west and the crew would lean hard, then he would return to his southerly heading as it dissipated, just to do it again moments later. With the help of the wind, the *Admiral* was making nearly twenty knots in the direction of Providencia's safe harbor. It was a constant struggle, however, to stay on course and not allow the wind to blow them due west into the exposed shoals and rocky shores of Nicaragua's coast. The Captain was far less familiar with that area and its dangers, preferring to steer toward Providencia and the perils there that he had experienced before.

The Captain's eyes moved constantly. He monitored the sails, the riggings, the four-to-six-foot swells all around them, and the array of instruments in front of him. The radar, GPS, and depth gauge occupied a portion of his attention. Red and orange blotches on the radar screen indicated heavier rain fall lay to their east, but would be upon them before too long. Somewhere within the next hour or so, the Captain knew the winds would increase and he would be forced to furl most of his sails and reduce his speed for the safety of all aboard.

* * *

London, England

   June 15, 9:49 p.m. London Time

Nic jumped in his seat as a hand clamped on his shoulder. "What the—?" he exclaimed breathlessly. Nic had been studying the storm's path as well as obsessively scanning for any hints of radio contact with the *Admiral Risty*. So engrossed was he that he didn't notice footsteps entering his cubicle, nor sense the presence of another human in his space.

"Easy there, chap. Just me," announced Alastair.

Nic's surprise deepened when he realized who it was that grabbed him and what time it was. "Whoa, I was not expecting that . . . not expecting anyone . . . Geez, don't ever do that to me again, Alastair." Recovering his wits, he added, "What brings you back to the office at this late hour?"

"Hey, you're not the only one who works late, Lancaster," said Alastair. His tone was artificially buoyant, the alcohol fumes attesting to the origin of such jocularity. "I've been monitoring the situation, as well. Just so happens, I was in the comfort of my own home, enjoying a lovely supper of toad-in-the-hole with brandy, when your text came in. It got me thinking about an old chum of mine. We go way back, we do. He's now an admiral in Her Majesty's Royal Navy with loads of experience all around the globe. Then it struck me: he spent some time in the region, dealing with many Caribbean states and territories. Maybe, just maybe, he could shed some light on things for us. So, I called him up, explained the situation, and asked him if he could provide some sort of guidance. Know what he said, Nic?"

"Haven't a clue. Tell me."

"He told me he'd get back to me. 'Right,' I said and continued my supper. Then you know what happened?"

"You polished off the brandy bottle and came down here to tell me this story."

"That I did, but first, my chum rings me back, gives me a name of a friend of his who just happens to be the new governor of the Archipelago of San Andres, Providencia, and Santa Catalina. Says he's already contacted his friend. The governor will see to it that every available resource is used in our search for these terrorists."

"What does that mean, 'every available resource'?"

"I asked the same question. It means he has a small fleet of ships stationed on the island and he will assign two of them to search for our sailboat. Fair enough?"

"It's not exactly fantastic now, is it? But I'll take it. It might prove to be a bit of a break and we need every break we can get, don't we?"

"That's what I thought, too," exclaimed Alastair as he plopped himself into a chair at the far end of Nic's cubicle.

"So, you got dressed in the middle of the night to relay this news in person? You couldn't just call me?"

"Two things, Lancaster: First, this governor is going to be calling me here at the office as soon as he has some news to relay. Second, I needed to get out of the house, know what I mean?"

"Yeah, yeah. That's great. Are you expecting that call to come in soon?"

"One never knows with these kinds of things, but I figured it certainly couldn't hurt to be ready," said Alastair as he rubbed his head and looked at the ceiling. "Got any aspirin here, Nic?"

"I do, actually." As Nic rummaged through his desk drawer, looking for the aspirin bottle he knew was in there somewhere, he made a mental note to remember this day. This day, he reckoned, marked the first time his boss was actually useful to him. It was worth noting. "Why the sudden change? How is it you have now thrown your support back into this case?"

"The FBI contacted my boss and asked for cooperation, stating that they had a reliable trace on the whereabouts of Collin Cook and wanted to know if we had any resources in the Western Caribbean to contribute to the hunt," explained Alastair.

"So that's why you're suddenly involved. McKnight rings you up at home and, voila, the case is reopened," said Nic.

"You have a problem with me helping out, Nic?"

"I'm glad for the help, but I have a sneaking suspicion that you're in it to be sure you're credited with breaking the case. Am I right?"

"Nonsense, Lancaster. It's a win for the team."

"Team? I bust my hind end for weeks on this case, even after you tell me not to, and now it's going to be a team win?"

"I didn't see you get in touch with your admiral friend and get put through to the governor of the island chain," said Alastair with relish.

"One bloody phone call and now it's a team effort," Nic mumbled as he turned back to his computer.

Chapter Fourteen

W*estern Caribbean, 40 miles north of Providencia Island*
June 15, 4:08 p.m. Caribbean Time

A melodic trilling once again caught the Captain's ear. At the same time, Stinky's herky-jerky movements caught his eye. Stinky was trying to dig the phone out of his pocket with his arm wrapped around the railing. Mounting waves tossed the boat about. Seawater sloshed and ran across the deck. Wind whipped rain pellets haphazardly, but Stinky was determined to answer the incoming call, even with his rain slicker providing yet another obstacle to his goal. The Captain watched Stinky pull out the bulky phone, encased in a thick, yellow plastic case with a chunky, black antenna the size of a thumb. He was familiar with that model of satellite phone and knew it was capable of transmitting and receiving a signal virtually anywhere in the world. Once the device was out of Stinky's pocket, he punched a button to answer it. When Stinky finally answered the phone after several rings, he was off balance and panicky. "Ya," he said, then stuck the forefinger of his free hand into his ear. His feet slipped out from under him, causing his cheek to slam into the rail as he landed on his knees. The fact that his elbow was wrapped around the railing saved him from skittering across the deck and over the edge. When Stinky recovered, he said something into the phone that seemed to be a request to give him a moment. He then carefully worked his way toward the cabin door, keeping one hand firmly connected to the rails. Stinky bounced side to side, hitting the walls of the stairwell with each shoulder, until he eventually pushed his way through the cabin door.

* * *

Collin had moved into position at the edge of the bunk bed, his feet set shoulder width apart under him, poised once again to pounce when something banged into the door of the cabin, then stumbled through. It was Stinky, trying to stay upright amid the constant pitching and heaving of the boat. He clutched a phone in his left hand.

Collin slumped back down and closed his eyes in defeat.

Without a word, Stinky motioned to Mr. Green to get up, then wrestled the wet raincoat off his torso and pushed it at Mr. Green. Mr. Green, as he staggered and swayed with the boat's movement, put the raincoat on and exited through the door and up the steps.

Stinky gripped a teakwood handhold attached to the ceiling near the dining table and braced himself as he held the phone to his ear. "Ya, ya," he started. He mumbled something Collin could not understand, then listened hard. "OK," he said.

Stinky calculated his movements and maneuvered across the cabin to another set of handrails bolted to the ceiling near Collin's bunk. He tapped a button to place the call on speaker mode and tossed the phone on the bed next to Collin. Stinky held on tight as the boat heaved upward again at an odd angle. Using his free hand, he managed to swing the Uzi, which was strapped around his shoulder and across his chest and aim it at Collin.

Surprised and flustered that his chance at freedom had again been snatched away, Collin stammered, "Hello? Who is this?"

"You need to ask?" The sound coming through the speaker of the phone had a tinny quality that echoed. This gave the tenor voice a smooth, mechanical tone, but there was still a hint of a British accent. "This is the owner of the $30 million you have hidden in Panama City. Who else?"

Collin took a deep breath. The words and the voice—so confident, so well-articulated—along with the timing, punched him like a fist to the gut. Everything froze and he could feel the color drain from his face. He shook his head and blurted out the first thing that came into his battered brain, "What are you talking about?"

The calm, refined chuckle exuded a regal authority, even with the disconcerting reverberation. "Surely you jest, Mr. Cook. I am not a fool and I am not amused by your games."

A flood of emotions came over Collin as his mind flashed through the past eleven months of his shattered life and the abuse of the past two days. The cold inside turned to rage. "I don't know what you're talking about, you arrogant prick. I could care less about the money. It won't bring my family back." Collin paused, trying to sort out his feelings and put them into words. "But I won't give it back, if that's what your insinuating. Not to the likes of you. I know what you're all about," he seethed.

"Insinuating? You think I called to insinuate something, Mr. Cook? I am simply requesting that you return that money to its rightful owner."

Collin waited a moment for the garbled metallic beeps and squawks to subside. "Rightful owner?" Collin spat the words out. His mind was in gear and revved up now. Something about the man's arrogance set the wheels spinning and loosened his tongue. "What makes you think you're the rightful owner? You're a blood-sucking scumbag." Collin paused, knowing there was a millisecond delay in the transmission. He spoke slowly and enunciated his words for optimal comprehension on the other end. "You and your insurance company take money from customers, then when you have to pay a large claim, you use any devious means you can to get your money back."

Another wave crashed into the hull of the boat, nearly propelling Collin off the bed.

The phone ricocheted off the wall and hit Collin's elbow as he leaned on it. He pushed the phone to the side where he could talk into it more easily.

"You surprise me, Mr. Cook. For a man of your limited education and resources, you sound all too sure of yourself." The voice, though hollowed by the satellite phone, carried a patronizing edge.

"It's called the Internet, you condescending sack of trash. I know about you and Tranquil Pacific Casualty. I also know how many of your claimants end up dead or in prison or mysteriously penniless within months of receiving settlements from your fraudulent company. Yeah, I know about you and your sinister tricks."

"Well, then, Mr. Cook, you must know that I would not approach you like this if I did not have leverage against you."

"What are you talking about, Penh?"

"I'm talking about your ailing mother, Mr. Cook. She is not looking too well these days, you know."

A lump formed in Collin's throat, trapping the torrent of foul words he planned to let loose. He squinted at the phone as he coughed out the words, "You're full of crap." His voice held neither volume nor conviction.

"Let me show you, Mr. Cook," Penh continued, smugger than before.

"Problem is, Penh, my hands are tied behind my back and we're in the middle of a raging storm, so—" The boat was once again pummeled from the side. This time both Collin and the phone hit the floor, sending a fresh wave of pain shooting through the ragged skin around his wrists and his aching shoulders. Stinky, now using both hands to brace himself, stuck a foot out to stop the phone. He re-aimed the muzzle of the Uzi at Collin and motioned for him to get up and get back on the bed before he bent down to retrieve the phone, his eyes never leaving Collin's.

"My men will set up a link to a computer and I will transmit a video clip." Penh added a few commands in a language Collin didn't understand.

Stinky responded by saying, "OK." Then he backed carefully toward the cabin door, never taking his eyes or weapon off Collin. He bellowed out the door and Long Hair appeared a few seconds later, dripping wet.

Fighting to keep his balance, Long Hair pulled a black briefcase from the closet and carried it to the table and went to work. After unlocking the case, he unzipped a rubberized lining and removed a sleek, ultra-thin laptop and began punching keys, unraveling and connecting a yellow cable. He plugged one end into the laptop and motioned for Stinky to hand him the phone so he could insert the other end into it. He muttered something and Stinky relayed something that sounded similar through the phone.

"It appears we are prepared to send you a nice little video clip. Enjoy, Mr. Cook."

Stinky waved the muzzle of the gun toward the table, motioning for Collin to move in that direction.

Collin struggled to his feet amid the tumult, leaning forward and using his shoulder to balance against the wall, then carefully moving across the floor to the table. Long Hair had stood and moved out of reach. Once Collin was seated, Stinky continued speaking into the phone, apparently explaining what had just happened. Stinky tapped a few keys and slid the laptop in front of Collin. There, on the screen in front of him, was a most haunting image: his mother duct taped to a chair. A thick strip of the gray adhesive covered her mouth. Her hair was matted down. The bones in her hands and arms protruded and the skin sagged. Her face was gaunt and ash gray. Collin opened his mouth, but nothing came out. Thoughts and words vaporized, and his tongue felt glued in place.

"Mr. Cook? Are you there?"

Collin grunted, "Mmm-hmm."

"Good. Now that I have your attention, allow me to explain."

* * *

Industrial Complex, 30 miles southeast of San Diego, California
  June 15, 2:09 p.m. Pacific Time

Sarah Cook found herself suddenly wide awake in a strange place, feeling spacey and detached from her body. Everything seemed to have a slight tilt or bend to it. Or maybe she was spinning. Or the room was. She closed her eyes, took a deep breath, and held back a wave of nausea. When it passed, she again tried to take in her surroundings.

Sarah found that all of her senses were alert as she began to orient herself. A spot on her arm burned. A man with tattoos was walking away from her with a needle in his gloved hand. He threw the needle against the far wall. It hit with a tiny pinging sound. The wall must be metal. She looked up. The ceiling was very high. The room was dark, except for immediately around her. A bright light pointed down at her from a stand. No, there were two of them; one on either side of a camera held up by a tripod.

She closed her eyes for another wave of dizziness to wend its way past.

Now an Asian man with a very colorful tattoo climbing his neck stood behind the camera. Sarah could feel her heart racing and her whole body shaking. Beads of sweat rolled from her temples. *What was in that syringe?* she wondered. Whatever it was, it was making her feel strange—hyper-aware and jittery, but heavy at the same time. She noticed everything but didn't want to move.

She was seated in a padded chair. Her arms were taped to the arm rests with multiple swaths of gray duct tape. Her mouth couldn't move freely, and she tasted the adhesive on her lips. She couldn't open her mouth and her jaw ached.

Another man approached her from the side. He held a fat, brightly colored phone in his hand. Someone on the phone addressed her. He had a pleasant voice, laced with a mild accent, and was very articulate. As the phone was brought close to her, she could see on the screen the man who was speaking to her. He was a handsome Asian man with perfect skin and a beautiful silk tie. She wondered where he was and where he got that tie. *I wish Henry had one like that*, she thought.

"Mrs. Cook, thank you for joining us," he said, then paused. He spoke in a commanding voice in a foreign language. The man holding the phone ripped the duct tape from her face with one jerky motion. Once the stinging abated, Sarah noticed she could move her jaw again. The man with the silk tie continued in his pleasant voice. "Is there anything you would like to say to your son, Collin?"

"Yes," she said, just above a whisper, her voice strained.

"Unfortunately, your son is in a very remote location. The Internet connection is not strong enough to allow us to do a live video conference, but we will allow you to talk with Collin and share a brief message. What would you like to say to your son?"

Sarah worked her sore jaw and tongue and tried to speak. Her mouth was so dry it made her cough and choke. Again, the man with the silk tie spoke forcefully in that other language and the man behind that camera came to her other side with a bottle of water, which he held for her while she drank. Much of it spilled down the front of her shirt, as he poured it into her mouth.

Sarah thought for a moment, cocking her head upward. "You'd better not harm my son." She smiled an airy smile at the camera, then at the man with the nice tie whose face smiled a tight smile at her from the phone held in front of her and slightly to her right.

"Don't worry Mrs. Cook, as long as you and he both cooperate, no one will be hurt."

Sarah opened her mouth and started to speak.

* * *

Western Caribbean Sea, 39 miles north of Providencia Island
June 15, 4:11 p.m. Caribbean Time

Collin was leaning forward, peering at the computer screen when it went dark.

Stinky stood at attention with the muzzle of his gun pointed at Collin. He stared at the blank computer screen and shifted his weight from one foot to the other until the satellite phone rang again. Nothing but white noise. He handed the phone to Long Hair and waited for it to ring again.

A few moments later, Penh was back on the line, calm and cool. "Mr. Cook. I want to assure you that your mother is doing well. She is being treated with kindness and respect—for now. You can understand the technical challenges of video communication and data transmission when you are hundreds of miles at sea, I presume. I believe we have remedied the situation now." He broke into his native tongue and commanded something. Stinky snapped back to full attention, gun at the ready, as Long Hair moved in and punched keys and adjusted the laptop's screen. Sarah Cook reappeared, unnaturally energetic.

Collin watched a recorded short message from his mother. The video clip lasted only thirteen seconds. Her words stuck with him. She knew what she was saying, even if she appeared to be out of sorts. Her message was simple: "Collin, your father and I trust you will do the right thing, the thing you know in your heart is best for everyone involved." She cleared her throat and added, "Do what Ronnie would do and remember I love you, son."

Do the right thing, the thing you know in your heart.

Collin remained silent, unable to speak as he processed what he had seen and heard. His mother was sending a message. Ronnie had to be Ronald Regan, their favorite US president ever. He would never negotiate with terrorists. Did she fully understand what she was saying? There was no way she could know about Tog and what these animals had done to him. Maybe she didn't realize what was at stake. Could she possibly know the consequences of not cooperating with Penh and how that could affect her and probably the rest of the family, as well? Why would she say that?

"You heard your mother. She said to do the right thing. Surely you know what the right thing is. Give us the computer so no one else gets hurt," Penh insisted.

"I want to speak to her again when she is not drugged up. I want to know that she is well and will not be harmed. If she is, there will be hell to pay."

"Are you really in a position, Mr. Cook, to make such demands? Or threaten anyone?"

Collin's chin sank to his chest and he heaved a sigh. "But what about her health? And her treatments?"

The line fizzled and a distorted, robotic voice answered. "Her health is in your hands, Mr. Cook. You cooperate with us and hand over the computer so we can transfer the funds and we will return your mother to the medical center. It's up to you how quickly that happens."

"I'll do whatever I have to do to make sure she's not harmed," said Collin, straining through his thickening emotions.

Penh interjected something Collin could not understand, and another video clip began to play. A pair of spiked wrist bands appeared behind his mother's head. The hands were on his mother's neck but not exerting any force. Collin

114

looked away and yelled, "Don't touch her."

"You don't want your mother to be harmed, Mr. Cook? Then give us that computer."

"I told you, I don't have it with me."

The hands on Sarah's neck began to tighten their hold until Penh yelled again.

With that, the call ended, and Collin was left to decipher the meaning of her last words to him. What was the right thing to do? How would Reagan handle these guys?

Chapter Fifteen

I ndustrial Complex, 30 miles southeast of San Diego, California
June 15, 2:12 p.m. Pacific Time

In her dream, she heard loud noises, followed by banging and rattling that came from somewhere in the distance, then up close, then in the distance again. Things were moving outside the cave where she was hiding. Then, someone was in the cave, stalking closer and closer, until she felt hands on her. They started at her feet, manipulating something at her ankles. They made a slow crawl up her legs. She tried to pull away. Next, she felt the hands at her waist. But it was happening in a dream. Until . . .

Emily's eyes shot open. She struggled to move and tried to scream. There were straps on her wrists and ankles and around her waist. Her mouth was taped. She couldn't scream, kick, punch, or get away. She was completely helpless; at the mercy of someone she didn't know and didn't understand. It was a foreign feeling and she abhorred everything about it instantly. Meanwhile, the hands moved up her body as she thrashed from side to side. She was staring into dark, demonic, narrow eyes. A stud poked through one of the eyebrows of the Asian man's face. A devilish snicker met her ears as he flicked his tongue out, as if it would turn her terror into desire.

Another voice from her left penetrated the tight space around her. It was sharp and forceful and, to her, unintelligible. The cackling and tongue flicking stopped immediately. The hands slid behind her and started tampering with the strap around her wrists. Next thing she knew, she was being yanked from the sitting position she had been in and dragged headfirst across a metal surface. Someone held her upper body under her arms while the man with the spike in his eyebrow held her feet. They plopped her in an office chair in the middle of a vast, empty warehouse.

The floor was bare concrete and covered in a layer of brownish dust. The ceiling was twenty feet or more above her head and insulated with aluminum-backed fiberglass that hung loosely in places. The walls appeared to be bare metal. The sounds of the men's feet shuffling as they worked echoed through the space.

The only other items she could see, other than the white van parked just inside a wide roll-up door to her right, was a camera on a tripod six feet in front of her with lights on either side. The young guy with the spike in his eyebrow approached from the side and fussed with her hair as the other man, who had a colorful tattoo crawling up his neck, stood behind the camera giving instructions. The young guy grabbed her cheeks and squeezed. He had spikes on his wrist bands and spikes on his belt along with the spike in his eyebrow. His eyes telegraphed his intentions, causing a cold shiver to run down her spine and across her entire nerve network until her whole body trembled. Emily considered herself as tough as any other woman on the planet, but the thought of being held captive, all alone by these two miscreants in this isolated warehouse filled her with dread and despair until she burst out sobbing. She hung her head and clinched her eyes shut.

The young man with the spikes stepped closer, speaking a language she didn't understand, and forcibly moved her head back into position as he pointed at the camera. He stepped behind her and held her head still, pressing it back into his mid-section. The tattooed one gave a thumbs-up and said, "Say hello, Mr. Cook."

She couldn't stop the sobbing. In fact, the thought of Collin only made it worse.

As if on cue, the spiked one held her chin with one hand and a cell phone in the other as his face moved close to her cheek. Emily tried to pull away, but the hand on her chin gripped her more firmly, holding her steady as he began whispering in her ear. Her sobbing became more intense. Then, as if to pacify her, he began to gently stroke her cheek, her ear, the nape of her neck with his tongue in an exaggerated act for the camera and for the phone he held in his other hand.

Angry protests erupted from the phone. It was Collin. "Get away from her. Don't touch her, you mangy dog. I swear, I will kill you for this."

Emily cried even harder at the sound of his desperate cries, knowing there was nothing he could do and no one who could help her.

The tattooed one barked and it all stopped. He stepped away from the camera and said, "OK. Good." But the phone was still on, still recording.

The spiked one was slow to move. He lingered in the moment, inhaling her scent with his nose touching her neck just below her ear. When the older, tattooed man commanded a second time, he pushed back and stood, still leering at her. She shut her eyes and turned away, trying desperately to control her emotions. Emily had never wanted to be dead before, but she was beginning to wish she could end it right now rather than have to endure whatever form of horrible, disgusting, degrading treatment these two had in mind.

* * *

Western Caribbean Sea, 38 miles north of Providencia Island
  June 15, 4:13 p.m. Caribbean Time

Penh's voice had lost its smooth veneer. It interrupted Collin's boiling thoughts with its gruff demand. "Mr. Cook, I am losing my patience. Give me the information I need to retrieve my money. Now."

"My mother told me to do the right thing. I don't think negotiating with a terrorist is the right thing to do. Giving you the money you need to bankroll your operation would be the exact opposite of the right thing."

Penh barked another command and the image of Emily weeping reappeared on the laptop's screen in front of him. He gasped as he saw his dear friend bound and gagged and weeping uncontrollably. He had never seen her show any sign of weakness, so this display jolted him to the very core. He tried to look away, but he couldn't. Morbid curiosity kept his eyes glued to the screen even while tears clouded his vision.

The video showed two men moving about in the background. The one with the spikes disappeared into the darkness. He reappeared a moment later with a long-bladed knife. He began speaking to the phone, but Collin could not understand his words. The sharp edge of the knife pressed against Emily's cheek and began a slow journey downward, leaving a trail of blood.

Emily's eyes went wide and her breathing became sharp and panicked. The knife skipped her neck and went to her chest, continuing a bloody arc until it stopped at the top of her blouse. In very deliberate fashion, it nicked the first button, sending it flying. The spiked face came into view. More words, spoken in a hushed, romantic sort of tone, and some tongue flicking.

Collin yelled, "Enough. Get away from her."

But it was in vain. The knife continued to the next button and flicked it into empty space.

Collin screamed again. "Stop. Don't hurt her, you animal."

Another voice emerged from the distance and the man with the tattoos on his neck stood behind Emily, holding her shoulders. The knife sliced off another button. The spiked wristbands appeared and pulled the blouse open before he stood and crossed in front of the camera's view, growing larger as he approached then vanished. Now the camera view was moving, panning left and right to show Emily and Sarah sitting side by side. When it settled, the camera took in a wider view. Both women sat with their arms wrapped in gray duct tape around the chair arms, straps around their waists and ankles, and a strip of tape across each of their mouths. Emily's blouse was open, and blood streamed down her cheek to her chest, slowly soaking both her beige blouse and her bra dark red.

The man with the tattoos stood behind them. He pulled back the action on his handgun, chambering a bullet, and held it to Sarah's head.

Penh continued the narrative. "You see, Mr. Cook, you have once again put people you care about in harm's way because of your stubborn lack of cooperation." His voice echoed with a metallic tone, but it retained a steely sternness. "What would you like to see first: my men enjoy the company of your beautiful friend? Or a bullet destroy your mother's head?"

Collin hung his head and clenched his jaw. He braced himself as the *Admiral* sluiced down another swell. He leaned into the edge of the table to help keep his balance. Stinky glared at him from his post on the other side of the cabin but said nothing. He held the satellite phone encased in thick yellow and black plastic. Everything was quiet, waiting for Collin to respond.

Collin's jaw muscles quivered as he fought to control the storm raging inside. What was the right thing to do? What had his mother meant for him to do when she said to follow his heart? That heart was useless at the moment. It was splitting wide open with anguish watching her and Emily being groped and threatened and hurt. At the same time, it was ready to explode with rage and desire for revenge. The same heart was sinking in despair knowing he had brought this misery and torment to the two women in his life who, in recent months, meant the most to him.

"Mr. Cook, I'm waiting," said Penh.

Collin hung his head in defeat. "Fine. You can have the codes. Just tell your men to get their filthy hands off my mom and Emily. Leave them alone."

Penh barked out more orders and the man with the gun lowered it. "Very well, Mr. Cook. You shall have your wish when I have mine."

"How can I be sure your two monsters there won't hurt them?"

"You hand over the codes, my men will leave them alone," said Penh in his icy, commanding tone.

"Why should I trust you?"

"Because, Mr. Cook, unlike you, I am a man of my word."

Collin snorted and shook his head, fighting back a million nasty words he wanted to unleash, knowing they would do no good. "Fine, but I want proof that they are all right."

"You will have your proof after I have the codes."

Collin sucked in a breath and bit his lip. "The codes are on my laptop. My laptop is hidden in a compartment behind me. Cut me loose and I'll get the codes if your dogs leave the women alone."

Penh laughed out loud. "Cut you loose? Why would we do that, Mr. Cook?"

"So I can get to my computer and get you the codes. But your men have to free my mom and Emily first."

"Not until we verify the authenticity of the codes, Mr. Cook." Penh then barked out commands. Stinky said "OK" after each one.

Stinky wagged his head at Long Hair across the cabin, keeping his eyes and gun trained on Collin as he did. With a hand gesture, Stinky commanded Collin to remain seated and pointed Long Hair toward the bunk where Collin had been held captive for nearly forty-eight hours. Stinky said something and Long Hair began to search the area all around the bunk.

Collin turned his shoulders, showing Stinky his bound hands. "Cut these things off and I'll get the computer out for you."

Penh's voice reverberated through the satellite phone. "Nice try, Mr. Cook, but your hands will remain as they are. I suggest you hurry and give my men instructions, or your mother and girlfriend will pay the price for your defiance." A beep came from the laptop on the table in front of him as another video clip started to play. The images were halting and intermittent but showed the man with the spikes moving into the frame, then kneeling beside Emily with his long-bladed knife in full view. The video feed stalled. The frozen image on the screen showed the tip of the man's knife moving Emily's open blouse.

"Fine," yelled Collin. "I'll tell them how to open the hatch. Just get that mutt away from Emily."

Penh's voice crackled as he barked out a command. The image on the laptop skipped and sputtered, but showed the man standing with the knife still pointed at Emily.

Collin began to explain how to open the smuggler's compartment. Long Hair followed Collin's instructions, finding the hidden buttons to release the secret hatch. It took some effort, but Long Hair extracted the rubbery sea bag, unsealed it, and pulled out the laptop.

Minutes later, Long Hair had Collin's spreadsheet open and was connecting his computer to the sat phone. When he finished, he tapped a button on the keyboard of the other laptop and turned the screen so Collin could see his mom and Emily, still bound and gagged, in the empty warehouse.

"Now, Mr. Cook. You will have the pleasure of watching me keep my promise to leave your mother and girlfriend alone, just as you wished. I will instruct my men to leave. If the information we have retrieved is bogus, however, they shall return, and I will be powerless to stop them from acting on their natural desires." Penh cackled as he commanded his men in another language. "You should know they really are all alone. There is not another soul around for miles." Penh's laughter rang in Collin's ears and in his head for hours afterward.

* * *

Industrial Complex, 30 miles southeast of San Diego, California
June 15, 2:18 p.m. Pacific Time

With Emily in tears and Sarah off in oblivion, the two thugs did as the big boss ordered and moved toward the van, preparing to leave. The man with the tattoos had to forcefully pull the younger one away from Emily's side. His eyes said everything in a way that twisted Emily's stomach into knots. The two men left the camera on, its red light blinking, as proof to Collin that Penh was keeping up his end of the bargain. The driver fired up the white Sprinter van's engine while the younger one pulled open the roller door of the warehouse. Brilliant light flooded the hollow cavern. The younger one made a slow, arcing circle around the ladies, talking softly and puckering his lips toward Emily as he did.

What's next? Emily wondered. In that same moment, she realized the van was pulling out of the warehouse and the roller door was closing. Then it was dark. Not quite pitch black, but dark enough. The only light in the building came in the shape of shafts and splinters from the sides of the roller door that had just closed and from one of those spinning roof turbines. She heard a lock snap shut.

As the sound of the van's engine faded into the distance, Emily could hear

Sarah breathing hard next to her. Sarah's hunched shape was roughly visible in the fractured rays of sunlight, head lolling to the side. And the only thing she could think about was Dr. Navarro's stern instructions that Sarah eat regularly from the prescribed menu. Emily's insides heated with fury. Sarah could die in here, next to her, and no one would know. At least not for a long time. Who could know how long it would take to find them? She was certain that they were in about as obscure a place as could be found. There were no sounds coming from the outside. No sounds from cars or trucks. No sounds from people. No sounds from machinery.

Isolated somewhere. Alone. Desperate.

Chapter Sixteen

*Western Caribbean Sea, 35 miles north of Providencia Island
June 15, 4:25 p.m. Caribbean Time*

The *Admiral Risty* leaned and yawed as wind gusts reached forty-five miles per hour. The rain pellets were becoming more constant, whipped sideways by the wind. The swells coming from the southwest had grown to six feet or more, slowing the *Admiral's* progress and complicating things for the crew.

Mr. Green kept one eye on the mounting sea and one eye on the Captain. He looked unwell as he gripped the railing around the cockpit.

Captain Sewell called to his men, who continued to lean out on the port side. He had to weigh the risk to their immediate safety with the risk of being caught in open ocean as the storm intensified. "Reel in the tethers. Return to your posts."

Rojas looked at him and shook his head. "Not yet," he yelled. "We're OK. Keep the hike on longer. We need the speed."

The Captain paused, admiring the courage of his crew. The *Admiral* was pushing along southward at twenty-two knots, a pace he knew he couldn't maintain for much longer. The winds remained at thirty to thirty-five knots—the upper threshold for full sails and tethered hiking like the men were doing. It was the fifty-plus knot gusts that worried him. They were increasing in frequency and duration. To remain at full sails much longer was tantamount to suicide.

Knowing from weather updates on his navigation system that the storm had gained in both speed and intensity across the warmer waters south and east of their current position, he knew it was going to be a close call getting to safe harbor, even at full sails. Likewise, being stuck out here in the worst of the storm was also suicide.

He nodded reluctantly at Rojas, who smiled back and gave him a thumbs-up.

At best, the safe harbor of Providencia was an hour and a half away. Most likely, it would take longer.

* * *

Collin watched as Long Hair fought to keep from falling off the bench as the boat continued to shift from side to side and bob up and down. At the same time, he held tight to the laptop and the other computer equipment he pulled from a nylon bag Collin had not noticed before. First, Long Hair slid a slim, silver device from one of the duffle bag's pockets and held it on his lap. He stuck wires and cables into the device, the laptop, and then into something that looked like a really old cell phone. It was big and bulky but had a touch screen interface with Chinese characters on it. This device he clutched between his knees.

There was a series of beeps and other noises, reminiscent of the days of dial-up Internet connections that lasted several minutes.

When all the chirping and whirring stopped, Long Hair closed the lid to Collin's laptop and muttered something. He disconnected the cords and stuffed everything, excluding Collin's laptop, in the nylon bag and placed the bag on the bench next to him. He put Collin's laptop back in the rubbery sea bag and sealed it shut.

Stinky replied and pointed to the stairs, apparently dismissing Long Hair so he could enjoy the weather up top.

Stinky then punched a button on the sat phone and Collin heard him speaking deferentially to Penh. When their conversation was over, Penh addressed Collin.

"Mr. Cook, we both now have what we wished for. My associates have successfully cloned your hard drive and transmitted that data to my servers. Now, I have the account numbers and codes to retrieve my money and you have your mother and girlfriend left alone, just as you requested," Penh said with an air of triumph.

A jumpy and jumbled video clip sputtered on the screen in front of Collin. The halting images showed Emily and his mother still taped to their chairs in near darkness. Emily's head swiveled from side to side and her body thrashed and pulled against the restraints. There was fear in her eyes.

A dull but powerful ache welled up in Collin's stomach. When he told Penh to leave them alone, he hadn't envisioned this scenario.

"Wait, your men are going to tell someone where they are, right? My mom needs medical attention. You can't just leave her there."

"Is this not what you demanded? You demanded we leave them alone, so that is exactly what we have done," said Penh with an air of triumph.

Collin instantly regretted saying anything. He thought things through as fast as his tired brain would spin. This was a far better outcome than having that mangy mutt pawing over Emily or touching his mom.

"Would you like me to send my men back to them? I can't guarantee they won't succumb to the temptation presented to them. That girlfriend of yours does present a sumptuous feast for the eyes, if you know what I mean."

"I know what you mean. Forget I said anything."

"Very well," said Penh.

Before Penh could start into his next soliloquy, Collin interrupted with a question. "So, what happens to the rest of us? Are you going to kill us now? Or wait until we get to Panama?" asked Collin.

"I have no interest in killing . . . have to kill." Penh's words were mottled and halting as the connection failed. The wind outside was howling and the intensifying storm was wreaking havoc on their satellite link as the rain beat down on the fiberglass hull of the boat, making it hard for Collin to hear. "I wish I could say it's been a pleasure doing business with you, Mr. Cook . . . different circumstances, I'm sure . . . gotten along quite well. It's a shame . .

. so difficult for yourself and those close to you. Our agreement is complete, is it not?"

"Wait, there's something you need to know," Collin yelled.

Penh's voice came back, "If you have nothing more to say, I bid you good day, Mr. Cook."

"There's something I have to tell you—" but it was too late. The line went dead, and Collin assumed he and those he loved would die soon, too, if he didn't tell Penh about the fail-safe security on the account in Panama.

Penh needed to hear what Collin had to say. Frantic, Collin shouted at Stinky. "Get him back on the line. I have important information I have to tell him."

Stinky raised an eyebrow but didn't move.

"I don't care if you kill me when this is all over, but it's not right for my mom and my friend to . . . Listen, I need to talk to Penh right now. If you want the money I'm sure he promised you, get him back on the line. Now."

Stinky looked at the phone and shrugged. He punched some buttons and waited. The fuzzy sound of an empty phone line was all they could hear.

"Keep trying," Collin insisted.

Stinky tried three more times with the same result. *The storm must be messing with their ability to connect to the satellite*, thought Collin.

Any minute now, Collin expected Stinky to either shoot him in the head or slice his jugular or get his goons to wrestle him topside and pitch him overboard. In any case, he didn't expect to live to see Penh's ultimate defeat.

* * *

Northbound Interstate 5, Southern Orange County, California
June 15, 4:05 p.m. Pacific Time

Rob thumped the steering wheel of his rented Ford Fusion, frustrated by the snarled traffic. Being a native, he expected it, but not this far south. It was unbelievable that five lanes of traffic could clog up so thoroughly and literally inch along slower than a man could walk. The lack of progress was making him crazy, but he had to keep himself together. He would be no good to the Cook family if he showed up in a crisis situation completely frazzled.

The lack of information was equally as frustrating. Lukas had given him hourly updates with scant details. The updates had come every hour on the hour. This one was late. Lukas was never late. He was as Austrian as they come: prompt, precise, and accurate.

It can't be a good omen, can it? Rob thought.

He checked his watch. He would still have time to visit briefly with Henry before going to the airport to pick up Collin's brother and sister. He had called both Richard and Megan and had spoken to each of them for the first time in nearly ten years. After hearing about their mother's kidnapping and the assault on their father, each made preparations to take the next flight into Southern California. It was important for the Cook family to be together and rally around their parents, they explained.

Rob had answered their questions about Collin as best he could, explaining that his last known location was on an island in the Caribbean, but that he was trying to avoid some very bad people. Rob figured the whole story would be a little overwhelming at this point.

Rob's phone finally rang. The sound of Linkin Park signaled Lukas's long-awaited call.

"Found her," Lukas announced excitedly. "Took a while, but we were able to trace a very weak signal from Emily's phone, the cheap one Collin gave her, to an industrial park eight miles northeast of Chula Vista. Apparently the whole complex is empty. Something to do with a federal lawsuit against the owners over environmental hazards. It's miles away from nowhere, very poor cell reception, very sparsely populated. Brilliant place for a hostage situation. But, that's beside the point."

"OK, I'm ready to go. Just give me the address. I'll be there as quickly as I can," said Rob. "And I'll need a gun."

"I'm afraid not, my friend," said Lukas. "It's way too dangerous. I'm sending in a strike team."

"I want to be there, Lukas. I flew out here from London, changed all my plans to help, so let me help. Please."

"I know you'd love to put a bullet in these guys. I would, too. But let's let the trained professionals handle this one. I'm going to need you later."

"Come on, Lukas. I can't just sit around doing nothing when my friends are in danger. You know I'm capable. You've seen me play all those simulated video games. You know I rock in combat situations."

"Very funny," said Lukas. "This is real life, not Xbox. I need your real-world skill set, not your virtual combat prowess."

"I know, but I want to help."

"You'll be no good to them or to me if you're the one that ends up with a bullet in you," said Lukas. "I'll let you know as soon as the mission is complete."

"What about Collin? What's going on with him?" asked Rob.

"It does not look too good," Lukas said with a sigh. "That storm took an unexpected turn northward and picked up speed. They are sailing right into it."

"I'm sure they'll be OK. You checked out Captain Sewell's background. The man has been sailing all his life. Certainly, he's handled storms like this before," Rob tried to assure him.

"Maybe so, but it's always risky dealing with Mother Nature. Besides, the area where they are heading is full of rocky outcroppings and shallow reefs. It's suicide for them to try to navigate through there in this weather." Lukas, the calm one of the group, was worried. It was obvious from his tone of voice. "The full force of that storm is going to hit as they are surrounded by these hazards."

"Captain Sewell must know what he's doing, don't you think?"

"My guess is that he's heading for a safe harbor on the west side of the islands. But I must also assume he knows about the reefs and rocks. I just pray he gets them there safely."

"How far are they from the island?"

"Right now, about ten miles."

"That's not close enough, is it?"

"No, and they are not making the same progress they were making before. They've slowed down as the storm has worsened and as the sun goes down."

"That's a prudent move, don't you think? Collin trusts him. We should, too."

"Trust in the Captain is not the issue. Besides, Collin has no choice at this point, does he? Dealing with the unpredictability of nature is the real problem right now."

"Let's keep in mind who we're talking about here. Collin is Mr. Resourceful, remember? He's a tough, do-what's-got-to-be-done-to-survive kind of guy. He survived a Category Two hurricane in a twelve-foot rubber raft. This is nothing more than a tropical storm. Easy for a guy like him. He's going to be fine. One way or another, Collin is going to be fine, Lukas."

"I wish I had your faith. And don't use my name."

"Oh, yeah, sorry. I guess the faith comes from Henry and Sarah. They always taught me that if I didn't doubt, God could do miracles for me. I know Collin believes that way, too. You should try it."

"Wish I could . . . I really wish I could," said Lukas.

* * *

London, England

June 16, 12:07 a.m. London Time

Nic's cell phone buzzed on the desk next to him. Alastair, who had nodded off temporarily, jumped at the sound. It was Crabtree.

"We just lost signal on Cook's phone," said Crabtree.

"We saw that, too. What do you reckon it means? Dead battery? Or downed ship?" asked Nic.

"My gut instinct is that it's a dead battery," said Reggie. "He probably hasn't charged it since they shoved off and that was more than forty-eight hours ago. If it's a cheapie like the one he gave his girlfriend, I'm surprised it lasted as long as it did, especially when it's constantly searching for signal out in the middle of the ocean."

"You're probably right," said Nic. "I've forwarded on the last known coordinates to our contact in the Colombian Navy. He says they'll begin their search at first light, after the storm has passed."

"I guess that's the best we can do at this point. I just hate being blind. Wish we had another way to track him."

"If it's of any interest to you," added Nic, "my contacts in Grand Cayman have been monitoring the radio transmissions for me. They haven't heard a word from the boat since they shoved off. Quite strange, he says, to have total radio silence like that."

"That makes sense. I'm sure it's a forced silence," Crabtree said, almost to himself. "Let's hope the Colombians help us out. That's all we've got going for us."

"Our contacts there are very high up and they have assured my section chief that they will do everything in their power to rescue these guys and keep them until our forces arrive to take custody," Nic said with confidence instilled in him by Alastair and his story.

"I just hope it's not too late. They are sailing into some hazardous waters at the height of this storm. Nothing can be guaranteed at this point," Crabtree said with a hint of exasperation.

Chapter Seventeen

*Western Caribbean Sea, 7 Miles north-northwest of Providencia Island
June 15, 7:12 p.m. Caribbean Time*

Collin's head felt like it was stuffed with dry straw—and it was smoldering. He couldn't think about anything but the intense thirst. Every fiber groaned, in need of something to drink. Stinky refused his repeated requests for water, telling him he didn't need it. *So,* he thought, *this is how it's going to end. A slow, torturous death by dehydration. Beats death by fire, maybe. And falling. A bullet to the head right now would certainly be better than this.*

Collin just glared at Stinky, unwilling to speak even if he could think straight. He was dying. He could feel his core temperature was rising. The beginning stages of heat exhaustion, beyond dehydration, were kicking in, but relief was not forthcoming. The only thing saving him was the cooler temperatures brought on by the storm and the obscured and sinking sun. Temperatures in the cabin still hung in the upper eighties Fahrenheit. Without water, Collin knew his time was short. It was surprising to still be breathing.

As his overheated mind spun in circles, he began to realize that he was not dead because Penh must still need him for something. That got him thinking about his mom and Emily, wondering whether Penh had kept his promise to leave them alone. Thinking of them being left alone in that abandoned warehouse brought little comfort, but them being alone was still far better than having that mongrel touching them. Collin closed his eyes and prayed for them harder than he had prayed for anything in recent memory. That prayer brought hope.

With his eyes closed, Collin felt the waves crashing against the boat and listened to the rain beating on the deck and the winds shrieking all around them. What he wouldn't give to have that rain landing on his face and in his mouth. The sound of water he couldn't touch, couldn't gulp, drove him crazy. It was so close, yet so far beyond his reach. Every thought led back to his dire need for water.

Just above the din, he could hear the Captain and crew shouting out instructions and responses. The pitch of their voices attested to the peril they all faced. As his body rocked and bounced with the boat, he realized the storm might kill him before the thirst.

With his impeccable timing, Penh decided to call Stinky at that very moment. Stinky shouted into the phone and, as nearly as Collin could tell, asked Penh to repeat himself several times. Then, as the boat swayed and jostled, Stinky lunged across the space between them and onto the bed next to Collin. He quickly regained what balance he could, sitting next to Collin, bracing himself with his feet spread wide on the floor in front of him. He pointed the Uzi at Collin's ribs with one hand and held the phone to his face with the other.

The unnervingly calm and precise voice of Pho Nam Penh blared at full volume with a tinny hollowness from the phone's speaker. "Mr. Cook, it seems our business together is not finished. How cunning and deceitful you are. It looks like I shall have to order my men to return to the place where they left your mother and that lovely female friend of yours. I'm sure they will see it as a gift to continue where they left off. She is indeed a beautiful woman in her prime."

Collin's blood boiled anew with the thoughts of Penh's goons harming Emily. He cursed himself for ever involving her.

"Mr. Cook? Can you hear me?"

A pause while Collin sucked in a breath and unlocked the pulsating muscles of his jaw. "I tried to tell you, but we got cut off because of the storm. Your man here tried three or four times to reconnect." Collin hated pleading for mercy, but knew for his mother's and Emily's sakes, groveling was a must. "Listen, you've got to understand. I tried to tell you. You've got to call off your dogs."

"It appears that a retinal scan is required to remove the money from your accounts. That is indeed a clever security measure, but I assure you, your beautiful friend and your ailing mother will pay the price for your trickery."

"Go to hell." Collin's voice was weak and the ambient noise in the cabin was deafening. He hoped the rat on the other end heard him.

"You lied to me," Penh bellowed. "And your ladies will suffer for it."

"I told you, the line went dead. I didn't lie to you. I just didn't get the chance to explain." There was a crackling and popping over the line. No response from Penh. In desperation, he added, "I'll do whatever it takes to keep them safe. When we get to Panama, I'll take the money out and give it to your men. That's the deal. That's the best I can do. There is no other way to do it. I tried to tell you that. Even with the codes, you'll never get the money without me." Collin was desperate. He knew it and he knew Penh knew it. A position he never wanted to be in with the likes of Pho Nam Penh.

"It's not that easy, Mr. Cook. You have attempted to make a fool out of me. If I look a fool in front of my men, I lose all power. That is not an acceptable alternative. There will be a reckoning. There must be. It is the only way. Now, my men will have their way with your doctor friend. But don't worry. They'll record the whole thing so you can watch."

"Don't. Don't hurt them. Hurt me. I'm the one who deserves it, not her and not my mother." Collin had his brave voice on, and it was genuine. There was nothing he wouldn't do to defend the people he cared for. "If your men touch her—"

A wave pounded the side of the boat, sending Stinky and Collin hurling off the bed and crashing to the floor where they both rolled and skidded into the opposite wall. Stinky was able to catch his fall with his hands. Collin was not. He landed on his face and shoulder and rolled. The phone, too, went flying. It slid across the wooden floor, banged into the wall, and bounced down the step to the galley.

While the men above them yelled and scurried across the deck, Collin and

Stinky struggled amid the continuing turbulence to gain traction and get into a ready position. Collin saw an opportunity to strike and went for it. He turned on to his back and kicked outward toward Stinky's head, hoping to crush it into the wall. But Stinky was too quick. Collin's foot slammed into the bulkhead instead, sending a shockwave jolting through his body.

Stinky reacted like a threatened animal. Any instructions from Penh blocked out while he focused on subduing his attacker.

With his hands tied behind his back and the plastic zip tie digging into his flesh, Collin was not able to maneuver his body into a defensive posture fast enough. Before he knew it, Stinky was on his hands and knees over Collin. He grabbed Collin's shirt collar and twisted it tight, but the constant motion of the boat caused him to lose his balance and fall onto Collin. Collin, however, had no leverage as Stinky's weight pressed down on his torso and legs. Another wave sent them both rolling again. As Collin struggled to sit up, he felt Stinky's arm wrap around his neck and his body being dragged across the floor as he gasped for breath and tried to get his feet under him.

It was no use. Stinky had the advantage. Thanks to the abuse he had sustained, Collin lacked the strength he needed to overpower his foe. The storm did the rest, keeping him jostling and unable to regain control. The two men lay on the floor, rolling and sliding together in a heap, as the boat continued to pitch and sway. Collin fought to stay conscious by thrashing back and forth to loosen Stinky's hold around his neck, hoping the next wave would enable him to work his way out of his enemy's clutches.

* * *

Industrial Complex, 30 miles southeast of San Diego, California
  June 15, 5:19 p.m. Pacific Time

Heat collected in the empty space. There was no movement of air, not even a hint. The arid desert summer penetrated the steel ceiling, the steel walls, the steel door, and pressed in from all sides against the two women bound to cushioned steel office chairs in the deserted warehouse. Stifling, dry air that hurt to inhale surrounded them and sucked the life force from their bodies. The silence that enshrouded them was almost as bad. With duct tape covering their mouths, it was futile to try to communicate. Making grunting noises only hastened the evaporation of their energy. So they sat in silence. Then the silence was broken by faint, distant noises. Sounds that were all too familiar to Emily. Squeaks, scurrying, and the pitter-patter of tiny feet scampering across bare concrete in search of something to eat, following smells that offered hope of a meal. Her stomach tightened and her pulse quickened at the thought of what was coming.

Emily tried to multi-task. Until the rats descended in droves, she had been trying to work one of her arms loose from the multiple layers of duct tape that bound both arms from the wrists to the elbows. It was impossible to reach with a fingernail, so she had attempted to pry it off by levering upward with her wrists and elbows as much as she could. It proved difficult and exhausting and not very rewarding. She had spent the hours since the two thugs left trying to free her arms. All that struggle had yielded only a few millimeters of play between the chair arm and the tape.

When the rats made their first timid arrival an hour before, she split her concentration between trying to scare them away and trying to get another millimeter of wiggle room. Now the rats were not so timid. They smelled something—her blood, her sweat, her fear, or the scent of the rats from the laboratory—she couldn't be sure. With her shins strapped to the legs of the chair, she was unable to kick outward more than an inch or two. The only thing she found she could do was to make her chair hop by thrusting upward with all her might, using all her strength. The legs of the chair would come off the ground maybe a quarter of an inch and crash back down on the concrete floor, compelling the rodents to retreat. The first half dozen times she did it bought her several minutes each of relief with the rats scampering back into the shadows. After an hour of this effort, she was experiencing diminishing marginal returns on her energy expenditure. What sent them shrieking away in chaos the first few times, now hardly slowed their advance.

Emily's chair hopped. The rats waited, then advanced. She hopped again. They waited again; moved forward a few more inches. And so it went until the dirty varmints were nipping at Sarah's feet.

And her energy was nearly gone.

In the pale, dust-filled shard of light that penetrated the dim, Emily hung her head and observed her own appearance as if doing so from outside her body. Her dress slacks were grimy and stained and damp from tears and sweat. Her silk blouse, ripped and torn and missing buttons almost down to her navel, clung to the perspiration on her skin except for where it had been pulled wide open by the man with the spikes. Blood and sweat had pooled in her bra, soaking it. The gashes on her cheek and chest had crusted over. The ones visible to her resembled the red lines on a map denoting a major highway.

It was no wonder the rats advanced toward them: blood. Both women had blood on them. Sarah's dripped from the spot where her IV had been inserted into her vein. A thin trail of it leaked to the floor. The rats now favored the more docile and still Sarah, the vulnerable one. They congregated around the drips and scurried around her feet.

Emily summoned all of her strength to once again make her chair hop in Sarah's direction. She found she had more strength than she expected and ended up hopping three times in a row, covering nearly a foot of ground and pivoting until she and Sarah were practically knee to knee. There was just enough slack in the tape on her legs to allow her to kick out an inch or two with each foot. She connected with the plump bodies of a few of them, but they continued to swarm, moving around to the back of Sarah's legs, out of range of Emily's feet.

Sarah was fading. Her eyes were hollow, and her head slumped to the side. She could barely lift it to acknowledge Emily. This concerned Emily more than being swarmed by rats or being suffocated by heat. And there was nothing she could do to help. She wanted to scream but chose not to waste the energy.

Chapter Eighteen

I ndustrial Complex, 30 miles southeast of San Diego, California
June 15, 5:31 p.m. Pacific Time

Emily's flailing efforts to keep the rats off of Sarah were exhausting and minimally effective. Although she continued to kick at them, they climbed up the backs of Sarah's legs and into her lap and across her torso to the bleeding arm. They climbed up her chest, across her shoulders, and into her hair. Sarah had gone catatonic. It appeared that she didn't realize what was happening to her. But Emily was distressed enough for the two of them. She knew the diseases feral rats carried, unlike her pristine laboratory friends, who only carried the diseases she and her team injected into them.

Panic hit full steam when the first rat made the jump from Sarah's lap to Emily's. No amount of hopping or erratic movement with her limited range of motion could shake them off. She felt their claws digging through the thin, silky material of her dress slacks and scraping the skin on her legs. Then they were climbing up into her blouse, scratching as they clamored up to the gash the knife had made on her chest.

Horror set in and she began to shriek through the duct tape covering her mouth as she realized they were doing more than scratching with their claws. They were reopening her wounds with their teeth.

The terror was real. Emily was sure she and Sarah would be reduced to skeletons before anyone discovered them.

* * *

So caught up in the terror of potentially being eaten by rats was she that Emily didn't hear or notice anything else. Her shrieking filled her ears and covered all other sounds. She didn't hear the engine as it approached the building or the crunching of the tires on the loose rocks strewn across the well-worn pavement outside as the van turned a wide arc into position and began to back toward the large bay with the locked roller door. She didn't even hear the *thunk* of the sliding steel bolt. When the large metal door flew up and bright light poured in, her heart leapt with relief and joy. The sudden clatter made Emily jump, but the rats jumped higher. In an instant, dozens of the horrid creatures darted off to their secreted hovel, out of sight under the wall of an interior office behind them. Emily dropped her head and began to sob. Someone had somehow found her and Sarah and had come to rescue them from the terror of the filthy rodents. The relief was overwhelming, but short lived.

Straining to see her liberators through the brilliant light, her excitement brimmed until her eyes adjusted and she saw the white van backing into the warehouse. Then the door rolled down with a raucous clanging, blocking out the light from outside and snuffing the hopes within. Now her eyes were wide and her face pale with dread and a morbid, sickening brand of fright as she watched the two Asian captors unload a sturdy wooden table and a roll of carpet from the back of the van.

Emily's heart grew heavy as she realized what was happening. The two men were rolling out the carpet, positioning the table, the lights, and the video camera as if they were arranging a movie set. The older one walked to the back of the van while the younger one adjusted the tripod that held the camera, craning it as high as it would go. The older one returned with two large cinder blocks, one in each hand. The younger one retrieved two more blocks from the back of the van while the older one brought a plywood plank that looked to be about four-foot square. They worked together to set up a platform upon which they placed the tripod, with the camera aimed down at the top of the table.

When the older one returned with thick nylon rope, her heart began to race, and fresh beads of perspiration trickled down her face. A cold wave of panic gripped her, cutting her breath into labored gasps, as she watched him cut the rope into lengths, tie them securely to each of the table's thick legs, and drape the ends over the corners of the table. Emily began to realize what they had in mind and it filled her with loathsome disgust. Her insides tightened and twisted, and she sensed that all the color had drained from her face.

Suddenly, she preferred the rats.

* * *

Western Caribbean Sea, 4 Miles North-northwest of Providencia Island
June 15, 7:40 p.m. Caribbean Time

Several minutes passed while the two men silently endured the jarring bumps and harrowing pitches. They were still intertwined. Stinky held Collin's neck in the crux of his elbow and started once again to hiss and pontificate in a venomous stream of well-rehearsed lines. Collin guessed that they were practiced and memorized from a propaganda leaflet. His words were vicious, laced with hatred and vitriol against Western society and its excesses. He jabbed a finger into Collin as if he was the one responsible for all of the injustices perpetrated around the world in the name of capitalism. Stinky promised Collin would beg for mercy and cry like a baby as he beheld his loved ones' suffering at the hands of Penh's organization, a group of pure souls who had vowed to right the wrongs done by Americans for so many generations.

"When my boss commands, I will bring you a fitting death. Fitting for a thief. Fitting for a greedy cheater," said Stinky.

"What makes you so sure any of that will happen?" Collin shouted above the storm. "You'll die first if I have anything to do with it."

"How can you say I will die first, Mr. Cook? You are in a position of extreme disadvantage. You are subject to the will of my boss. He has power over your fate, not you. He has designed it to be this way and so it is."

"Go ahead and believe that if you want," said Collin as he tried to wiggle free. "I don't believe any of your nonsense. Someone else taught you those words and you spew them out as if they are absolute truths. But they're not. They're twisted to make you angry and to make you hate and you are too weak minded to know the difference between truth and the bald-faced lies that snake Penh wants you to believe. I have my own designs. Who says they won't come to be?"

"Our cause is just; yours is not. We seek to pull down the greed and pride and arrogance of your country and bring prosperity to all the world, not just one rich country. You only seek to keep the money that you stole from us. We will prevail. You and the other American scum will not. You will all be brought down to the dust to beg for mercy. And we shall laugh."

"How can you say your cause is just? All you want to do is harm and kill and steal, you lunatic animal."

As the waves smashed into the *Admiral*, the two men continued to tumble together in the cabin.

"You shall think differently when this is all over. When our plans are complete, you shall see our triumph," Stinky said. "This will be after you watch your mother and whore girlfriend suffer in a most cruel fashion. First, my fellow team members will enjoy the companionship of your beautiful friend. They have been waiting to do so all day and have a special plan for her. When they are through, your mother will be sacrificed while your girlfriend watches. She will be as helpless as you. And you will have a perfect view. You will beg me to kill them first, and then you."

"You're deluded," hissed Collin.

Stinky broke concentration during his speech. Collin felt the slack in his arms and took advantage during the next slide across the floor. He broke free and used his feet and legs to scrabble to the opposite side of the cabin.

Collin's eyes were fixed on Stinky's through the dim light spilling from a single, plastic-covered bulb mounted on the ceiling above the galley sink.

The rage inside burned with a ferocity Collin had never in his life experienced. Stinky was inexplicably passive about his escape. An air of superiority enveloped his countenance. He was full of some sort of philosophical confidence, which perturbed Collin to no end.

Stinky fought for balance so he could regain higher ground. First, he crawled on hands and knees to the salon table. Then he scrambled to a sitting position on the bench and glowered downward at Collin who was leaning against the bulkhead near the steps to the hatch.

The ship was being tossed about in the roiling sea, making it difficult for Collin to keep his intensity as he struggled to maintain an upright position.

"I wish the boss would say it is time right now," said Stinky. He raised his Uzi and pointed it toward Collin's face. "I will enjoy seeing your face when they ravish your girlfriend."

Another powerful wave propelled Stinky face first from his perch on the salon bench, knocking the gun out of his hands, and sending the two men careening toward the front of the boat across the wooden floor. They skidded in a jumble, aimed directly at the two steps leading down to the galley as the boat raced down the face of a towering wave. Stinky banged his shoulder against the wall before going head long down the steps. Collin managed to catch his balance just before plunging into the same low spot with Stinky by pressing his legs against the cabinet on one side and the wall on the other side of the steps to the galley and pushing his back into the floor.

Stinky scrambled to collect himself, but his weapon was behind Collin, and Collin blocked his path. The boat quickly changed angles as it climbed toward the crest of the next gigantic wave. Collin was now sliding backward toward the hatch and the steps leading up to the deck. The Uzi ricocheted off the wall and hit his bound hands as he slid toward the rear of the boat. With some effort, he was able to grasp it with his right hand by the stock. At that moment he sensed movement coming in his direction. It was Stinky making a last-ditch effort to seize the weapon. Collin hit the bottom step with the middle of his back and fought off the pain to stay in the moment. As Stinky left his feet, the step gave Collin just enough support so he could lift both legs in the air and kick out.

It wasn't a solid hit, but it did the job. One foot connected with Stinky's left arm, the other grazed his ribs on his right side. The impact, though not injurious, knocked Stinky's trajectory toward the steps instead of directly at Collin. One knee just missed Collin's left leg, but Stinky's left shoulder barreled into Collin's stomach, knocking out his breath.

The next moment, both bodies were slipping toward the kitchen and its precipitous step again. Collin struggled for air as he skated on his back. Stinky, dazed from the head-first collision with the steps, was tumbling on his side, shoulder over shoulder until he slammed against the base of the cabinet. Collin was heading toward the opening where the steps to the galley were located. This time, however, the boat pitched to the right. Collin's left foot made contact with the cabinet and the inertia from the boat caused him to slip under the dining table to his right. Stinky followed, his head hitting Collin's thigh as Collin's shoulder crashed into the bulkhead below the dining room's bench seat.

Collin still clutched the stock of the compact submachine gun.

As the boat began another steep ascent, the two men slipped along the floor as one tangled mess toward the rear of the boat again. Without hands, Collin's ability to fight was severely impaired. Stinky thrashed his arms in an attempt to commandeer the gun.

"I warn you," Collin growled into Stinky's ear, "given the chance, I *will* kill you."

"You won't. You have no guts. You are no killer."

"Believe that if you want," Collin barked. "I'll kill all of you if I have to."

* * *

Industrial Complex, 30 miles southeast of San Diego, California
June 15, 5:41 p.m. Pacific Time

Emily had closed her eyes to summon her strength and hide her fear. When hands gripped each arm above the elbow, she flinched. One of the men cut her feet free, then each man held her down more tightly on each side while they cut away the duct tape from her arms. Together they yanked her out of the chair and dragged her toward the table. She wanted to kick, but she couldn't move her legs. They had been bound in the sitting position for too long, too stiff to move.

The men lifted her onto the table and pressed her down on her back. The younger one climbed onto the table, straddling her with his knees and pinning her arms down over her head while the older man worked quickly to tie down her wrists first, then her ankles. She tried to resist, but her stiff muscles had very little strength or coordination.

The spiked eyebrow moved in close to her face, whispering something she couldn't understand in her ear. A demonic grin spread across his face as he pressed himself against her. Emily again closed her eyes, trying to block out the looks from the man as he leered at her. Her attempts to wrestle free were vain. The man was thin, but muscular. Every struggle to break free caused him to apply more pressure and snigger more obscenely.

Emily felt a tug on her left ankle and realized the older man with the tattoos on his neck had finished tying her down. When he stood, he raised his voice and wrestled the younger one off Emily. She imagined him saying something like "Not yet, but you'll have your chance later," as the two men moved back toward the van.

Emily had never felt so vulnerable in her life. Tied to a table with her shirt ripped open, dried blood on her face and neck, and fresh blood mixed with rat urine dripping down her chest, she experienced a level of humiliation and degradation she had never imagined possible. Being at the mercy of these two miscreants conjured feelings of helplessness and hopelessness more overwhelming and dehumanizing than anything she had ever thought possible.

Though her eyes remained closed, Emily could sense them moving and could hear them talking. The young one was anxious; she could tell by the tone of his voice. The older one was trying to settle him down.

She ventured a look as the voices grew distant. They were dragging

Sarah's chair closer. Then she heard a slapping sound and tried to scream. The younger one was slapping Sarah's face to wake her up. She was not responsive, so he began to shake her and scream. Powerless to stop them, Emily could only watch as the young bully grew more impatient. Finally, the older one showed up with a syringe in hand. After he injected her arm, Sarah's eyes popped open and she began to bob and sway in an agitated frenzy.

Emily's eyes met Sarah's, which were wide open and darting about in a frenzy until they locked in on Emily. She watched Sarah's brow furrow and a look of sorrow and pity overtake her countenance. Sarah's head shook and her mouth moved. Unintelligible sounds came through the tape, though it was obvious that Sarah wanted these two men to stop what they were doing.

The older one with the tattoos was holding the younger one with the spikes at arm's length and speaking strong words to him. Then a phone rang somewhere in the background and both men moved toward the sound. A conversation ensued that Emily could not understand, but yet she could. Instructions were being given by the man in charge for how this torture and assault would go down and how it would be filmed. They were going to show it to Collin as a means of punishment. The thought wrecked her. Anyone seeing her like this would be the ultimate disgrace, but for Collin to witness what was about to take place would completely undo him. She was supposed to be helping him. How could she be strong knowing what was coming and knowing Collin would be forced to watch it?

Chapter Nineteen

W*estern Caribbean Sea, 3.5 miles north-northwest of Providencia Island*
June 15, 7:45 p.m. Caribbean Time

The sun hung above the western horizon, though they could not see it. The storm had swallowed nearly all of the sunlight by day's end with its ominous black clouds and heavy showers. The *Admiral* slogged through thickening darkness and relentless wind and rain. Only through the miracle of modern technology and the gadgets onboard, along with Captain Sewell's knowledge and experience, had they managed to make it this far in these conditions.

Less than four miles to go. Three and a half treacherous, perilous, life-threatening miles. At their current rate, it would take roughly half an hour to reach the harbor. That felt like an eternity to Captain Sewell as he fought through the mounting swells and the lashing winds. He had ordered all sails furled and all hatches battened down, choosing instead to use engine power. It was the only safe way, if you could call it that, to navigate in these conditions. Their progress would be, necessarily, much slower. He threaded the *Admiral* through the maze of shoals with the hearty fortitude of an old sea dog. But it was a wearying task.

The swells came at the *Admiral* head-on and had grown to ten feet in height. In the shallow water around the shoals, the waves were amplified, being squeezed up from the rising ocean floor and pinched on the sides by the reefs and rocks. Climbing the face of each wave and fighting the increasing current, had slowed progress to a crawl.

Although the *Admiral Risty* was well-equipped for severe weather, including some retrofits to the bulkhead and mast for storm-ready sails, the winds had become too powerful and unpredictable for sails. The Captain and crew, like the ship itself, were experienced and prepared for such weather; their captors were not. The three hijackers above-decks clung to the railings near the cockpit, trying to maintain a vigilant guard. Guns drawn and ready, they let the Captain know they were wary and ready to shoot.

Noting their vigilance, the Captain, using a mix of nautical terminology and dialectic Spanish, spoke directly to his crew, warning them to be careful. One wrong move would spell disaster for them all.

The real danger now was the natural surroundings. So far, they had successfully navigated through several miles of shoals and reefs but were still surrounded by multiple rocky spits and islets, barely discernible on the Captain's instruments. The waters were shallow, the winds blew at gale force from the east, and the seas were rougher than ever. The peaks and troughs were closer together, making the swells steeper and more treacherous to navigate, and much less comfortable for all on board.

* * *

Below-decks, neither Stinky nor Collin had the strength to continue their fight. Stinky rolled to his side and retched violently. Although exhausted and parched, Collin had managed to land a knee to Stinky's gut as the two tussled about on the floor of the cabin, causing the intense reaction. When he was done, Stinky struggled to his knees, braced himself against the bunk, shimmied his way to the galley, and found the store of water bottles in the refrigerator. He gulped one down, then opened another. He drank another mouthful, then crawled to where Collin lay half unconscious.

Stinky grabbed Collin by the shirt and pulled him close as he wrested the Uzi out of Collin's feeble grip. While bracing himself and holding Collin steady amid the jostling of the sea, Stinky studied Collin's face, paying particular

147

attention to his eyes. "My boss says you must live," he muttered as he began pouring the water on Collin's face. At first, Collin gagged at the stench emanating from Stinky's mouth as he spoke. His breath was hot and foul, his face far too close to Collin's. But Collin's need for water was powerful enough to overcome the gag reflex. Instincts kicked in and Collin opened his mouth to catch every drop possible, licking and lapping like a starved dog.

The water was refreshing and renewing, but far from adequate. He needed much more. "Thank you," he said sincerely.

"You have been very clever, Mr. Cook," Stinky said. His energy was zapped, and the statement hung in the air. "But my boss is cleverer. You will not beat him."

"I don't feel the need to." Collin was lying, but his lack of vigor hid that fact. He sounded desperate and beaten, much like Stinky.

"You should not have hidden his money. My boss is a very stern man. He will do bad things. Your mother and your girlfriend will suffer and so will you. I will kill you then, slowly."

There was a period of silence between the two men, filled only by the sounds of the intensifying storm outside, the clanging of objects in the cupboards and closets, and their labored breathing.

Collin spoke slowly and clearly, his voice loud enough to be heard over the din, but hoarse and strained. "Only I can get the money out in person. Without me, the computer codes are useless. That account has no Internet access. I wanted it to be completely secure, so a retina scan is required. Then the codes. When we get to Panama City, I will get the money. But only if my mother and friend are released, unharmed. I told you guys this."

"That is for Mr. Penh to decide."

There was pause in the conversation as the ship slid down the face of another large wave, then up the side of the next. Both men were braced on the floor, using each other, the walls, and the table legs for leverage to prevent themselves from careening out of control. "Why does he want my money?" Collin asked. "He's shown that he can skim money from any major bank in the world. I'm sure he has plenty of money for his little cyber jihad. Why can't he leave me alone? I'm a nothing."

Stinky's voice was harsh and condemning now. Any trace of humanity or compassion had vanished. "That is not your money. You must first realize that fact. You must also realize that Mr. Penh does not tolerate thieves like you. You have proven that all Americans are filled with greed. Money. It is your god. Your family and friends will also pay for your greediness."

"I am not the greedy one here," Collin said with more strength than he thought he had. "And my family and friends should be left out of this. Justice was served and Penh's insurance company paid what was agreed upon as compensation for my loss and the neglect of his client. All of this," he said with a wave of his head, "is proof that your boss's greed is far more insidious than any greed you might think I have."

"You are wrong, Mr. Cook," Stinky snapped. "Americans are all greedy. They steal from poor countries like ours so they can get richer." His eyes bored into Collin's. "We must bring it to an end. Our cause is just. You are an American scum—a thief and a cheater. You and your family are like vermin that must be exterminated."

Another wave hit the boat from the side and the two men were knocked from their positions of balance into each other. They clamored and kicked as they slid, banging into the opposite wall then back again.

"I will watch you suffer, Mr. Cook. You, your mother, and your whore girlfriend." Stinky's words spewed out like foaming acid that burned Collin's insides, making him sick to his very core.

Collin shook his head slowly and clinched his jaw. The two men glared across the cabin at each other, bracing against the constant rolling action of the sea. Neither spoke another word.

The Captain's voice above them grew in volume and urgency. His orders were crisp and clear, fueled with authority. Those orders were followed by indiscernible activity on the deck. Scrambling, knocking, and whirring. Metallic pings. Ropes whistling through pulleys. More clanging. More yelling.

The *Admiral* pitched forward, leaning hard to the left. It was then thrown upward, bending sharply to the right.

These motions repeated themselves over and over for what felt like interminable hours, although it was only minutes.

Collin saw Stinky's eyes widen and his body tighten even more. His face had become ashen. He looked up and all around as everything inside the *Admiral Risty* banged and clattered with the violent motions of the storm-whipped sea. As if a thought struck him, Stinky whipped his head in all directions, searching for something. He crawled across the floor on hands and knees, eventually standing and stepping down into the galley. Emerging with the satellite phone in his hand, Stinky studied its screen. He tapped on it and muttered to himself as he turned and pointed the device to the sky in all directions, presumably trying to find signal.

* * *

Industrial Complex, 30 miles southeast of San Diego, California
 June 15, 5:56 p.m. Pacific Time

Emily's body went rigid and her insides turned cold when the warm sweaty hands gripped her ankles. Her eyes instinctively shot open to see the young one with the spike in his eyebrow holding her and the older one climbing onto the platform to adjust the camera. He had a phone to his ear again and seemed to be answering questions. The two men had been talking together and to someone on the phone for several elongated minutes while Emily lay tied to the table, filled with fear. A red light atop the camera began blinking as the man with the tattoos stepped down and moved close to her. He held the phone near her ear.

"Good evening, Emily," came a silky voice with an aristocratic accent. "It's so nice to have you with us. My men have been anticipating this moment since they first saw you. I wish your friend Collin could join us. After all, he is the one who has brought us all together here. We have him to thank for the pleasure of your company, which we are all about to enjoy. It is unfortunate that your friend is unavailable at the moment. He is apparently preoccupied or too ashamed of the actions he has taken, which have placed you and his mother in my care. But rest assured, my dear Emily, we will record the proceedings and share them with your friend at a more convenient time. Who knows, we may even find a website willing to pay us for such footage. You may become famous, Emily." Penh's cackle echoed in the hollow warehouse.

The voice returned to its previous suave and regal tone and said something in another language. The tattooed man nodded to the younger one and he began moving his hands tenderly up Emily's legs, massaging her calves as he licked his lips and whispered in a pseudo-romantic tone.

The older man barked something, and the younger man's hands stopped and let go. He moved in front of Sarah. Emily couldn't see what he was doing, but his frame was moving in an agitated fashion. Then she heard another slap, followed by muffled crying.

When he moved away, Emily could see a bright red mark growing on Sarah's cheek and tears welling up in her eyes. Emily shut her eyes and tried to contain the sobs, but it didn't work. Pent-up emotions, spiked with horror and dread, burst out. Her own tears began to flow, and her stifled snivels made it difficult for her to breathe.

The hands returned to her ankles, but instead of the gentle rubbing and attempted sensuality, the firmness of the grip alarmed her all the more. Then one hand forcefully grabbed the hem of her pant leg, tugging at it so hard it hurt, while the other held up the familiar knife blade—the same one he had used to cut her—so Emily could see it. He said something, then turned to show the blade to the camera. The carnal look in his eyes and devilish grin on his face when he turned toward her terrified Emily to the point her entire body started shaking uncontrollably.

* * *

Western Caribbean Sea, 2 miles north-northwest of Providencia Island

June 15, 8:08 p.m. Caribbean Time

Captain Sewell checked his glowing instruments again, the only discernible light in the tempestuous night, and confirmed out loud to his crew that they were now less than two miles from the shore of Providencia Island and its safe harbor. He hoped Collin heard him below and that it would keep his spirits up.

They were about to sail between two rocky islets, each one roughly the size of a short city block. Knowing that they were approaching Providencia from the west, the channel between these two tiny islands would essentially squeeze the waves into an even tighter area, further amplifying their height and power.

As he started the turn into the channel, the Captain shouted as loud as he could. "Brace yourselves."

The crew hunkered into position in anticipation, a mixture of dread and adrenaline pulsing through them with the rhythms of the sea.

While this storm was not the worst Captain Sewell and his crew had encountered in their years of sailing together, he knew it was the most dangerous. To sail through this area was distressing in the best circumstances. With night approaching and in the pouring rain, battling fierce winds, it was downright terrifying. Being a proud man, he projected the eternal air of calm and control. Yet he seethed at the notion of having his boat hijacked and his passengers and crew members threatened. One had been killed and thrown into the sea like refuse. An unpardonable offense.

It was bad form to come aboard a boat without permission. It was even worse to wrest control away from the Skipper and force him to sail into bad weather. Still worse, however, was to hold a gun to him and coerce cooperation by threatening evil things. Nothing irked Captain Sewell more than bullies and thugs. The worst, however, was Tog's murder. It weighed on him and on his crew like an anchor. There would be retribution. The Karma of the Sea would see to it.

The Captain clicked on a small but powerful flashlight and shined it through the darkness until he counted all six men on deck—three of his crew members; three hijackers.

When Sewell flashed the light at the longhaired man, he reacted by holding his Uzi in the ready posture. Since he used nothing more than his foot wrapped around a railing post to hold himself in place, he was not properly braced. The Captain's attention was diverted for a moment as he pointed to the man's foot and started to caution him. That's when a giant wave hit the boat sidelong. A torrent of water rushed over the deck. The hijacker was knocked sideways from his post on the port side, three feet to Captain Sewell's left. He caromed into the Captain's knees. The Captain was cut down and toppled forcefully to his left. Holding the wheel grips firmly as he tumbled sideways, the wheel rotated in the same direction, turning the *Admiral* sharply into the next steep, cresting wave as she scaled toward its peak on a diagonal across the curling wall of water.

Chapter Twenty

I ndustrial Complex, 30 miles southeast of San Diego, California
June 15, 6:09 p.m. Pacific Time

Again, the young spiked one had stepped away when the older one called to him, pointing at the phone, and the two men conferred, leaving Emily in agonizing anticipation for what felt like an eternity. They loitered around the van for quite some time, allowing Emily's hopes to rise briefly.

When they returned, the young one made a big show for the camera, waving the knife blade and talking in a low, sultry voice. He approached Emily from the side facing the camera and began to kiss her neck and ear, moving his body closer. One arm on each side of her head, his chest leaning into hers, his hands teasing her hair. Then he stood and let his eyes dance their way down her figure as he walked toward the end of the table again. He glanced seductively at her while he removed her shoes.

Her expression of disgust, though involuntary, did not please him. His face hardened. He grabbed the pant leg again and tugged it upward, the hem dug into her skin.

The long, sharp blade glided easily through the soft synthetic material of Emily's pant leg. She felt the cool, smooth steel of the knife's spine against her skin as it moved upward, which sent foreboding tremors throughout her body. When he reached her thigh, it stopped, and a boisterous laugh echoed through the building. The spiked tormentor was again playing it up for the camera. Emily could tell that he was going to make sport of her misery by the way he watched her face and smiled whenever she winced or let out a sob. This torture and agony was going to drag on and on. He seemed to be very amused by her distress. After a crude display with his tongue, the spiked one turned the blade perpendicular, cutting the pants off to become shorts, baring her shapely legs. Taking his time, he repeated the process on the other leg, allowing his hands to linger and make contact with her skin as he sliced. This made her cringe even more, if that was possible.

After cutting off the second pant leg to her mid-thigh, the young captor with the spiked eyebrow turned toward the camera on the platform, which was to Emily's left. He displayed the material and the knife for the lens as he talked in a sadistic tone. As he spoke, Emily heard two simultaneous sounds. One came as the back door of the warehouse blew open with a muted *phhhtt* sound. The other from a side door to her left, twenty yards behind the camera. These noises were followed by a sudden booming echo that filled the whole building with raucous clatter. Within seconds, twelve military operators in desert fatigues and full battle gear rushed in through each door in protective formation. Two soft *thwaps* followed a split second later. The spiked one's arms flew outward as his body was launched backward out of Emily's view and into one of the light stands, knocking it over with a thunderous crash. At the same time, the upper body of the one with the tattoos on his neck slammed into the table near Emily's left elbow, then fell to the ground with a dull thud. She felt something warm and wet land on her bare stomach and legs, on her blouse and arms, causing her to jerk against the ropes and scream through the duct tape. Sarah, seated to Emily's right, was also screaming. Checking to see what landed on her, Emily realized it was blood, bone, and brain matter. It was splattered on Sarah as well.

Within seconds, Emily saw the powerful lights atop the helmets and affixed to the rifles of the commandos as they spread beams of light in all directions. The ten men and two women swept through the dark, open space, systematically assessing any and all threats between them and the two bedraggled women—Sarah bound to a chair and Emily tied to a table—in the middle of the cavernous warehouse. Finding no additional threats, Emily heard men call "clear" from the area of the van and other men making the same call from the office to her left before four others moved quickly to the two women.

The relief this time was real. These people were true saviors. Emily, who was not given to the gushing of emotions, could not contain the flood. As soon as the ropes were cut from her wrists and ankles and she was helped to a sitting position, Emily collapsed into the arms of a woman who wore the red cross of a medic on her uniform. The other members of the team quickly and efficiently unpacked and unfolded equipment and supplies. After a comforting embrace and encouraging words from the medic, Emily turned to Sarah, who was being helped onto a short-legged, portable cot.

As she was helped off the table by her female medic, Emily was amazed at the efficiency of this group. These people were equipped and experienced. Before she was able to speak, Emily noticed the enormous pack that gaped open beside the medic who attended to Sarah and determined that was the origin of the cot. She also noticed three other massive camouflage packs in an array nearby. Each medic was assisted by another member of the team. Looking beyond their immediate area, she observed two sets of lights moving toward the front, where the roller door was, and another pair moving in the back, near the door they had burst through. A third pair stayed near the side entrance and the fourth pair inspected the van inside and out.

Before she could speak, Sarah's medic answered the question Emily's face must have asked. "They're securing the entrances," he said. "We have an assault team on the roof of this building and another on the roof of the building across the way." He pointed with two fingers, jabbing the air toward the front door. "No chance anyone else will hurt you again. At least, not today." The young Hispanic man with the dark, clean crew cut was warm and professional. The name embroidered on a patch above his breast pocket said Garcia.

"Thank you," muttered Emily, her gravelly voice low and strained. "How did you find us?"

"Apparently from your cell phone signal," he said. Garcia never stopped working. His hands glided in and out of the open pack, pulling out items, ripping open packets, and setting things in place.

"But they threw my phone out the window," said Emily, puzzlement twisting her expression. "I saw him do it. The guy with the pierced eyebrow. He threw it out the window on the freeway." Her words came in short bursts and her countenance carried that far away, frightened look.

"That's all I can tell you, Dr. Burns." He hung the IV bag on the shorter than usual IV pole he had connected to the corner of Sarah's cot.

"How do you know my name?"

"It came with the mission intel we were given," he said matter-of-factly as he attached the blood pressure cuff to Sarah's arm and started pumping.

The female medic who had embraced Emily, a Corporal Hanes, put her hands on Emily's shoulders and steered her toward a cot similar to Sarah's that was set up and ready for her. Emily resisted. "We have to get her to the hospital. Right away. The Scripps Cancer Research Clinic. In La Jolla. She's a cancer patient there. Dr. Javier Navarro. He needs to see her. She must get proper care." Emily was agitated, spacey. Shock was settling in.

"We are aware of her condition," said the female medic as she moved Emily into position on the cot. Smiling, she added, "You're safe now. You can relax."

"She's stage three. This stress, it can't be good . . ."

"We know, Dr. Burns," the woman said, smiling. "We will transport her there as soon as we get the 'all clear.' Don't you worry. We'll take good care of the both of you." Corporal Hanes handed Emily a water bottle. "First, we need to get you both cleaned up and hydrated. It's hot as hell in here."

After hours of bravely battling to protect Sarah from the rats and steeling herself for the two goons' torture, Emily slumped into a regressive, almost catatonic state, letting the military rescuers assume full responsibility for the situation.

* * *

Western Caribbean Sea, 2 miles north-northwest of Providencia Island
   June 15, 8:10 p.m. Caribbean Time

The force of the sudden erratic turn against the power of the breaking wave sent the *Admiral Risty* toppling over on its side. Captain Sewell reached for something to hold. His fingers grazed the edge of the bulkhead near the pilot's chair. The boat pitched at such a severe angle that his whole body went airborne as he and the long-haired terrorist tumbled toward the edge of the boat. He collided into the gunwale, first with his shoulder and second with the side of his head, as he catapulted into the dark, churning water.

The three crew members, cosseted with protective life jackets and recognizing the danger, launched themselves into the sea as the boat tumbled. Miguel, closest to the water when the boat tipped over, tried to get as far from the toppling vessel as possible, knowing the masts and sails presented deadly traps. Jaime, who was near the bow, launched himself forward of the boat. Rojas, the man nearest the stern, jumped off the back away from the hull. Jaime and Rojas, positioned on the uphill side, fell a long way before finally hitting the water.

The other two terrorists held on to the railing with everything they had, not sure what else to do.

The *Admiral* was rolled and tossed by the monster wave, like a pair of pants in a front-load washing machine. Its masts protruded deep into the water as it tumbled and sifted through the surf like a rake, slowing the rate of spin.

Below the surface, seven bodies either thrashed or floated under the surface of the turbulent sea, arms and legs in all directions. Some kicked wildly. Some moved quickly and with purpose. Others remained deathly still while the ocean carried them in suspended animation.

* * *

Collin faintly heard the Captain's voice. Something was wrong, he could tell. There was panic in that normally calm baritone. Suddenly, he and Stinky were shot through the air from the steps near the hatch toward the bunks on the port side. Collin curled into a ball the best he could. His side slammed into a hard surface with a jarring thud. Again, the wind was knocked out of him and searing pain burst through his ribs, hip, and shoulder. He was pinballed between hard and soft objects repeatedly before falling a few feet and landing with his back against the ceiling of the salon, above the dining table. Everything in his world was rotating.

Struggling to gain a sense of what was happening while pain enveloped him, he noticed a flowered shirt bouncing near him. With a shake of his head, he realized the boat was capsizing and tried to anticipate the boat's next movement. Disoriented and bruised, Collin couldn't get into position before the next violent revolution of the boat. He bashed into things and rolled uncontrollably. Out of the corner of his vision, he noticed the flowered shirt mirroring his movements.

Another wave hit the side of the overturned boat, causing more tumbling. The lights went out and Collin was plunged into total darkness, then cool wetness.

* * *

Miguel, the crew member positioned closest to Captain Sewell before the *Admiral* turned over, opened his eyes underwater and began to search for the surface. With the churning action of the waves, it was nearly impossible to tell which way was up. In the semidarkness, he could only make out shapes and masses. The long pole-like structures protruding through the water, he knew, were the masts. What little ambient light there was in the water glinted in wavy, silvery lines off the aluminum tubes. They moved in an agitated, unpredictable fashion. He needed to steer clear of them, so he began to kick and pull his way through the water in the opposite direction as his life jacket began tugging him upward. There were dark objects ahead of him, floating and tumbling through the water. Unsure what they were, he propelled himself away from them.

Miguel was so preoccupied with avoiding the dangers he had identified, that were now behind him and to his right, he didn't notice what was in his path. He bumped into something that spooked him. At first, the something brushed his cheek, then it made more solid contact with his shoulder. The fright caused Miguel to blow out some of his precious breath. He turned to look at the strange object, and pushed it away, when he realized it was the motionless body of Captain Sewell. The flashlight was still on, dangling from his wrist. It spun a beam of light through the dark water.

With the buoyancy of his life vest dragging him toward the surface, Miguel was fortunate to grasp a handful of shirt and to hook a foot under an arm. As he rose, Miguel clamored to get a better hold, but he was moving too fast and the sea was too turbulent. He managed to drag the Captain with him for several seconds but lost his grip before he breached the surface.

* * *

In the darkness, Collin's senses heightened. The sounds around him were terrifying. Water gurgling in, air whooshing out. Pots and pans and boxes and books striking hard surfaces, then splashing. Lots of splashing. Collin glimpsed Stinky flailing across the cabin, a scene of desperation and panic. Stinky's terror-stricken screams rent the chaos-filled space.

The feel of the water, salty and cool, soaking his clothes as he lay on the ceiling, sent him scrambling. Collin struggled to a kneeling position as the boat gyrated. The water quickly reached his ribs. The coolness felt good on his tied and swollen wrists bound behind his back, but the sense of sinking was terrorizing.

Light flickered on, a pale blue glow from the bunk area in the rear. Then another appeared from the kitchen, illuminating Stinky's panic-stricken countenance. His head turned in all directions, as did his arms and legs. He quickly locked onto Collin and lunged toward him in a violent series of frantic movements that resembled swimming strokes. Collin knew his intentions and acted on his primal survival instincts, sucking in as much air as he could and diving under the water, the surface of which approached his chest as he stood on the ceiling. Using his head as a battering ram, Collin threw himself into Stinky's gut, driving him through the water-filled cabin as he scissor-kicked with his legs. Stinky froze momentarily as the two of them sloshed about without footing or balance. Collin had only his feet, legs, and head as weapons. He also had no idea where the Uzi had gone.

Stinky, however, had use of his hands and began tearing wildly at Collin's head and back as Collin's momentum and the agitation of the sea propelled him underwater, back-first into a wall in the galley. Air bubbles escaped Stinky's mouth at impact and he began to sink, motionless. Collin whirled his body around, pointing his feet toward Stinky, and thrust them into Stinky's ribs and throat as hard as he could through the water. This was a kill-or-be-killed situation. Instinct and adrenaline were in full control. The contact with Collin's feet propelled Stinky the short distance into the wall behind him, magnifying the force of the blows. Another stream of bubbles, much smaller ones this time, poured out.

Collin kicked to the surface, took two deep breathes, and went back under. He found Stinky coming to and fighting his way to the surface for more air. Collin didn't get to him in time. As Stinky focused on air, Collin positioned himself for another crushing blow. He knew Stinky was struggling to breathe. Stinky clutched his throat with one hand and kicked with his feet until they found purchase on the edge of one of the bunks. With his other hand, he steadied his weight by pushing on the floor above him.

Collin's next strike was again on the money. The heel of one foot charged powerfully into Stinky's groin, the other slammed his kneecap straight on. Stinky was caught mid-breath and hurled face first back into the water. He was doubled over and appeared to be gulping in water. Collin surfaced and used his head to brace himself against the ceiling as he pushed down on Stinky's shoulders and back with his feet. Stinky struggled to break free, but before he could reach the surface, Collin worked one leg around his neck, then squeezed like a vice with the other leg in Stinky's back. Stinky fought and struggled desperately. His convulsions pulled Collin back underwater, but Collin had a full breath and Stinky had none. Collin pushed harder with his legs and twisted his body to keep Stinky off-balance and underwater. He thrashed again in an attempt to maintain leverage, but he had none.

* * *

As soon as he felt air and refilled his lungs, Miguel began to tear off his life vest. This was no easy task in the midst of the wind, rain, and waves. He fumbled with the buckles until all four of them released. That was the easy part. Removing his arms from the armholes proved more difficult. As he struggled to break free, he felt someone wrap their arms around him. It was Rojas.

"Take it easy, man, you're OK," yelled Rojas. "You're going to be all right."

"No. The Captain. He's down there," shouted Miguel.

"The Captain? Where?"

"Get this thing off me," screamed Miguel as he continued to thrash.

Rojas held the jacket and Miguel squirmed free, gulped a lungful of air, then disappeared below the storm-tossed waves.

Rojas waved his arms and hollered to Jaime, who had surfaced some distance away. Jaime rotated in a circle but disappeared behind a wave. Rojas continued to call out and kept one arm raised until finally Jaime spotted him and swam toward him.

"Where's Miguel?" asked Jaime.

"Down there. He's going for the Captain."

At that moment, Miguel resurfaced fifteen yards away. He was straining. Rojas and Jaime paddled through the surf and huddled around Miguel, helping him pull his load up to the surface. Rojas grabbed the Captain's arm and fought the waves until he had him wrapped up under both arms and around his chest. Jaime helped Miguel get his life vest back on.

The three men worked together to get the Captain's face out of the water. They clung to each other and to the Captain. Knowing their best chance of survival was to stay together. Rojas squeezed the Captain's chest, moving a fist into his diaphragm and continually jabbing it inward. After repeating this several times, the Captain spit and sputtered and came to life. He looked around, eyes wide and wild.

"What? Where am I?" he said, still dazed. His head spun around in all directions, trying to ascertain his surroundings. Relief spread across his face as recognition of his friends and crew members dawned. "I thought I was dead."

His three crew members nodded to him and to each other, as traces of smiles worked their way up. Shouts of gratitude, relief, and hope boomed within the circle of men bobbing amidst the torrent. They held on to each other and to their Captain, a newfound appreciation for life and for each other taking hold while the bleakness of their situation retreated.

"Together, we can survive," said Rojas.

The Captain's smile faded. "Where are the bad guys?" he asked.

"We've been looking, but we can't see them," Rojas said. His face, too, grew dim.

"Keep looking," demanded Captain Sewell.

"Aye, sir," they replied, almost in unison.

"Where's Collin?" shouted the Captain.

The four men bobbed and dipped in the waves. The three crew members took turns diving down to search for their missing brother while the other two held the Captain. When one man exhausted his energy, the next removed his life jacket and dove down for as long as he could and searched as far as he could. This continued until they were all so stripped of energy that they could not stay under for more than a few seconds at a time, frantically searching for their missing client and friend. It was no use. The sunlight was gone, the sea was too fierce, and their own lives in imminent peril. They were compelled to focus on keeping the Captain afloat and themselves clear of the hazards surrounding them, as they negotiated huge swells.

The seas calmed as the waves and current pushed the huddle of men westward, out of the channel. They were surrounded by four–to–six-foot swells now, instead of twelve–to–fifteen footers in the channel. The *Admiral* appeared, bottom up, near the rocky edge of the channel. Wave after wave pushed and rolled the boat toward the rocks. The Captain eyed the vessel that was both his home and his livelihood with a melancholy expression as the waves continually swept over its barnacled underside, two hundred yards to their north. His mouth pulled tight and he turned away.

* * *

Stinky continued to twist and punch and pry. His hands tore at Collin's knee and ribs simultaneously. Collin felt he had an advantage thanks to all the years he'd spent surfing and building up his lung capacity to help him endure underwater after a wipeout. Collin held tight at first, but Stinky dug the tips of his fingers into a pressure point along the saphenous nerve of Collin's inner knee until Collin's leg muscles involuntarily released their captive.

Stinky clawed his way to the surface before Collin, and in a torrent of wild movement, managed to cuff Collin across the face and knee him in the chest. As Collin tried to recover and kick to the surface for air, he realized Stinky's hands were bearing down on his shoulders with tremendous force. Collin tried to wrestle free of Stinky's grip but couldn't. Every time his feet were set under him, Stinky would kick them out and knee him in the face or chest or back. Stinky's hands were on Collin's shoulders, then his neck, pushing down, holding him underwater.

Collin's lungs burned. Every cell in his body screamed for oxygen. Things were turning gray and cloudy at the edges of his vision. He felt like an old sock in an old washing machine, being shaken about in an agitated pool of murky water.

The need for air was all consuming, but without hands, Collin couldn't do much to free himself. Stinky's hands and legs continued to push Collin down with surprising force. Collin struggled to get his feet set on something below him, but the constant convulsions of the boat and the roiling water made it impossible. Stinky maintained the downward pressure while Collin's eyes began to bulge. Lungs, veins, brain all screamed for air he couldn't deliver.

Collin felt his eyes close. His body began to slump down toward the ceiling. A sweet, inviting peace washed through him. He was almost done, ready to let go of all the hurt. And rest.

Chapter Twenty-One

ashington, DC
June 15, 9:11 p.m. Eastern Time

"Stay in position. Keep a perimeter until I tell you," Lukas instructed calmly. Then he listened for a moment. "I know, but let the drone do one more pass before we move. I want to be sure there are no reinforcements patrolling the area. The last thing we want is a chopper shot while transporting patients."

Lukas paused and cupped a hand over the earphone.

"What's that? Shine some light on it so I can see it better." Lukas said as he tapped the keyboard to zoom in on the live feed.

Another pause to listen.

"Did that camera capture you guys? Is it recording?"

Lukas again listened to the assessment coming in from the field and looked at the images from the helmet camera.

"Get your Comm Engineer to create a loop to overlay those few minutes and feed it back into the camera," said Lukas. "While you're at it, have him copy the signal and clone the IP address of the computer it's linked to."

After the man on the other end of the conversation confirmed, Lukas replied, "The mission was to rescue the hostages and retrieve any and all actionable intel we could. This is a fortunate find, indeed . . . We need to get as much information from that phone and camera as we can."

Lukas listened again.

"Let's keep a team there for stealth security. At some point the guy at the other end will realize they're not coming back. He'll send in a backup team to recover the equipment, I'd imagine. Let's be ready for that, too."

* * *

Northbound Interstate 5, Southern Orange County, California
  June 15, 6:12 p.m. Pacific Time

"They're airborne, en route to Scripps Clinic," Lukas said as soon as Rob answered the phone, breaking the agitated silence Rob had endured for over an hour. "Should only take ten minutes by medivac helicopter."

"That's good to hear. What took so long?"

"Had to secure the area and make sure no more bad guys showed up. Frankly, we expected them, but they never came."

"Maybe they got caught in traffic, too. It's a nightmare out here," joked Rob.

"The important thing is that both Emily and Sarah are safe. They've been through a lot, but they're going to be fine," said Lukas.

"You had me worried, pal. Wasn't sure you'd be able to get a team in place on such short notice."

"It helps when you report to the director of the NSA," said Lukas.

"Probably helps that he thinks you walk on water," said Rob.

"Yeah, probably. But you should get Henry and take him there to see her."

"Good thing I followed my own best instincts," said Rob.

"What do you mean?"

"I mean it was driving me crazy to just sit around waiting for something to happen, so I decided to head up to Huntington Beach to see Henry," said Rob. "I'm glad I left when I did. With this horrible traffic, it would've been midnight before I made it back down to San Diego."

"Where are you now?" asked Lukas.

"Nearly to John Wayne Airport to pick up Collin's sister and brother. Megan landed fifteen minutes ago, and Richard's flight is due in about twenty minutes."

"Perfect. What about Henry?"

"Interesting story. I got to the hospital and discovered that his room is being guarded by FBI agents. Imagine that. They show up now that he's in the hospital and Sarah's gone."

"It's not their fault. Penh got the jump on all of us. He's been a step ahead of us since Collin showed up in Grand Cayman," said Lukas.

"No matter. I was able to gather the information I needed another way."

"What other way is that?" asked Lukas.

"I found a friendly young nurse who thought I was one of Henry's doctors—"

"I don't think I want to know the rest."

"OK, but to answer your original question, the hospital tells me they are ready to release him as soon as there's a family member to release him to," said Rob.

"How's he doing?"

"The nurse says he basically feels all right—bit of a headache and some painful bruises on his face. The whole situation doesn't sit well with him. He feels terrible that he wasn't able to defend his wife and, as you might imagine, he's sick with worry and anxious to see her. In fact, he's been so restless the nurse had to sedate him to keep him from walking out of the hospital when she turned her back."

"That sounds like Henry. What's your ETA to get him back down to Scripps to see her?" asked Lukas.

"With traffic, probably two hours at least, if everything goes smoothly at the hospital."

"That should be OK. I'm sure it will take some time for the doctors at Scripps to work on Sarah and Emily before they'll let anyone see them," said Lukas. "Do the best you can, but hurry. The medics tell me Sarah's been asking for him already."

"Will do. How's our friend, Emily, doing?"

Lukas gave Rob the run down, telling him what was happening when the rescue team rushed in and found her tied to the table. "She's pretty traumatized by the whole thing, not talking much at this point. Apparently, she's really worried about the rats. She keeps mentioning them and pointing to her chest."

"Sounds awful. The poor thing. Maybe it will help her to have me there," said Rob.

"I'm sure she could use a friend right now. Having someone she knows and trusts there will do a world of good, I'd imagine."

"Thanks for doing all this, Lukas. Pretty amazing stuff."

"Just happy it all worked out. Glad I'm in a position to make a difference for my friends," said Lukas.

* * *

Scripps Cancer Research Patient Clinic, La Jolla, California
  June 15, 6:33 p.m. Pacific Time

Sarah Cook whispered to Emily in the bed next to her. After cleaning the two of them up, giving Sarah some much needed nutrition, and bandaging and disinfecting Emily's wounds, the clinic staff had put the two together in a room on the second floor where a nursing staff kept watch twenty-four hours a day. Typically, the most critical patients were kept there overnight during their treatment sessions. Dr. Navarro and Emily had discussed this option for Sarah two days prior but had determined that she would be better off at home. Little did they know at the time the trouble that awaited.

Now they waited for Dr. Navarro.

"Emily, are you asleep?"

"No. What's the matter?"

"I can't sleep."

"Me neither."

Emily heard sniffling, so she crawled out from under the covers and made her way to Sarah's side, carefully maneuvering between the wires and machines and pulling her IV stand with her. Her tattered and stained clothes had been replaced by a fresh clean set of light blue scrubs. She had recovered from the shock, but still felt numb and oddly disconnected from the rest of the world. She couldn't be sure exactly what she was feeling. It felt almost as if she hovered above her own body, watching herself from a distance. Her mind had not yet processed all that had transpired in the past several hours and no one had asked about how she was coping with the trauma or what it was like going through it. Who could she talk to other than Sarah?

The room was mostly dark, illuminated by only a few shards of fading sunlight sneaking in through the gap at the top of the heavy curtains and the green, pulsating lights from the medical machines hooked up to monitor Sarah. Emily touched Sarah's shoulder and said softly, "What is it, Sarah?"

In the pale light, Sarah stared at her hands clasped tightly together on her lap. When Sarah tried to speak, no sound came out. She cleared her throat and tried again. "Collin," was the only word that made its way out. Sarah's voice was thick and hoarse.

Emily hesitated, not sure what to make of it. "Collin's not here, Sarah. I'm not sure where he is." She didn't want to say, "I'm not sure he's alive." She helped Sarah drink from a cup of water placed on the nightstand next to her bed.

After taking a pull on the water, Sarah tried again. "He never wanted you to get hurt. I know that much. But it's my fault. I got you involved."

"It's nobody's fault," said Emily faintly. She tried to fight through her feelings of detachment. "Bad stuff happens."

"I wish those bad things didn't happen to you."

"I know, Sarah, but I don't want you to worry about me. You've been through a lot in the last twenty-four hours. You need to rest and get your strength back."

"We both have, but we'll get past this, Emily."

"I hope you're right."

"We will. Together. I promise." Sarah reached for Emily's hand and grasped it.

The two remained connected, though wandering alone in their own thoughts for a long moment.

"Would you mind if I prayed for you?" asked Sarah.

Emily, whose eyes were full, stared blankly at her for a moment. Not knowing what else to say, she whispered, "That would be nice."

During the prayer, Emily fought through many competing emotions, but was struck the most by the juxtaposition of Sarah's comfort and familiarity with talking to God and her own clumsiness with it. This was something new and foreign to her, but not to Sarah. It seemed as normal and routine as brushing teeth or combing hair for her. In Emily's memory, not once did her parents even mention the word prayer, let alone bow before their Maker like this. To Sarah, however, this was apparently commonplace.

During the prayer, Emily cocked her head at the thought of Sarah thanking God for His goodness and blessings after what they had just experienced. Nonetheless, Sarah thanked God for His protection and their deliverance from evil, thanking Him for the valiant efforts of those who rescued them. She went on to express faith that Collin would be spared from his current predicament and returned to his family. To Emily, the whole experience was odd, but oddly comforting as well.

Emily watched Sarah as she lifted her head and met Emily's gaze. She remained hushed, unsure of what to say and afraid of ruining the moment.

"Well," said Sarah. "I feel much better; don't you?"

A tear ran down Emily's cheek. She dropped her head but didn't bother wiping it away. "I don't know what to feel," she quietly muttered.

Sarah took in Emily's far away gaze and returned it with perhaps the sweetest, most serene expression Emily had ever seen. "I know now everything is going to be all right. I feel it clear through to my bones. Don't you?"

Emily sighed. "Frankly, I don't know what to think," she said. "All I know is that the two of us have been through a lot and—"

"Didn't you find it strange how we were rescued all of a sudden?" interrupted Sarah.

Emily raised her head, fixing her eyes on Sarah as she spoke slowly and introspectively. "I don't know. The medic told me they followed my cell phone signal, but the guy with the eyebrow piercing threw it out the window. I watched him . . ." Her voice trailed off as she remembered things. "It is strange. I hadn't thought about it, but the soldiers found the cheap flip phone Collin gave me in Chicago. I had stuffed it in my lab coat pocket along with some papers and bag of carrots. That creepy guy tore the lab coat off me in the back of the van and left it there." Emily paused, mouth agape. "I don't usually carry that phone with me because I don't want to lose it and I don't want other people to see it. But that's how they found us."

"It's a blessing you had it with you, don't you think?" said Sarah. "I think it was an answer to prayers."

"Or maybe a coincidence."

"It's easy sometimes to mistake the two," said Sarah with a wink and a sage smile.

* * *

London, England

June 16, 2:35 a.m. London Time

Nic returned to his desk from the break room with another cup of bad coffee. He'd lost count of the number of refills during the night. For what it lacked in taste, it made up for in potency. He'd tracked the Caribbean storm through the night as it intersected the suspect sailboat's supposed path toward the small cluster of Colombian islands. The signal from Collin's phone had gone dead earlier in the night, but there was no doubt that Collin and everyone aboard that sailboat was caught in the storm's clutches. It had unexpectedly gained speed as it continued to surge west by northwest, hooking toward the Cancun peninsula, directly in the sailboat's last known path.

Alastair had retired to his office sometime around one a.m. where he slept on the floor. Nic had not seen Alastair this involved in a case since his earliest days in the department. He had learned that Alastair had a strange inconsistency about him, cycling between intense engagement and cold detachment.

As Nic sat staring at the Doppler radar images on his monitor, the phone rang. It was an officer from the Colombian Coast Guard, calling at the request of his admiral to inform Nic that as soon as the storm passed the islands, they would restart their patrol and report their findings to him. They anticipated launching no more than three hours from now. A crew was prepped to search the area where a blip on their radar had stopped moving before it reached the northern apex of the island. Nic would have an update by 5:30 a.m. London Time.

In his frustration, he decided to call Crabtree and share the news.

"That's bloody three hours from now. What am I to do, just sit around waiting for these guys to do something?" cried Nic, his voice pitching higher with each syllable.

"Unless you think you can command the Colombian Coast Guard to risk it all for you," Reggie replied.

"Maybe *I* can't, but I think I know someone who might . . ." Nic said, the scheming mechanisms in his mind clattering to life. "I'll call you back."

Nic hung up, whirled around in his chair, and stood up in one fluid motion, heading full steam for the opening of his cubicle. A coffee mug attached to an arm was coming right at him, but he couldn't stop before he collided with it. Piping hot coffee seared through the front of his shirt and the skin of his forearm. "Watch where you're . . . Ah, Alastair, just the man I wanted to see." Nic's tone and expression changed instantly as he tamped down the anger. He sucked in a breath between clinched teeth, waved his arm about, and pulled at his shirt. The pain wouldn't last long. He needed a favor of his boss, so a little burn and another stain was a price worth paying. Nic turned back to his desk and rummaged through a drawer until he produced a wad of rumpled napkins and started wiping his arm and dabbing his abdomen.

"Yes, well, I've come to check the status of things with our man, Cook," said Alastair as he produced a handkerchief from a pocket and began blotting the coffee from the sleeve of his tweed sport coat.

"Sorry about that, but you came at a good time. The Colombian Coast Guard just informed me that they are sitting in port, doing nothing, while this storm threatens to kill our quarry. Talk about indolent," squeaked Nic.

"I'm sure they have concerns for the safety of their crews—" Alastair started.

"Our Coast Guard don't rest when there's a storm. They're out there risking their lives to save people. That's what they do. That's what they train for. How can these guys hole up when there's a boat full of people in serious trouble near their island? One of them is an international fugitive and they're worried about getting wet?" Nic's voice pitched higher and his face turned redder as he worked up a good mad.

"What would you suppose they do, Detective Lancaster?"

"Their bloody jobs, that's what. They are the bloody Coast Guard. They are sworn to protect their shores from threats by sea and yet they sit on shore while a bloody terrorist approaches their territory. It's unbelievable." Nic's face and neck flushed a pale magenta as the emotion ran through his strained vocal cords.

"Now there, Nic, keep in mind this is dangerous business we're talking about. Caution and prudence must come into play in these situations. Nonetheless, I'm sure we can find a way to work this out," Alastair said. "Let me make a call or two and see what can be done."

Chapter Twenty-Two

W estern Caribbean Sea, 2 miles north-northwest of Providencia Island
June 15, 8:12 p.m. Caribbean Time

As Collin felt himself slipping away into another sphere, there was a violent knock that exploded from somewhere to his side. The next thing he knew he was tumbling through space. The pressure was gone. He was moving freely, no more hands or legs pushing on him. He was being tossed about like a child's toy, knocking into hard surfaces and bumping repeatedly into another body.

But there was air. He felt it on his face as he was being whipped about. Collin pulled in a quick breath as he collided with something hard and rolled into the water again.

The power pushing the boat around quickly subsided, as if a driver had taken his foot off the gas pedal. A loud groan echoed in the water. There was still plenty of motion and agitation inside the cabin, but the rolling had stopped. Collin was able to get his footing on something and peek his head above the surface. As he was enjoying the sensation of breathing again, something hit him from behind, square in the back, and pushed him forward under the surface. It was Stinky tackling him and wrapping him up with both arms.

Collin thrashed and kicked as best he could, but Stinky was strong and determined, like a bull refusing to give up the fight. The two twisted and lashed at each other in a tangle under the water. Stinky squeezed around Collin's stomach, forcing out the air. Collin responded by kicking and gyrating like a fish in a net until his feet and knees and elbows collided enough times with Stinky's soft spots that he could feel the pressure ease.

A few more violent spasms and Collin was free and heading for the surface to replenish his lungs with oxygen. He caught one breath before Stinky's hands were on him again, dragging Collin down as he tried to pull himself up. Collin knew Stinky had the clear advantage, but he couldn't let that continue. Flailing his knees and feet in a desperate struggle to regain the access to air, Collin landed a few heavy blows. One he could tell must have been Stinky's chin. It hurt his thigh as he made contact. Another, he thought, must have been ribs against his foot.

Collin reached the shrinking pocket of air as his head hit the floor of the cabin above him. One gulp and he headed back under to find his target. In the bluish light coming through the salon windows above the dining table, Collin could see Stinky was struggling to reach the surface as he tried to recover from the multitude of dizzying blows Collin's feet and knees had inflicted. Collin continued his assault, burying his feet into Stinky's midsection with every ounce of energy he had. Stinky's trajectory shifted sideways instead of upward. Collin dolphined his way into position to strike again and again, his feet kicking out full force and landing crushing blows to his assailant's face, head, ribs, legs—wherever he could make contact.

Collin's air supply was exhausted. He surfaced for one last breath, kicking Stinky downward as he did. With a lungful of oxygen, he went in to finish the job, knowing deep in his subconscious that if he didn't Stinky would finish him instead. He was locked in a struggle for survival and he knew he didn't want to lose.

Feeling Stinky's labored movements near his kicking feet, Collin steadied himself. A plan bloomed in his mind, becoming clearer each time his feet made contact with Stinky's body. He allowed his body to sink in the still-churning water. One foot was already holding Stinky's flailing body down. Stinky's hands were thrashing, alternating between trying to strike Collin's legs and crawl to the surface. Collin used his other foot to pummel Stinky in

176

the gut one more time. He then pulled himself closer but wedging his foot in an armpit as he maneuvered his body into position. He hastily wrapped one leg around Stinky's chest and brought the other around his back. Collin locked one foot around his other ankle and began to squeeze, using his own weight to bear down as hard as he could. Stinky's arms were pinned to his side, his whole body locked in place between Collin's knees.

Though his hands were still tied behind his back, Collin was able to grasp something that felt like the edge of a bunk to hold himself and his battered captive under the water. Collin increased the pressure until his muscles trembled under the strain. Stinky's movements through the churning water grew slower, more lethargic, and uncoordinated. A stream of air bubbles escaped from his mouth.

A brief flurry of sympathy and guilt swelled inside Collin. He pressed his eyes shut and let recent memories reel through his mind: Stinky's venomous tirade about Collin's family, particularly his mother; his promise that Penh would kill them all while Collin watched; his repeated slaps and punches and spitting on Collin; and, just moments ago, his holding Collin underwater with every intention of killing him. This man wanted Collin and his family to suffer painful deaths, and if Collin allowed him to live, surely he would follow through on his vituperative threats.

As he felt Stinky's body growing limp, the crushing horror of his culpability in another human's death tugged at him to let go and save his captor and tormentor. But, before that instinct kicked in, the image of his mother and Emily bound, gagged, and held captive flashed through his mind. If Collin let Stinky go, Stinky would surely turn the tables on him and suffocate Collin. His ignominious demise at sea would certainly lead to his mother's and Emily's tortured deaths. No way could he let that happen. One bad man dying was better than three good people dying.

It was a matter of properly setting his priorities. Saving those two was more important than the horror of killing another human. He could live with that, but not with causing the deaths of the two most important women in his current life. Collin knew he had to first finish the task at hand, then break free and tell Lukas to find his mom and Emily. Surely Lukas would know how to do that. Nothing was beyond Lukas.

Collin shook off the soft feelings and steeled himself, tightening his leg muscles with renewed energy to put more pressure on his victim's diaphragm. This had to be done. There was no other way to save his own life and the lives of his loved ones. Collin's survival depended on him seeing this through, despite how repulsive it was.

For good measure, Collin twisted himself to and fro, eliminating any leverage Stinky might have been able to gain, and continued to press his legs around Stinky's rib cage. After what felt like an hour, Stinky stopped thrashing and went completely motionless. Collin didn't release his grip until his own lungs burned for want of oxygen.

Collin pushed up from the ceiling, his head hitting the floor of the overturned vessel as he breached the surface and sucked in air. Water was now up to his neck. His feet found the underside of the table and he stood on it, panting. His head felt like it might explode, and his eyes burned. He was exhausted. One bright spot, he noticed, was that the wave action had died down considerably. The boat was still being jostled about, but not with the same destructive force.

Collin gulped air and tried to reorient himself. He had no time for remorse or contemplation. Yes, he had just killed a man, something he never imagined he would or could do. He knew the guilt would catch up to him at some point. But at the moment, he had to move in order to save his own life. Getting out of this sinking tomb before it was too late was his first priority now.

As the oxygen flowed back to his brain cells, Collin realized the next task: he had to free his hands. The galley below him was fully stocked with all manner of utensils and cutlery. Surely, he could find something there to cut the plastic zip ties that held his wrists bound behind his back. As he dove down, he realized for the first time that everything in the cabin had broken free from its normal place. A menagerie of objects lay strewn across the ceiling of the cabin, swaying and rolling with the tidal action. Books, cans of soup, silverware, sodden rolls of paper towels, floating articles of clothing, the Uzi, Collin's backpack, cups, plates, pillows. It was a jumble of items that were useless to him at the moment. He needed a knife or scissors ASAP, but he was having trouble locating anything in the clutter. With no hands to move things around, he was reliant only on his vision to spot his quarry. Twin LED emergency lights at opposite ends of the cabin had come on and cast a dim, bluish glow—just enough to make out objects, but not bright enough to see under or around them. Collin swam toward the galley. He knew there was a drawer full of knives and hoped he would be able to locate one in the mess. He was out of air.

He rose to the surface, using the lip on the underside of the counter to stand on. Since the galley was two steps lower than the rest of the cabin, there was a larger air pocket there. He inhaled as much of it as he could and dove again to continue his search. As he scouted the area around the galley, he noticed a few objects he hadn't noticed before. The Captain's stateroom was adjacent to the galley, so some of his things had splayed across the galley's ceiling. There were a couple of shirts and shoes, but most notably, there was a dive mask and snorkel, a fin, and a compass. He knew there had to be more, so he continued toward the Captain's room.

The Captain's bed looked like the gaping mouth of a whale shark as gravity had unlocked its hinges. It yawed in the dark, while all the contents of the compartment under the bed, which was now inverted, lay scattered about. Collin kicked and wiggled his way through the space, fighting to stay down where he could see better, hunting for the items he knew would accompany the mask, fin, and snorkel: a scuba regulator, a buoyancy compensator, lead weights, the other fin. At last, he located the one thing he needed above all else at the moment—the Captain's dive knife, still in its rubbery sheath. It tumbled back and forth, knocking against the cabinet that normally was above the Captain's bed as the boat rocked forcefully in the surf.

Water was still flowing into the overturned boat and now reached Collin's mouth as his head met the floor. He took a few quick breaths, then returned to the ceiling below the Captain's bed where the knife lay. In the swirling tug of the tide, Collin struggled to position himself directly over the object he needed, turn his body around, and get his restricted hands on it. The continual sloshing and jostling pushed him this way and that. Holding himself steady enough to grasp the handle, the sheath, or the straps on the sheath in the tumult proved frustrating and difficult. Each time he gained a tenuous grip, he would fumble the slippery, narrow, and surprisingly heavy knife. Although panic lurked at the edges of his consciousness, he had to push it back. He was running out of time and air. He had to stay focused.

It took him five attempts and all of his breath, but finally he met success and surfaced with the knife clutched in his fingers.

Collin worked his way back into the galley and again perched atop the underside of the counter, balancing himself with the other foot on the bottom of a cabinet which was normally above the sink.

Setting himself as best he could, Collin first removed the blade from the sheath and grasped the handle. A wave struck the boat, tipping Collin sideways. As he caught his balance, using his outstretched elbows, Collin felt a fiery streak along the underside of his forearm. He'd cut himself with the sharp serrated edge of the knife. Blood trailed through the water like a red ribbon in the breeze. Something he'd learned about sharks being able to detect blood in the water from a mile away caused a shiver to run through him.

Shutting out the rising pain in his arm, Collin concentrated on regaining his balance, keeping his head above the waterline, and continuing to saw at the thin, strong bands around his wrists. Another wave struck, but this time the knife was pointing away from his body. Collin recovered and resumed, trying to find the notch he'd started. He got three or four more short, sawing strokes on it when another surge came. This time he was prepared and braced himself for it, not wanting to lose valuable time recovering after each surge.

The ever-shifting watery environment, coupled with the awkward angle and lack of leverage, combined to make it a difficult, if not delicate, operation to cut through the tougher than expected plastic restraints. After two more waves, the plastic snapped. At last, Collin's hands were free. As he moved them, he was struck first by the stiffness of his shoulder muscles and second by the flapping of his own skin from the tear in his left forearm as it moved through the water. Blood streamed out from the open wound, but he didn't have time to think about that—or sharks—right now.

Collin dove down again and quickly found what he was looking for: one of the Captain's shirts among the clutter below him. He tore it with the knife, creating a long, thick strip of cloth. He wrapped the strip around the wound several times, tied it off, and continued to think through his exit strategy as the boat shuddered with each new wave and his air supply dwindled.

* * *

Even from two hundred yards away, the Captain and his crew could hear the ocean beating on the side of the *Admiral Risty*. With the concussion from each successive wave came an additional cracking or snapping or banging sound; a glugging noise, followed by a whoosh, followed by a little less of the boat's bottom showing above the surf in the diminishing twilight. Their attempts to swim toward their ocean-bound home were futile. With the Captain drifting in and out of lucidity and in need of help keeping his head above water, they had no capacity to rescue anyone else. It required the combined strength of the three remaining crewmen and the buoyancy of their life jackets to keep the Captain from sinking under the billowing surge. Add to that the wind and the force of the current dragging them westward, away from the boat and the rocks, and they didn't stand a chance of swimming back to the boat, although Miguel and Jaime tried. With the *Admiral* sinking, there was nothing they could do to help anyhow.

The Captain, despite his hazy mental state, kept asking about Collin. Rojas assured him that they were doing all they could to help. His fellow crewmates looked at him with mixed expressions of sorrow, helplessness, frustration, and desperation. The three sailors knew they were lucky to have survived, as was their Captain.

"Did Collin make it out?" asked the Captain again, straining his voice above the wind and waves. "I need to know. Where is he?"

"He will be OK," said Rojas, staring longingly at the sinking *Admiral*. "That man knows how to survive." After waiting for another swell to crest and move past them, he added, "And God is with him."

"But do you see him?" the Captain asked again, determined to keep trying.

"It's too dark, Captain. Can't see anything," said Rojas.

"We need to find him. He has to survive," pleaded the Captain.

"We can't, sir," said Rojas. "The current is too strong. We can't swim back."

The Captain turned toward the whitish reflection from the hull of his boat, which now was nothing more than a crescent-shaped hunk of flotsam, rising and falling in the six-foot swells. He bit his lip as he watched, hoping to see Collin surface or to hear him call out. As the distance between the men and their boat grew wider, he lowered his head. "God help him," mumbled Captain Sewell, barely audible.

Chapter Twenty-Three

H*untington Beach Hospital, Huntington Beach, California*
     June 15, 7:07 p.m. Pacific Time

Rob, Megan, and Richard were having a conversation in the car while Rob drove. He was turning into the parking lot of the Huntington Beach Hospital where Henry was reportedly very eager to get out when Rob's phone buzzed, and a Linkin Park tune rang out. Lukas's ring tone. "Hang on, let me park the car," he said. Looking at Richard and Megan in turn, he said, "Why don't you guys go get your dad while I take this call? I'll wait right here." They both nodded and climbed out of the car.

Rob returned to the call. "What's up, buddy?"

"Listen, Rob. We've got problems," came Lukas's hurried voice.

Plugging his ear to hear, Rob replied, "What kind of problems?"

"Collin's phone stopped," said Lukas, keys tapping relentlessly in the background.

"Dead battery, maybe."

"No, it's still transmitting, but it is no longer moving."

"Maybe they've arrived at a safe place."

"No, it stopped about two miles from a harbor on the west side of the island of Providencia, in the middle of a shallow, rocky channel."

"What're you saying?"

"I'm saying this doesn't look good and I don't know what to do. It appears their boat sank or it's grounded or something. Apparently, someone high up in Interpol has somehow convinced someone high up in the Colombian Coast

183

Guard to go against their protocol and hightail it to the spot now. They've decided it's a top-priority international search and rescue operation. There's talk of apprehending terrorists, including a high-value American target. Looks like they'll arrive within half an hour."

"A rescue is a good thing, though, right?"

"Not if you're Collin, it's not. The last thing he needs is to be thrown in a Colombian prison awaiting extradition to the US. Plus, I'd be willing to bet that Penh will have someone combing the wreckage, assuming that's what happened, within a day. Two at the most."

"Why would he do that?"

"Because he knows Collin has everything on the hard drive of his computer—all the account information, routing numbers, PINs, and balances. He's figured out by now that he couldn't replicate the entire hard drive. I'm sure he ran into the registry which pulls data from the second, separate drive—the one they would not have been able to see or copy. So now he knows there's more information hidden there, and he needs to physically access the rest of the data from the original drive. If he gets that computer, he gets more than just the money. He wins and Collin dies."

"Not necessarily. Collin can still hide and live to fight another day."

"It's more complicated than that."

"How so?"

"I would assume that Collin hid his phone as well. With that phone, Penh would also be able to track you and me. Once he hacks into that phone and the computer's hard drive, he'll know of my involvement and yours. He'll be able to hunt us, too. More importantly, he would likely figure out how to worm his way into the NSA computer network. That would allow him to wreak all sorts of havoc within the United States. He could potentially get into some very sensitive national security info . . ." Lukas blew out a long breath between his teeth.

"Why would he be able to do all that?" Rob asked, not quite following Lukas's high-speed train of thought.

"I set up that computer for Collin to be able to IM me, right?"

"Right."

"The security protocols it runs basically tap into the government's secure network and allow the two of us to communicate in the blind. No one else can see it or interfere with it," Lukas explained.

"So, what's the worry?"

"I never worried about Collin going beyond the firewalls and virtual private network I set up for the two of us, and because I never worried, I didn't make it hack-proof. It's secure, but someone like Penh could blow through it eventually and enter the NSA's network and troll around undetected from there. He could unlock all sorts of doors," Lukas groaned. "I shouldn't have been so lazy."

"Lazy? You're far from lazy, man," said Rob, trying to console him. "Remember, you only had a few hours with him to put that whole thing together and teach him what he needed to know about it."

"That's true, but still, if that computer gets hacked, we're all in trouble."

Without hesitation, Rob asked, "What do you need me to do?"

* * *

Western Caribbean Sea, 2 miles north-northwest of Providencia Island
  June 15, 8:18 p.m. Caribbean Time

The three crew members and Captain Sewell were being swept through another channel between rocky islets by a powerful current. Rather than expend precious energy in a vain attempt to reach the shore of one of the islets, they huddled together in silence. Dark thoughts traced their way through the empty spaces within and between this tight-knit team. The absence of Tog and Collin tugging at their insides the way the current pulled at their collective mass.

Unspoken horrors threatened to swallow the men each time they felt a bump from below or looked back toward the floundering *Admiral* or surveyed the brooding horizon in any direction. The growing unease weaving its way deeper into each man's thought processes was if or when they would be rescued—and by whom.

The winds had calmed but were still blowing at twenty-five–to–thirty knots. The tail end of the storm was passing overhead. They were four men with three life jackets tossed about by a vast, angry ocean, unsure where the currents might take them. Curling white-capped waves continually washed over them. The constant effort required to keep themselves and the Captain above water zapped their energy and their morale. How long they could last was the unspoken question. Light rain continued to fall intermittently.

The Captain began to stir and come around. He tried to engage his men in conversation, but no one was in the mood to talk. When it grew quiet, he dug out an orange device from his pocket and began pushing buttons. It was his waterproof GPS unit. Jaime asked what he was doing.

"I'm checking our position," he replied.

"What does it matter?" Jaime asked dismissively.

"It's always good to know where you are. And I'm marking the spot where we went down."

"Why?"

"So we can go back."

"Why would we go back?"

"We must find his phone," said the Captain.

"Why is that important?" asked Jaime. "Why risk it to get a phone?"

"If Collin is dead, we must return him to his home," said the Captain resolutely. "His family's number will be on the phone."

Jaime nodded his head in the murky starlight.

"I must call his mother. She needs to know," the Captain said grimly. He patted at the pockets of his coat. With a sigh of relief, he produced his satellite phone in its compressed waterproof bag. He crammed it back in the pocket.

Silence. Long minutes passed with no sound other than the lapping of the swells, the pattering of the rain, and the breathing of four men struggling to find a bright spot, a reason to propel them through the unknowns lurking in their future, altered as it would be.

At last, Rojas muttered, "That's the right thing."

* * *

Collin struggled to maintain his balance as he attempted to catch his breath. Even after taking several desperate gulps of air, his head was not feeling any better. That's when the burning in his throat reminded him of his dire thirst. The irony was thick: surrounded by water, but he was dying of thirst. He needed a drink. There had to be some more bottled water somewhere on this boat. *Where did Stinky find that water?* He dove down and tore frantically through the refrigerator, the cabinets, and closets, all of which were mostly emptied. No water bottles. Then he remembered the hatch under the kitchen floor, which was now above him. He resurfaced and pulled on the metal loop, twisted it and jumped back as a bevy of packaged food flooded out the trapdoor. Canned fruit, beans, and chili; packets of ramen noodles; bags of dried fruit and nuts; and bottles of water still bunched together in a tight plastic cocoon. Along with the food, two large mesh bags dropped through the opening—a red one and a yellow one.

Collin dove down and, in the ghostly light, found the nearest cluster of water bottles and ripped into it. He emerged with a bottle in each hand. After draining both bottles, he went back down and stuffed two more into his pockets. He came back up toting the two mesh bags. He yanked open the draw string of the first and rummaged through the contents. Perfect. A full complement of scuba gear: mask, fins, snorkel, and dive octopus, which included an air regulator for breathing air off a tank as well as a depth gauge, compass, and dive computer. The second bag had neoprene dive booties, gloves, and an underwater watch in a clear plastic cube. He had already attached the Captain's knife to his leg using the straps on the sheath. These items completed the set-up he would need to escape.

The last item at the bottom of the bag was as important as any of the others: a dive light. This wasn't the cheap kind that he had once owned. No, this was the good stuff. Two ultra-high-density LEDs boasted 825 lumins in a dual-reflector system to optimize the brightness and power of the beam. It had a high and low setting to save battery power when needed. He switched it on and let out a yelp of elation when it worked. The whole cabin lit up as the high-powered beam shone through the turquoise water.

Everything he needed for a successful dive was either in the bags or in the mess below, except an air tank.

Collin's joy was short lived. No sooner had he turned on the light than a terrible jolt rocked the entire hull of the *Admiral*. Collin realized that something had given way and the boat had slammed against rock. Terrifying scrapes, snaps, and groans shook everything around him. His whole environment shifted, and the clutter below rolled and bounced to one side. The wave action was more violent now as each wave pushed the boat against the unforgiving rocks.

Time was short. Collin knew the boat could not stay intact much longer. He knew he had to get out—and soon. The thought crossed his mind that rescuers would likely appear at some point in the near future. This sent a cold chill through him. There would be too many unexplainables, too many complications, and too many risks to his freedom and, therefore, his loved ones. He had to stay free if he was to have any hope of stopping Pho Nam Penh from carrying out his murderous plans. No, he mustn't let anyone rescue him and he mustn't let them see him, either. His survival would have to be on his own terms in order to save his family and Emily.

That meant he had to fetch the rest of the dive equipment he would need so he could remain unseen underwater and find his way to one of the nearby islands. From there he could contact Lukas. He'd know what to do next.

Collin dove into the Captain's quarters and began gathering the other items he knew he needed, like the buoyancy compensator and lead weights. The last item necessary was a tank, but he had no idea if there was one onboard or where to find it. As quickly as he could move, he searched everywhere in the Captain's stateroom, shining the powerful beam of light into every corner, cabinet, and drawer. Nothing left in the closets or under the bed.

The pounding of the waves and the banging of the hull against the rocks and the groans and cracks continued as Collin frantically searched, impeding his progress.

As he rummaged for an air tank, he grabbed food items and pushed them into the yellow mesh bag. Things like cans of chili and fruit and water bottles.

When he surfaced in the galley, his air pocket was all but gone. There was only enough space to press his face against the floor to draw in a few lungfuls of air while trying to steady himself. Panic crept closer. The cramped space. The sound of the hull breaking and crunching. The absence of air. The boat teetering on the rocks as the waves continued to beat on it. His breathing rate escalated, fueled by the panic, as all of these variables raced through the narrowing field of his mind. It felt like everything was closing in, including his own doom.

Pushing away the fear that threatened to paralyze him, Collin tried to slow his breathing. He had to stop the panic by thinking logically about saving himself. He went through a checklist of the items he had gathered: regulator—check; mask, fins, and snorkel—check; knife—check; compass and dive computer—check; buoyancy compensator—check; weights—check; air tank—still unchecked.

Drawing in one long breath, Collin dove down to where his gathered items lay more or less together. He shoved all the items he had into the red mesh bag, except the vest that was the buoyancy compensator, which could be blown up to help a diver float. This he wrestled on, pushing his arms into the armholes so he wore it as it was intended, almost. With the red mesh bag cinched tight, he attached it to a clip on the shoulder of the vest to keep his hands free. The yellow mesh bag with the food in it he attached to a similar clip on the other side of the vest.

Collin pushed up to the air pocket one last time, knowing he needed as much oxygen as he could get while he thought through his action plan.

With his lungs full of air, he used the dive light strapped to his wrist to fill the watery space with its intense light. Thinking and hunting, Collin began to work his way through the cabin, unsure of what he'd discover, but hoping he would find an air tank.

Chapter Twenty-Four

Western Caribbean Sea, 2 miles north-northwest of Providencia
Island
June 15, 8:21 p.m. Caribbean Time

Another wave crashed into the side of the boat, unsettling and destructive. Collin had forced himself to move forward, resisting the urge to shut down. He was surrounded by water, trapped in the dimly lit cabin of the *Admiral Risty*, facing an unwitting burial at sea.

In this dark moment, a ray of hope struck through the mental fog, the fright, the paralysis and opened his mind. For the first time in two days, he felt 100 percent clearheaded and focused. In that instant, images of himself opening the storage compartment below the second bunk and finding an air tank flashed across his mind. With astounding clarity, he knew an air tank, the last remaining item he needed to make his escape, would be there. Images of him releasing the back panel of the microwave to retrieve his iPhone in its lunch-bag-sized waterproof pouch ran through his mind as well. Prior to this split-second vision, Collin had worried about not being able to open the hatch and gain access to the outside. Thanks to the mysterious preview, he was certain he'd find his way safely out of the cabin and into the blessed air outside.

He had no time to ponder or appreciate the significance of this series of images that came to him or give thanks for the confidence they instilled. He only knew he had to act on the impressions, and he had to act now.

Infused with new inspiration and courage, he picked his way forward.

With the vision of what he needed to do clear in his mind, Collin plowed through the watery cabin, shining the dive light toward his first goal, the iPhone secreted behind the back wall of the microwave. He grabbed it and stuffed it in one of the mesh bags.

Next, the storage compartment under the bed. As he approached the darkened bunks, he didn't waste any time fumbling to figure out how to open the inverted storage compartment. With remarkable ease, Collin adjusted to the upside-down configuration, found balance, and performed the tasks he needed to perform, one by one, calmly and efficiently. He was able to carry out the entire sequence with only the air in his lungs.

There was only one surprise during the process. As Collin tugged the air tank out of its storage compartment, something large and squishy bumped him from behind with unexpected force. His elbow knocked it back, but the contact with the mass felt grotesque, prompting him to examine it. He reeled around, pointed his light to see, and realized what it was. He jumped back with fright. Stinky's lifeless body floated through the cabin amid a myriad of other objects, twisting and turning aimlessly. His hollow eyes stared forward, vacant and fixed, the terror of his final moments permanently expressed on his face. Sickened, Collin pushed the lifeless, spongy corpse away and shook off the shock. He had no time for distractions, even horrific ones.

Collin headed to the doorway, moving quickly and carefully in the unstable boat's cabin.

When the hatch released, the door swung open to a dark and forbidding cavern-like space between the *Admiral* and the slope of a rising pile of rocks. It was filled with water, barnacled boulders, kelp, and a few broken pieces of the boat scattered around. Collin crouched in the doorway, balancing himself and the load he carried. The boat listed at an odd angle. That and its continual shifting and swaying made his exit treacherous. One misstep or loss of balance and he could be pinned between the hull and the jagged rocks. Overshooting his target could send him careening into oblivion.

Moving his weight, with all the items he carried with him, altered the boat's delicate equilibrium. He repositioned and prepared himself to drop through the open doorway, down past the cockpit, and onto a rock ledge five feet below him. Using the handrail by the steps for balance, Collin dragged the dive tank through the opening with his free hand. The dive light spun on the strap of the wrist holding the rail, making it impossible for him to see where he was going.

At that moment, a wave hit the boat and it rocked violently, throwing Collin's back against the wall and knocking his feet from their purchase on the threshold. He dangled there, hanging by the handrail with one hand, holding the tank in the other, unable to see below him as his flashlight twirled above his head. He couldn't let go of the tank. It was essential equipment for his escape. He kicked and flailed with his feet, trying to find a foothold. Using the tank like an extension of his arm, he sought a surface he could use for leverage to hold himself in place. There was nothing that gave him more than a second or two of relief. His feet and the tank kept slipping in the agitated surf.

When the next wave hit, he lost his grasp on the rail and began to plunge into the depths below. His knees bumped a solid object. His arm struck the steering wheel and nearly caught on it. All the weight he carried pulled him downward at an alarming rate. He was in free fall with the steel tank, which he gripped fiercely, leading the way. Desperately, Collin stretched out with his free hand until it caught on the serrated, barnacle-encrusted edge of a boulder, tearing the flesh of his palm and fingertips. His feet swung under him, slamming his knees into the same type of sharp surface. Two new trails of blood swirled in the water, possibly alerting more hungry sharks to the presence of wounded prey. What he imagined might be the equivalent of a dinner bell. Or the smell of fresh bread coming out of the oven. A signal that food was ready.

Despite the pain, Collin was able to jam one foot into the seam of a rock and hold onto the lip of another with his free hand to arrest his plunge. Then the other foot soon found the horizontal seam as well, allowing him to rest the tank on a surface so it would stop dragging him downward.

Collin's lungs burned. He looked up and saw the *Admiral* above him, swaying and creaking in the surf. To the right of the stern, the glint of moonlight shone faintly. Without hesitation, Collin began to scramble upward and to his right, feeling the burden of the load as he climbed.

As he scampered past the *Admiral*, he swept the light to his left and realized things were even more precarious than they had sounded inside. Collin could see in the beam of the Captain's dive light, the masts and bow of the *Admiral Risty* wedged in and among rocks, jutting down through the murky water. The long aluminum masts were bent and misshapen, but lodged in the darkness below, caught between car-sized boulders dozens of feet down. The entire weight of the *Admiral* pivoted mostly on the main mast, but the other two provided some additional support. For the moment, the boat tottered back and forth, its hull slamming on submerged boulders as the waves pushed and rising as the next wave advanced. This, he knew, couldn't last in the relentless surge. It would all break to pieces before too long.

He never stopped moving upward, despite taking quick glances to his left to survey the sunken ship he had come to love.

As he hefted the load, clawing his way up the rocks past the jammed vessel, Collin realized that all of his years of running, surfing, and working out with weights had prepared him for this. His breath hadn't failed him, and his strength had proven more than adequate.

It wasn't until he breached the surface and drew in fresh air that Collin realized what he had just done and how long his breath had held out.

This was not the time to celebrate or commend himself, however. Collin gasped for air as he knelt on a round, half-submerged boulder, clinging with all his might against the sucking of the outgoing wave. He moved rapidly to stabilize his balance on the rocks and haul up his load so he could rest for a moment. The relentless waves wouldn't allow him to relax just yet. Using the tank almost like a cane, he waited for the rise of a wave and pushed himself upward to a higher ledge, set his feet, then pulled the tank up next to him and leaned against it. He repeated this action, bracing each time for the next wave, until he was beyond the waves' reach. As he scuttled up the piled rocks, the flashlight dangled from its strap around his wrist, shooting light in all directions as it spun, while Collin positioned the tank safely on a long flat boulder.

Darkness was closing in. The sun, long hidden behind the thick piles of clouds, had disappeared altogether. The moon's glow coming from just above the horizon was diffused by the thinner, wispier clouds that now passed overhead.

Collin hoisted himself and his load of gear up to a polished, mossy boulder out of the water's reach, switched off the light, and collapsed onto the rock, breathing heavily. His whole body shook as he held his head in his hands. Reality crashed into him like the waves that pounded the rocks below his perch. He had narrowly escaped death, holding his breath far longer than he ever believed possible. He had survived ruthless beatings and physical trauma. He had melted under the mental and emotional barrage from Pho Nam Penh. He had been forced to behold his frail mother and his dear friend Emily subjected to the whims and unspeakable barbarism of two of Penh's mangy miscreants. Buckling under the pressure, Collin had felt the need to give his enemy the computer that held the key to his new life in order to save two lives that were important to him.

But of all the life-altering events of the past two days, most devastating to his soul was the inescapable fact that he had taken another man's life. There was no reversing his actions, no do-overs. This wasn't a video game or a movie. This was reality and nothing he did or said would ever undo what he had done. The man was dead, dead because Collin killed him. Despite all of his justifications for doing it, he had killed someone. This was not something he had ever considered in his former life. Never needed to. Moving past it was paramount to his survival, but he knew that at some point, he would be required to deal with this fact head on.

This new life of his now seemed destined to be marred by death. And this time, he was the one to blame. To him, the man didn't even have a name. But certainly there were people somewhere on the other side of the world who would miss him, maybe even mourn him.

These thoughts consumed Collin, leaving him short of breath and trembling.

The image of his mother bound to a metal chair in some deserted warehouse in the middle of nowhere, looking pale and feeble and pathetic, flashed across his mind and chased away the guilt. He thought about the pierced guy and his despicable display with Emily. He thought about the gash that barbarian had left on Emily's cheek and chest and the rage welled up anew. Recalling that video made his blood boil and pushed away, at least for the moment, any remorse for killing the unnamed man.

A renewed strength filled the emptiness that, just moments ago, had made him feel like he might break into shards of glass. A raw vibrancy took hold, pushing him to his feet. There were two more animals out there that needed to die. The world would be a better place without them.

Somewhere in the recesses of his mind, Collin knew his parents were praying for him. A thought he chose not to dwell on. Somehow he knew that they knew he would return to them when this was all over. For the first time since the death of his sweet wife and children, he wanted to go home. He wanted to heal and to restart his life. But first, he had to finish the business Penh had started. The running and the chasing and the hiding and the hurting would end. Then his new, new life would begin.

* * *

Rojas held Captain Sewell's head out of the water with his arms woven through the Captain's armpits. Jaime held one leg under the knee; Miguel held the other. With their spare hands, Jaime and Miguel clutched the life vest of the man next to him in order to keep the group together and increase their communal chance of survival. The four men had once again receded into their own thoughts as they bobbed together in the choppy swells. The storm had moved to the northwest, but a light rain continued to fall.

Nothing, it seemed, could or would penetrate through the darkness of their collective mood. It was heavy and thick, as was the silence that enshrouded the four men. There were so many unknowns, so much sadness and loss to contemplate. And nothing they could do to further help themselves or save either of their fallen friends.

That's when they saw it. A flicker in the distance, coming from the east.

It disappeared as quickly as it appeared. It returned, briefly, and was gone again. Rojas almost said something to his friends, then decided not to raise false hopes. The beam of light came again. This time it lingered, dancing unsteadily as if it was unsure of itself, sweeping left and right, before hiding once more. As soon as it was gone, it reappeared. Rojas's smile mirrored the light's movements, coming and going in a whimsical ballet.

The silence was broken when Jaime asked, "Did you see that?"

Rojas jerked his attention to his right, where Jaime's voice was. "You saw it, too?"

"Yeah, what is it?"

"I'm not sure, but I think it might be a flashlight," Rojas said.

"Isn't that where the *Admiral* is? Over there?"

"I think so."

"Then that could be Collin. Maybe he's signaling to us," said Jaime, the hope in his voice rising.

"Maybe."

"Maybe? But you're the one that said he would survive because God is with him."

After a moment of reflection, Rojas admitted, "Yes, that's true. I said that. And now, I want to believe it, I really do, but that's a lot to hope for."

"If it's Collin and he's alive—"

"We mustn't breathe a word of it to anyone," interrupted the Captain. "It would be best for him if his enemies think he's dead."

Chapter Twenty-Five

W*estern Caribbean, 2 miles north-northwest of Providencia Island*
June 15, 8:28 p.m. Caribbean Time

Collin's moment of contemplation was long enough for him to catch his breath and hatch a plan for his escape. Action would be the ultimate antidote for the overwhelming angst that threatened to paralyze him. Standing tall against the breeze was a good start. The need to create an action list had been instilled in him by his father and was a natural part of his being. It kept his mind from getting stuck in neutral in difficult situations. "Find your starting point. Figure out what needs to be done first. Get it done and move on to the next." How many times had his father said that to him growing up? How many times had it helped him solve problems? Too many to count.

Even after racking his brain, Collin's list consisted of only one high-priority item: to call Lukas and ask him to find and rescue his mom and Emily. That was all he needed. With a starting place in mind, he pulled out the waterproof pouch and dug out his phone. He unlocked it and tried to call Lukas but was not surprised to find that there was no signal.

Now he switched his thinking to focus on finding a place with cell signal. He returned to the pouch for the yellow handheld GPS Captain Sewell had given him when he fled in the dinghy during Hurricane Abigail less than two weeks earlier. Stinky's surprise attack had left many things undone and unsaid between Collin and Captain Sewell, including returning the GPS and the dinghy. It was a good thing, though. He needed that GPS now to guide him.

The fierce winds had calmed to blustery gusts. Light rain, soft as cotton pellets, glided down, barely noticeable. The swells looked no larger than four feet, their white tips curling and splitting innocuously in the breeze. Moonlight shone through billowy, silver-streaked clouds above. It appeared the storm had delivered its punch and exited the arena, perhaps seeking other victims. Dripping wet and wearing only the shorts and T-shirt he had changed into before the Asian men showed up, Collin began to shiver in the wind.

He picked up the GPS unit and switched on the power. Once it locked into the satellite signal, a map appeared with a blinking red dot in the middle of the vast sea of pale blue. Collin adjusted his eyes and oriented himself quickly. East by southeast of his position was a cluster of long, thin islands stretching southward. Surely there would be inhabitants and, being the Caribbean, surely there would be tourists. If there was civilization, there would be cell reception. With cell reception, he could call Lukas. Lukas could find his mom and Emily. Priority number one could be checked off. Then, he'd have to sort out the next priority.

Collin set the destination on the handheld GPS, then went straight to work assembling the scuba gear, piece by piece. This he had done a hundred times. His moves were fast and fluid, but thorough. Each piece of equipment was familiar to him in its shape and function. He wasted no time, but double checked everything he did to make sure it was done properly.

First, he removed the buoyancy compensator vest, positioned the Velcro strap-and-cinch system on its back, and clamped it around the tank. Then he connected the regulator and checked the air flow. With the connection made between the regulator and the tank, he checked the air pressure in the tank with the gauge on the regulator. It was gratefully full, showing over 3500 psi of air pressure. In his experience, he could make that much air last ninety minutes in shallow water.

Collin attached the dive computer that included a compass, timer, and depth gauge. He marked his bearing at 150 degrees on the compass, a south by southeast direction, matching what the handheld GPS told him. After attaching the buoyancy compensator to a hose from the tank, he pushed the button that allowed air to flow into the vest, partially inflating it with three short bursts of air. He placed two of the large lead weights and two of the small ones into their pouches attached to the vest with Velcro. The others he left on the rock.

Collin located the fins, mask, and snorkel next and put them on. The Captain had larger feet than Collin, so he adjusted the straps on the fins, then removed them again. That's when he remembered the dive boots. He fished them out of the red mesh bag and tried them on. They were too large, but he wore them anyway knowing they would prevent blisters and chafing on his feet and ankles. After adjusting the mask and snorkel, he reattached the strap for the dive light around his wrist and tested its beam. He sat on the rock in front of the outfitted tank and donned the vest, tightening the straps and adjusting the weights. With the buckles snapped, everything felt as it should: snug but not restrictive. Feeling as prepared as he could under the circumstances, he stood and braced himself on the rocks before moving carefully toward the water's edge beyond the stern of the *Admiral*, where he had emerged.

Three minutes had elapsed since he started assembling the scuba gear. Quick but confident. Cautious but experienced.

Without ceremony, Collin climbed into the water, bracing himself against the tidal surge. He pulled the mask over his eyes and adjusted the rubber gasket before sucking in slightly to seal it against his skin. He moved the snorkel into place, put the mouthpiece between his front teeth, and took two quick test breaths. When he was waist deep, he slipped on the fins.

Before launching himself into the surf, Collin took one last look at the GPS. It showed 2.1 miles to the tip of the closest island. Not knowing the strength of the current, he wondered how long it would take him to traverse that distance. He pushed off the rocks in the direction of the island, having one finger on the button of his vest, which he pressed to add air to the buoyancy compensator until he could feel himself floating near the surface. With the snorkel in place, he pumped his legs in the water, feeling the fins propel him forward, breathing through the snorkel to save air in the tank as long as possible. Collin fine-tuned the angle of his legs and feet and positioned his body to maximize the thrust of the fins. Before long, he felt himself skimming along the surface.

* * *

Scripps Cancer Research Patient Clinic, La Jolla, California
  June 15, 7:52 p.m. Pacific Time

The humming and beeping of the medical equipment was interrupted by a soft feminine voice. Emily bolted up, still jittery. The voice came from three feet to her right. A nurse was standing next to Sarah's bed.

"Mrs. Cook, someone is here to see you. Someone you asked me about earlier. Mrs. Cook, please wake up and say hello to your very special visitors," the short dark-haired nurse said as she leaned in close and gently shook Sarah's shoulders.

Emily looked on in silent anticipation. Sarah's eyes were slow to open. It was as if she needed a crowbar to pry her eyelids apart. Her focus adjusted and she let out a joyful squeal as her tall white-haired knight stood at her bedside smiling down at her. His big hands scooped up hers and held them tight.

"I'm so happy to see you, dear," Henry said. "And so sorry I couldn't fight those animals off. They caught me completely by surprise—jumped out from behind the trash bins as I came around to your door. I'm so sorry I let them take you." His eyes were moist, and his voice choked. One of those eyes was circled in a bright purple ring and one of his cheeks bore a bruise and a scrape as proof of his scuffle.

Sarah took in the battered face of her husband with doleful eyes and swallowed hard before she attempted to speak. When she did, it was just above a whisper. "No, no, Henry. Don't you blame yourself. Those monsters ambushed you—us—without warning. It wasn't a fair fight to start with. I'm

200

just glad you're all in one piece."

"I'm so sorry, dear," Henry repeated.

The two kissed and held onto each other's hands like they were hanging from a building. Twenty-four hours' worth of stress and anxiety pooled up like rainwater in a storm, then seeped below the surface.

Emily looked at her hands instead of watching Henry and Sarah. She felt like an intruder. Her own loneliness, like a whirlpool, threatened to pull her down into its inescapable depths.

Richard, the oldest Cook child, moved to his father's side and caught his mother's eye. Her surprise turned to elation. Henry stepped back as she reached for their son. When their embrace ended, Sarah looked to her left where another concerned figure stood in anticipation. Megan, her only daughter, burst into tears and practically launched herself into her mother's arms, holding on until they both stopped sobbing.

While the Cook family huddled and hugged, Emily caught sight of another figure moving through the dimly lit space at the foot of Sarah's bed. A man stepped over to the side of Emily's bed as she looked down at her hands. His sudden presence surprised her. "Emily Burns? You look marvelous," he said in his best imitation of the Billy Crystal character who made the phrase popular back in the day.

"Rob Howell? What are you doing here?" she said.

"I came home when I heard about Sarah's health issues. Figured I should add whatever support I can in Collin's absence," he said smiling. Then he looked at Emily's bandaged cheek and spoke in an almost reverent tone. "I'm sorry about what happened to you two. I feel awful knowing that if I had gotten to your office just a little sooner, you and I would have been at lunch somewhere instead—"

Rob's cell phone started playing Linkin Park. He fumbled it out of his pocket with agitated haste. Glancing at the screen, Rob apologized to Emily for the interruption, explaining that he had to take the call and excused himself from the room.

Emily shook her head softly and tried not to look as awkward and alone as she felt.

The Cook family continued to talk, and Megan continued to cry, not noticing Rob's exit.

When Rob returned to the room moments later, the Cook family circle had widened to include Emily. Henry stood between the two beds, holding a hand from each of the ladies. He smiled at both of them. Without Henry speaking a word, Emily knew he cared, like a father, and that simple gesture pulled her back from the edge of the whirlpool.

Rob moved to the far side of Emily's hospital bed and attempted to contain a smile. Emily tried to read the eager yet subdued expression on his face. "What is it, Rob? You look like you have some good news."

He grinned at her and said, "Later. For now, I want to make sure you're OK."

* * *

Western Caribbean Sea, 2 miles north-northwest of Providencia Island
   June 15, 9:03 p.m. Caribbean Time

When he felt he had been swimming for a respectable amount of time, Collin stopped to survey his surroundings and his watch. In the darkness, he could just make out the white hump of the *Admiral*'s hull sticking up out of the water behind him. Ahead, tiny yellow specks of light twinkled just above the horizon. The GPS indicated he had traveled four-tenths of a mile. His watch indicated twenty-five minutes had elapsed since he reentered the water. Fighting the current and the swells was hard enough. Dragging all that weight was slowing him down, making him work harder than he should have to. Survival was paramount, which is why he loaded up on provisions before exiting the *Admiral*, but time was of the essence. A quick mental tally of the items dangling from the mesh bags told him he would need to dump the canned food and anything that was not essential. He could survive without food. Sparing only two water bottles and the GPS, Collin emptied everything out of the yellow mesh bag clipped to his buoyancy compensator and let them sink to the bottom of the ocean. It was now slim enough to wedge into his vest to make him more streamlined. Less weight and less resistance should speed things up.

Despite his frustration at making such slow progress toward the Island of Providencia, Collin put his face back in the water and continued to battle the current. Recalling his scuba training from years before, however, he chose to turn himself forty-five degrees to the pull of the current and swim for ten minutes. After the ten minutes was up, he turned ninety degrees and paddled and kicked for another ten minutes, again at a forty-five-degree angle to the current. After half an hour, he noticed he had covered significant distance. He was now halfway there.

After another ten minutes, something changed in his watery world. In the distance, a muffled hum grew steadily louder and stronger. Collin stopped to survey the horizon, rotating in a circle. That's when he saw it approaching from the three o'clock position. Two spotlights scanned in all directions from either side of the bow of a swift-moving boat. The beams of light stretched and retracted as they swept across the water's surface. Although the oncoming vessel was still an estimated quarter of a mile away, Collin's heart jumped to his throat. It was probably a Coast Guard boat from who knows where. If they saw him, he could say good-bye to his family and his freedom. Upon learning the fate of his men, Pho Nam Penh would surely show no mercy on Collin's mother and Emily. Would Penh stop there or hunt down the rest of his family? The thought made him shudder and produced a surge of adrenaline to power him forward. He had to alert Lukas and soon.

Collin had less than a mile to go before he reached the island. As near as he could tell, he had been swimming hard for about an hour and five minutes. At this rate, he had another hour to go. He was exhausted and breathing hard, so he knew that even if his considerable stamina held up, the air in the tank would not last him the whole way. But he had no choice; the boat approached unexpectedly fast. Diving below the surface and hiding underwater to avoid being picked up and interrogated was his only option.

Collin fumbled for his regulator, put it in his mouth and pushed the air release button on his buoyancy compensator to allow himself to sink as the speeding vessel with its search lights raced toward him. Holding his nose and blowing out to relieve the pressure on his ears, Collin dropped quickly below the water line just in time to look up and see the lights from the boat panning in every direction, followed by the hull and the propeller, and then the wake straight above him as it left a contrail of shimmering silver moonlight on the surface. The propellers were no more than ten feet from his head, bouncing up and down in the swells, as they charged toward the wreckage of the *Admiral Risty*.

It was a close call. He easily could have missed the warning signs in his state of concentration and physical exertion. All of his and Lukas's efforts over the past six months would have been knocked over and sunk like the *Admiral Risty*. And only a handful of people on the planet would have known how close Collin and Lukas had come to their goal of ending Pho Nam Penh's threat to the American way of life and averting the calamities Penh had cooked up for the Western world.

In the eerie darkness, Collin waited to make sure the boat with the lights would not turn around, sensing life and movement all around him as he floated. Knowing the scrapes on his knees and hands were seeping blood, as well as the poorly bandaged gash on his arm, he feared what he couldn't see yet figured must be lurking somewhere close by. He forced himself to count to thirty as a precaution before he turned on the dive light to behold his fate.

With the dive light on low beam, he found himself in a strange aquatic world with fish he'd only seen in dive magazines. They were brightly colored and mysterious. A few hefty but harmless ones had moved in for a closer look, curious about this alien. For the most part, the other fish carried on as if he wasn't there. When he started to move again, after checking his dive compass and getting his bearings, it was like a curtain of fish opened to allow him passage through their tight formation. It was a peculiar and exciting phenomenon. The big guys peeled off in search of something more to their liking. The little ones moved alongside him, aimlessly, for a while, then disappeared.

Retreating back into his thoughts, his heart began to ache fearing he wouldn't make it to land in time to warn Lukas of Pho Nam Penh's intentions and threats against his family. In Collin's absence, he knew Lukas could do something to protect them. But he had to know what Collin knew in order to act. There was no time to rest. Ignoring the fatigue, the bruises, the torn flesh, the scent he was leaving behind in the water, and the growing hunger, Collin pushed himself forward through the water faster than before. Either the current was not as strong below the surface, or his determination and adrenaline had helped him find that extra gear. He knew he was making progress.

Twenty minutes later, Collin noticed he was swimming over a reef. It gradually rose to meet him. Then the ocean floor turned to a mix of sand and rock. He surfaced and found himself within a few hundred yards of land. It was mostly dark. To his left, he spotted a few lonely lights that seemed to follow the curve of the island as it bent away from him. Straight ahead, he could see what he figured was a cluster of small buildings with orange-ish lights that oscillated in the night sky. Beyond them, to his right, was mottled darkness. The moon and stars struggled to cast enough light through the dissipating clouds for him to discern the existence of anything other than trees and bushes. From his vantage point, the land seemed to be flat to his right and there seemed to be an accessible, though rocky, beach. That was the direction he headed.

Chapter Twenty-Six

L ondon, England
    June 16, 4:30 a.m. London Time

Nic's hand and head felt heavy as he placed his phone back in its cradle. He rubbed the other hand across his face and sighed. Another blow to his career. Another failure to complete the simple assignment Alastair had given him six weeks ago to track and capture this nobody named Collin Cook. Despite his bitter disappointment, he was obligated to inform his counterparts in the FBI. Nic checked the time in Los Angeles. 8:30 in the evening. He knew Reggie would still be working.

"I've good news and bad news, Reggie."

"Why don't you start with the good news?"

"OK. The good news is the Colombian Coast Guard have picked up three Asian men floating in the Caribbean a few miles off the coast of Isla de Providencia. They're unarmed and in pretty bad shape. Glad for the rescue, I'd imagine, but not talking. The Colombians also picked up four sailors who claim to be the Captain and crew of the *Admiral Risty.*"

"What's the bad news then?"

"The bad news is that Collin Cook was not one of the men they rescued. He was not with the other men and could not be found anywhere near the shipwreck. The Captain thinks he died below-decks when the boat capsized. The Colombians have ordered a dive team to search the area of the wreckage at first light." Nic paused, not so much out of grief, but more like placing a divider between tasks on his list of things to accomplish that day. "I'm really sorry to pass along such horrible news, Reggie. Since you've got a relationship with them, will you talk to his family?"

"I'll wait to hear back from you before I do that," said Reggie. "Knowing his mother, she won't believe he's dead until we produce a body for her to examine."

"Right. I'll be in touch again once the Colombian divers report their findings." Nic's voice conveyed a hint of his eagerness to wrap this thing up, cut his losses, and find a more fruitful field to plow.

"Thanks, Nic. And good job. I'll let Alastair know what an important asset you've been throughout this whole investigation," added Reggie, knowing he needed to keep Nic's spirits up. "This thing isn't over yet, Nic. We have to either recover Cook's body or find him alive. You understand that?"

"Yeah, I understand," said Nic, trying to hide his disappointment.

Crabtree continued. "You've proven to be a valuable contributor through-out this case. I know it's dragged out and we've been left holding the bag a number of times, but we're not done yet. Not by a long shot. We're going to need you and your skills as the next phase of this hunt begins." Crabtree paused while Nic absorbed the message. "I assume you've coached the Colombians on interrogating the Asians they picked up. They ought to be able to provide information that will lead us to Pho Nam Penh. They could be very useful to your search for him and the solving of some very far-reaching crimes, know what I mean?"

Nic rallied, forcing optimism into his tone. Maybe, just maybe, there was still a sliver of hope, a chance at redemption. "Yep, I'm planning to do just that. We'll see what we can get from them. The larger question, however, is what if they don't find Cook's body? What if he got away again and by not searching until morning, we've given him several hours' head start?" Nic's forceful breathing betrayed his inner frustrations.

There was a pause on the line. Reggie didn't reply at first but let out a long sigh. He sucked in a quick breath and began, as if thinking out loud, "I guess we'll have to deal with that when it presents itself. It really wouldn't surprise me either way. If he survives, he will undoubtedly be wanting to talk with his mother. I just got word that our rescue team has returned her to the hospital.

We'll meet with her and the girlfriend there as soon as possible. Meanwhile, we are monitoring all of their incoming calls, texts, emails, tweets, posts, messages, Instagrams, Snapchats—you name it, we're watching it. We'll know the minute he surfaces. If he surfaces."

"Wonderful. Just bloody wonderful. I'm left once again with nothing to show for my work," huffed Nic. "This case has been a bloody nightmare."

"And it's not closed yet," said Crabtree. "We've still got work to do, so keep your wits about you. Think outside the box, like Collin Cook would do."

* * *

Western Caribbean Sea, Providencia Island
   June 15, 10:28 p.m. Caribbean Time

As he drew nearer the island, Collin came to the surface and used his snorkel to conserve air in his tank. It was down to 600 psi, just 100 psi above the critical stage where the diver knows he needs to get to the surface as soon as possible. Lost in his thoughts and worries, and glad for the faster pace of swimming underwater, he hadn't paid much attention to his air supply. He swam hard and fought the current to move southward toward the flat, vacant area on the island he had spotted.

The journey was slow and painstaking. Collin measured his progress against a stand of trees on the shore. It was gradual and tiring, especially since the current continually tugged him westward.

Above his own splashing and the rumbling of the surf against the pebbly sand in the distance, Collin heard another mechanical noise. This time, it was coming from above. When he turned toward the sound, it was too late. The pontoon-equipped float plane was diving straight at him. It looked to be no more than twenty feet in the air and a few hundred yards away. The plane wiggled its wings as it approached. It took a few seconds to register in Collin's panic-stricken mind, but the friendly gesture finally dawned on him.

The plane's pontoons bounced lightly on the tips of watery peaks before settling down and gliding toward Collin. The engine shut off and the plane came to rest within a hundred feet of Collin's position. With the island as a shield, the sea was much calmer here. Before the plane stopped, the door swung open. The pilot pulled his headphones down around his neck and yelled out to Collin, "Hey, your German friend, some dude who goes by Billy Bob, sent me out here in the middle of the night to track your cell phone signal and pick you up. Said something about you need to talk to your mom right away."

The words didn't sink in at first, but Collin's bewilderment soon turned to joy. Billy Bob was a nickname Collin gave Lukas in high school after Lukas declared his undying love for Angelina Jolie. The thought brought a grin to his weary face. "I need to talk to my mom?" called Collin over the noise. Collin smiled a wide knowing smile as he began to paddle his way toward the plane.

"Come on, let's get you in here," said the pilot as he waved a hand toward the door on the passenger's side.

The pilot had gray, curly hair sticking out from under a baseball cap and a handlebar mustache that matched. It was all accented with a thick soul patch of similar color in roughly the shape of an arrow below his bottom lip. The gray hair stood out from his tanned, leathery skin. He spoke with that familiar Texas drawl.

Exhausted, Collin struggled to pull himself into the plane. His weight and the push of the waves nearly tipped the plane over.

"Bring me your vest on this side," yelled the pilot, a look of worry spreading across his face as he surveyed the waves. They were pushing the plane toward the shore and making it unstable.

Collin swam to the other side, unclipped the mesh bag and handed it up, followed by his dive light, mask, and fins. Then he unzipped the vest and wiggled his way out of it. The pilot grabbed the vest's looped handle behind Collin's head and yanked the vest off Collin and set it on the pontoon. It was an awkward and heavy load and it nearly pulled the pilot out of the plane, but he managed to regain his balance, open the back door of the plane, and shove the load in the back seat.

By the time the pilot had secured the buoyancy compensator and tank assembly, Collin had pulled himself into the plane on the other side and sat dripping in the seat next to the pilot.

"Welcome," said the pilot, taking in Collin's bedraggled appearance. "You look like hell."

"Thanks. I feel like it, too."

"Buckle in. We gotta get outta here." The pilot was already firing up the engine and working the switches and controls to get the plane ready to go.

Soon enough they were charging forward in the surf, headed out to sea. The ride was bumpy until the plane started to gain altitude and slowly rose above the waves. It leveled out at about forty feet, though. The pilot signaled for Collin to don the headphones hanging on a handle in front of him. Once he did, the pilot spoke into his microphone and Collin heard it through the headset. "This is known as flying under the radar, son," the pilot replied to Collin's unspoken concern. "Hopefully, no one saw me coming or going. A sleepy resort island like this—chances are good we're safe."

"Where are we going?" asked Collin once he regained his mental footing.

"That's up to your friend. Here, I've got him on the line," the pilot said as he flipped a switch connected to his headset.

"Collin, this is Billy Bob. How're you doing?" Lukas's soft Germanic accent was like soothing music. Collin closed his eyes and took a deep breath. It was the sound of security, a blessing from above. He knew he could relax now.

"All right, I guess . . ."

"Good. The pilot wants to know where to go. I've just texted him the coordinates of the wreck. He's taking you there now, but you don't have much time. You have to hurry."

"Wait . . . what are you talking about?"

"I assume you left your computer on board the boat. Am I right?"

"Yeah, I didn't even think about it. Why?"

"You can't leave it there. There is too much valuable information on it. You're going back for it before the Colombians get there. Now hurry."

"Colombians?"

"Yes, they own the islands you just swam to. Their Coast Guard is patrolling the area, looking for boats in distress. They know about you guys. Interpol alerted them. They've already picked up seven people and are heading back to the islands."

"That must be the boat that almost ran me over."

"Probably. Their communications indicate they spotted the wreckage as they searched for survivors. Found them drifting a few miles away. You've got to get in and get out as quickly as possible. You can't let them see you. This is risky enough as it is, but we have to retrieve that laptop."

"OK," said Collin, his voice hesitant and shaky. He shot a look at the pilot, who was pointing straight ahead at the sliver of white peeking above the surf. It was the bottom of the *Admiral Risty*. "But it's got to be wrecked, right? It's been in the water for hours now."

"The hard drives I installed are solid state drives. Very durable. Maybe not waterproof, but surprisingly tough and resistant. If you know what you're doing, the data can still be retrieved from them, and if they got in the wrong hands that would be a very bad thing."

"But I think they already cloned the drive. They hooked it up to some sort of modem-looking thing and a satellite phone. They already have all the data," said Collin.

"They may have gotten some of it, but they couldn't have gotten it all. Not without my knowing," said Lukas. "I installed a phantom drive as further protection."

Collin shook his head, remembering his one and only priority at the moment. "But what about my mom? The pilot said something about talking to her," said Collin. "But I need your help to save her from—"

"No, you don't," said Lukas. "She's already been saved. A group of Marines from Pendleton air-lifted her to the hospital already."

"But—"

"Don't worry about her or Emily, Collin. I've been tracking them both and sent a team in as fast as I could. They're safe and doing fine. Right now, your focus needs to be to get that hard drive. Good luck, Collin."

"Thanks. I'll need it."

The pilot signaled with his hand to interrupt the conversation. "Listen up, boys. I'm sure you've got a lot to discuss, but for now I'm gonna have to land this plane for you—out there a ways," said the pilot, pointing to an area ahead on the right. "You gotta swim about two hundred yards. I just can't get any closer—not with those waves and rocks. You OK?"

"I guess I'll have to be," sighed Collin, the sense of security already banished.

"Good," said the pilot. Collin looked out the window at the fast-approaching tips of the waves. "I'm going for that calm water over there, to the north. See it?"

"Yeah, I see it."

"That little rock island is creating a nice little runway for me in the water."

Within a minute, the pilot brought the plane down the short distance to the water, spun it around, taxied toward the *Admiral*'s sunken hull, and turned away from the islet with the nose heading back the way Collin escaped.

"Well, you best be getting started. We oughta be outta here in five minutes or less," said the pilot, gesturing with a thumb toward the dive equipment crammed in the rear seat.

Collin climbed into the seat behind the pilot and began putting his gear on. He was back in the water, head still reeling, ninety seconds later. Just before he dropped below the surface, the pilot rolled his hand as one does when trying to hurry someone along.

With the dive light on low beam, Collin dropped under water and headed toward the boat. A wall of silvery fish parted like a curtain as he kicked and pulled himself toward the submerged vessel. As he approached, the sounds coming from the *Admiral* were haunting. A low moan, followed by a splintering sound, permeated the water.

Chapter Twenty-Seven

W*estern Caribbean Sea, 2 miles north-northwest of Providencia Island*
June 15, 10:34 p.m. Caribbean Time

Collin had no time to think or worry. He knew what he had to do, dangerous as it was, and knew why the risk was necessary. Nonetheless, the noises coming from the leaning boat gave him pause. Switching the beam on the light to high as he approached the sunken hull, he was alarmed by the angle at which the boat slanted downhill. Time was running out. He swam straight to the open doorway of the upside-down cabin he had escaped from two hours earlier. Clouds had moved in again to obscure nearly all light from the moon and stars overhead. Twelve feet underwater felt like a closet. An inky blackness enveloped the space he had occupied for most of the last three days, making it as dark a place as he had ever been.

Getting inside proved to be a tight squeeze through the hatch door with the tank and dive gear on, complicated by the surging tide. Once inside the cabin, he realized all the lights were now out. The flashlight's beam created an eerie, turquoise glow as it reflected off the white fiberglass walls and ceiling.

Moving cautiously through the inverted cabin, he swept his light left, then right to orient himself. As he rotated to his left, and swept the light farther, the grayish-blue skin of Stinky's bloated face surged at his, bumping into his cheek, as the boat rocked to its starboard side. The wide-open eyes and ghastly expression of terror made Collin jump back and scream through his regulator in an explosion of massive bubbles. He turned away and shut his eyes and used the nearest object he could find to push the body toward the front of the cabin.

Despite knowing Stinky's body was still nearby, it surprised him with its sudden appearance. Collin's heart hammered in his chest and his breathing was out of control. As Collin worked to regain his composure and slow his breathing, he stared at the lifeless corpse. Something inside him drew his attention to the body. Was it morbid curiosity or some sort of sick pleasure in seeing the man he had killed? Was it a primal need to glory in his triumph over the mercilessness and evil that Stinky had come to represent?

No, it was something else, something more substantial. It was as if Stinky was posthumously taunting him with a secret. A scene flashed in Collin's memory: Stinky holding the phone in front of Collin's face as Penh spoke with his mom and Emily. His jaw muscles tightened, and his stomach quivered at the thought. But he replayed the scene again. His mind was drawn to something else, something beyond the image on the screen. The phone call. That was it. The phone. That phone had been in contact with Penh. That phone could be a treasure trove of useful information that Lukas could use. Yes, he needed that phone.

Wasting no time, Collin swam toward the bloated mass as it moved away from him. He grabbed one of its ankles. The squishiness of its flesh made him convulse, but he kept dragging it toward him, manipulating it until he was digging through the pockets and at last extracting the phone in its waterproof case.

Collin stuffed the phone in his own pocket as he pinched his eyes shut and fought back the urge to regurgitate.

His next thought was of the Colombians and how they may be patrolling the area again soon. Collin went straight to the secret compartment where he had stashed his sea bag that still contained cash and other items he used to live his fugitive life. These things would all be necessary, he thought, so he pulled the bag out and set it down next to him. Lukas never mentioned the money, but as long as he was here, there was no sense in leaving behind half a million dollars in cash.

Now he had to find the laptop. Think, where did he see it last? He remembered watching Long Hair deposit the computer in a nylon gym bag, but the bag wasn't readily visible.

As he began to paw through the debris scattered across the ceiling, somehow the boat felt even more unstable than it had prior to his escape. Each wave that slammed against the side of the hull caused it to rock harder and move more fluidly than before. There was more motion inside. The debris piled on the ceiling had rolled to one side, creating mounds stacked up against the walls on the downhill side of the boat, adding to its instability. Collin struggled to hold himself in place close to the ceiling below him as he searched through the litter. The wave action kept knocking him off balance.

Collin searched the entire cabin for the nylon bag. It was nowhere to be found. Panic began to build. It wasn't safe in the boat; he could feel it. Then he thought about the closet next to the bunk. That's where Long Hair had stashed it before, so he tried it. It did not open easily. The jarring turmoil to which the boat had been subjected had lodged a bevy of heavy objects against the door, blocking its intended movement. By shifting some of the items around, Collin was able to grab the edge of the door as it popped open just wide enough to insert his fingers and pry. As he applied leverage, gradually pressing with all of his strength, the boat teetered harder than ever into the rocks and Collin lost his grip and drifted back into the cabin with the current. He repositioned himself and went at it again with the same result. His fingers weren't strong enough to lever open the door with all the weight pressing against it.

He stopped and tried to think through the problem. Moving the heap of items would take too long and use up all of his air. Since he wasn't positive the bag was in there, he didn't want to spend all that time for nothing. That's when he remembered the Captain's rifles under the bunk. He levered that compartment open, caught one of the rifles as it dropped through the opening, and moved back into position. With renewed zeal, he approached the closet and searched for a way to put pressure on the door in just the right place. Finding it awkward to maneuver with the fins on his feet, he removed them. With his booted feet, he was easily able to get in a position where he could use his legs for maximum strength as he held the rifle in place like a crow bar and exerted force upward and outward until there was just enough movement to allow Collin to insert an arm into the gap, push outward a little more, and shine his light inside the closet. The nylon gym bag's fluorescent striping gleamed, so he pried a little more until he could grasp a handful of the gym bag and yank it from its pinned position. He continued to tug and pull until one edge of the bag poked through the opening. With both hands firmly gripping the corners of the bag, Collin again used his feet and legs and heaved with all his might until the bag broke through the door.

As he pulled the gym bag free from its lodging, there was a frightful crashing sound reverberating through the water. He hurriedly stuffed the rubbery sea bag into the mostly empty gym bag. As he did so, Collin realized it was more than just the breaking of the door hinge. Something had come loose with all of his prying and yanking. His weight and exertion, along with the power of the ocean waves, had snapped something and the entire boat was now dislodged and tumbling through space. Collin sensed a flowing, cascading motion until there was a jolt. Everything inside the boat was tossed up or out. The heavier objects crashed into walls or floors or ceilings. The lighter ones swirled weightlessly in the cabin. Collin, like the other heavy objects, bounced and collided with the hard surfaces around him as other hard things pummeled his body.

The boat was plunging deeper into the ocean and bouncing on rocks.

Panic flashed through his mind as he assessed his situation. The gym bag was tucked under his arm and the door to the outside was open just a few feet from him, but he was battered and disoriented. When he kicked toward the opening, he remembered he had no fins to propel him through the water. The additional weight and bulk of the gym bag made it difficult to swim quickly enough to free himself from the fast-sinking boat. Instinctively, Collin kicked with his finless feet and pulled with his free arm against the current toward the opening. Without hesitation, he wiggled through.

The surge of adrenaline brought a flash of brilliance to his mind: If he filled his buoyancy compensator and dropped the lead weights, the flotation device would bring him to the surface much faster. A quick shot of air in the vest helped him start to rise. As he struggled through the murky water, he managed to tug on the Velcro weight holder on the right side of his vest with his free hand. The first lead packet came loose and fell into the abyss below. That prompted him to pull the bag's strap over his neck so he could use his other hand to let loose the other pouch of lead. With the bag in place, he first gave his vest another short burst of air by pressing on the inflator button and felt his body begin to rise more steadily. That wasn't enough, so he added another short burst. That accelerated the ascent, but he needed more. His hand went to the second weight pouch, but before he yanked it free, he attempted the third burst of air in the buoyancy compensator. When he did, all he heard was a feeble whoosh. That was it. No more air. Collin sucked in on the mouthpiece, but there was nothing as he tried to breathe through the regulator. He was experiencing every diver's nightmare: his tank was completely out of air and he was far below the surface, unsure where it even was.

Collin was rising steadily through the dark water, but not rapidly enough. He hadn't taken more than a normal breath of air before he ran out, so his lungs were already aching. Looking up to see how far he was from the surface, he realized he was heading into the flapping, swirling, entangling sheet of the mainsail. It had come unfurled and was billowing through the water. Before he knew it, he was wrapped up in nylon. His upward progress stopped, and a gentle tug downward began to pull him with the boat as it descended.

* * *

Scripps Cancer Research Patient Clinic, La Jolla, California
  June 15, 8:41 p.m. Pacific Time

Rob Howell stood next to Emily's hospital bed and took in the scene. He listened, with the rest of the Cooks, to Sarah's harrowing story as she recounted what she remembered from her kidnapping experience. Of course, she told them, she couldn't recall much because they had drugged her. She had reached the part where Emily had suddenly appeared across from her in the cargo van. Then Sarah tightened up. It was as if she was reliving those moments of being bound and gagged. She stopped talking midsentence and grew silent and still.

"My heart dropped when I saw you there, Emily," Sarah said, a tightness in her voice choking the words to just above a whisper. "I realized it was my fault that you got involved in this whole thing." Sarah looked at Emily tenderly, the corners of her mouth drawn tight. She then looked at her hands. "I know I said this already, but I hope you won't blame Collin for what happened. It was my fault, not his."

Emily nodded her head and forced a half smile that faded quickly. The emotional numbness had not yet worn off.

Rob stood next to Emily and put a reassuring arm around her shoulder. He wondered what his high school friend was thinking and feeling. As her friend, he wanted to help. As Collin's friend, he wanted to wait and let Collin be the one to offer a shoulder to cry on. No way did he want to get between those two.

Sarah restarted her narrative, skipping to their arrival at the abandoned warehouse.

Rob's phone started to blare Linkin Park, the telltale ringtone for Lukas. Rob blew out a sigh and said, "I'm sorry. I have to take this one. Anyone else and I would ignore it, but I can't ignore this one." He ducked out of the room and into the mostly empty hallway.

"Listen up," said Lukas. "The FBI are on their way to the hospital right now. ETA is about five minutes. You've got to get out of there. They can't see you. If they do, they'll start asking questions and things will get messy real fast."

"Roger that. I'll say my good-byes and go."

"I'd imagine they're both mad and embarrassed about letting Emily out of their sight. Tell her not to say anything about you, OK?"

"OK. What about Sarah and the others?"

"They've all seen you?"

CHAPTER TWENTY-SEVEN

"Yeah, we're all together in the hospital right now," said Rob.

"Oh, great. That's not going to fly." Lukas hesitated a moment, then came back. "Don't worry about the others. The FBI are going to be more focused on Emily, I think. Just tell her and get on the road."

Stepping back into the room, Rob apologized for the interruption. "Something's come up and I'm needed elsewhere. I will catch up with you all later." He nudged Emily, pointed with his head, and gestured with his eyebrows for her to follow him out to the hallway.

She slid off the bed and made her way out of the room while the Cooks all looked on with confused expressions.

"Emily, the FBI will be here shortly. They're going to want to get a statement from you with as much detail as you can give them. The only thing I want you to leave out is me. Please don't mention me, OK?"

She looked at Rob with the look of a lost but obedient puppy. Her pain was evident as her understanding. "I won't say anything. Don't worry about me. If you've got to work or meet people or whatever, go ahead and do what you've got to do." She shrugged and gave a blank stare toward the elevator. "You best be going."

"It's not like that Emily. This is not work related, but I don't have time to explain right now. I'll touch base with you later. Probably tomorrow. Get some rest. You'll feel better in the morning."

Emily's mouth opened, but nothing came out.

Rob paused. "I promise, when this is all over, we'll talk. Promise." With that, he turned on his heels and speed-walked to the stairwell at the other end of the hall, in the opposite direction of the elevators. He opened the door, smiled, waved, then disappeared.

Chapter Twenty-Eight

Western Caribbean Sea, 2 miles north-northwest of Providencia Island

June 15, 10:39 p.m. Caribbean Time

The rippling white nylon sail enveloped Collin's upper body as it dragged him toward the sea floor. Instinctively, he swung his elbows out to create a cocoon of space around his torso. This was a natural, life-saving reaction. His survival instincts were firing on all synapses. The next thought that flashed across his mind was the Captain's dive knife strapped to his leg. Kicking and flailing, he unsheathed it and began to rip and tear at the fabric that threatened to entomb him. After several desperate swipes, he cleared a hole big enough to fit through. He struggled to break free of the sails, frantically beating his legs and thrashing with his arms. The problem, he discovered, was that one of the ropes had twisted around his ankle.

Collin forced himself to calm down and think. With his lungs burning, he was in full panic mode, so it required every ounce of energy and discipline he had to fight it off. He knew he had only seconds to act or he would be dragged to his death. He bent down, pushing away a sheet of nylon from his face, and held the rope with his left hand. Sliding the knife between his leg and the rope, sharp side up, he sawed twice. The rope fell away from the razor-sharp blade, allowing Collin to free himself. With a few kicks of his legs, he broke away from the last entanglements and continued his ascent to the surface. But his breath was gone. Blackness encroached from all sides of his vision and he felt himself slipping into oblivion.

Seconds later, Collin's limp body, pulled upward by the air in the buoyancy compensator, breached the surface like a shot. The jolt and the night air reawakened him, causing him to spit seawater and gasp for the sweet humid oxygen. A few breaths and a shake of his head revived him physically and mentally. Collin leaned his head back and panted, clutching the gym bag around his neck with one hand, the serrated dive knife in the other. A sense of accomplishment and relief took hold and he let out an emotionally charged laugh.

In the distance, Collin heard the plane's engine start up and watched it taxi toward him before he had fully regained his bearings. Dazed and panting, Collin instinctively swam in the direction of the plane. He and the pilot nodded at each other as the pilot's door swung open. They repeated the same drill they had done just a few minutes before. Piece by piece, Collin handed up his gear, starting with the loaded gym bag.

When Collin climbed in the passenger's seat the second time, dripping and out of breath, he was spent. Exhaustion, mental and physical, overpowered him and he closed his eyes.

"Don't go to sleep just yet. Billy Bob's on the line again and wants to talk with you," said the pilot.

Collin wrangled the headset over his head and ears clumsily. "I'm here," he said, still breathing hard. "And I've got the laptop."

Lukas's voice was again reassuring but focused on the business at hand. "Good. Just in time, too. The Colombians should arrive onsite in less than ten minutes. Take a look at it and make sure both hard drives are still in it."

"Now?" asked Collin. "You want me to check it now?"

"Why not?" said Lukas. "What else are you going to do between here and Honduras?"

"Honduras?"

"Yeah, we have a safe house near Puerto Lempira, on the southeastern coast."

"Safe house? Am I in the witness protection program now?" Collin could feel himself recovering. Oxygen was flowing, restoring normalcy to some extent—at least enough to restore his wry sense of irony.

"Not quite, but close," said Lukas.

"Ha ha, very funny. What's really going on?"

"You're going to a safe house on the beach in Honduras. You'll like it. Trust me. Right on the beach. Fabulous view."

"When can I call my mom? I need to talk to her. And Emily, too," said Collin.

"Soon, but not yet," said Lukas. "Let's check that laptop and make sure the hard drives have not been tampered with."

Collin reached into the back seat and pulled the gym bag close. He removed the rubbery sea bag, then raked his hand through the bottom of it, rummaging through cables and smaller components that looked like external drives, modems, or routers. After checking through the contents a second time, exploring every inch of the bag and its contents, he stopped and uttered, "Oh, crap."

"What, Collin? What's wrong?" asked Lukas.

"The computer is not in the bag."

* * *

Scripps Cancer Research Patient Clinic, La Jolla, California
June 15, 8:44 p.m. Pacific Time

An authoritative knock on the door announced the arrival of Special Agents Reggie Crabtree and Spinner McCoy, who didn't wait for a response before entering the crowded hospital room. Two nurses had joined the Cook family and were busily attending to Sarah and Emily. The older one, an African-American in her forties, turned toward the entering visitors and said, "Visiting hours are long over. You'll have to come back tomorrow. All of you. These two lovely ladies need time to rest and recover."

Reggie flashed his badge and said, "We need to ask them each a few questions, then we'll let them rest."

The wise and experienced nurse, who looked as if she had seen and heard it all before, put her hands on her ample hips, tipped her head, and arched an eyebrow. "Visiting hours are over. You'll have to come back in the morning."

"I don't think you understand," started Reggie.

"Oh, I understand all right. It's you who's not understanding." Her arms were out wide as if to herd and corral the whole group out of the room.

"We will be providing protective detail for these two lovely ladies," said Crabtree matter-of-factly. "They've been through a lot already. We don't want anything more to happen, now do we?"

The nurse wasn't backing down. She continued to round up the visitors and move toward the exit with them in front of her.

Reggie side-stepped her outstretched arms and added. "You don't want the bad guys to get in here, do you?"

The nurse just stared at him, her expressionless countenance giving way to exasperation. "You have five minutes. After that, you can do your protecting out here in the hallway. Understood?"

Chapter Twenty-Nine

Over the Western Caribbean Sea en route to Puerto Lempira, Honduras
June 15, 10:55 p.m. Caribbean Time

Collin spent the few moments of quiet time after his initial conversation with Lukas staring out the window to his right, taking in the vast pool of dark water only fifty feet below him. The single engine prop plane droned along at top airspeed of ninety miles per hour on a bearing of 290 degrees. The pilot explained that he needed to conserve fuel, so he was going to keep the speed down a bit.

Collin was spent. He tried not to think about what he had seen, the things he had done, or what might happen next. Guilt worked its way to the surface of his consciousness, but he continually batted it away. The terror of almost being dragged to the ocean floor swept in, replacing the guilt. Images of his mother crossed his mind and a new kind of angst took over. Seeing her so weak and frail, bound to a chair, stirred a deep, foreboding wrath that threatened to consume him. Evil thoughts of revenge and how he might exact it spun in his mind like the stout, sticky strands of a spider's web.

Worries about her well-being and safety were dispelled by his belief in Lukas's words that his mother was safe and in good hands.

Thoughts of his mom tied up brought with them images of that pierced and malevolent degenerate licking Emily's cheek. This brought his blood to a boil and increased the speed and noise level of his breathing. His whole body tensed. His fists balled up and he leaned forward. Even the pilot noticed his anxiety, giving him a long sideways look. Collin just waved him off and turned his face toward the side window as he forced himself to think about something else.

The only other image to cross his mind was that of Stinky's distended gray face. The ghastly, haunting figure floated through his mind the same way it floated through the boat's cabin—aimless and unfettered. Guilt and remorse flooded in and out of his weary mind, like the tidal surge—alternately pushing him against the rocks, then threatening to drag his soul to the bottom of the sea.

Again, the dark desire to do the same thing to Pho Nam Penh as he had done to Stinky swelled like thunder clouds in the mountains, black and ominous.

In the midst of these mental convulsions, the pilot smacked Collin on the arm. "Hey, man, your friend's on the line again."

"Collin? This is Billy Bob. Do you read me?"

"Yeah, I read you loud and clear." After a brief hesitation, he added, "Billy Bob?"

"Yes, that's my handle for this mission. We don't use real names," said Lukas.

"Got it, uh, Billy Bob."

"Okay, here's the new plan," said Lukas. "We're going to drop you off at the beach house in Honduras where you're going to get some much-needed rest. Then, as soon as we can get them there, we're sending a dive team down to the wreckage to retrieve the laptop."

Collin shook the sinister thoughts out of his head and said, "You've got a dive team in the area?"

"No. They'll be coming out of Houston, through Guadalajara. Should be there within twenty-four hours, if all goes well," said Lukas.

Collin contemplated this for a moment. "Do you know for certain the laptop is still on the boat?"

"Yeah, that's what I've been doing the last few minutes. I pinged the locator beacon and retrieved the coordinates. It's either on the boat or somewhere near where the boat sank. The coordinates are within two hundred feet of the boat's last known location," said Lukas. "That means that it is still operable and has not been severely damaged."

Collin asked, "What do you think Penh will do in the meantime? Wouldn't you think that he's found where it is using the locator, too?"

"Yes. That would be my guess. I would also guess that Penh is amassing a team to go in as we speak."

"Then why wait for your dive team to show up?"

"Because it's a risky operation, my friend," said Lukas warily. "Don't get any ideas in your head now. That boat is in at least one hundred feet of water. It may be as deep as one hundred twenty-five feet. We don't know what kind of shape that wreck is in. Plus, we're going to need to go in under cover of darkness. That's a very technical dive, so I want a trained team going in there."

"But wouldn't it be really bad if Penh got ahold of that computer?"

"Extraordinarily bad. With the codes and protocols I have built into that hard drive, he could worm his way into the NSA's network and access all sorts of top secret information," said Lukas.

"So we've got to retrieve it before he does. Waiting twenty-four hours is practically like inviting him to a veritable feast of national security secrets. Why wait for these guys out of Houston? I'm right here. All I need is a refill on my air tank and I'm good to go," said Collin.

"Too dangerous," said Lukas. "You've put yourself in harm's way enough already."

"Come on, Lu—Billy Bob. You know it only makes sense, given the timeline. I can do it. Won't be that hard."

"Won't be that hard? Who are you trying to kid? You won't have a dive partner, you're not in top shape because you've been through hell the past two days, and I'm willing to bet you don't have that much deep-water wreck-diving experience."

"I realize this is not a perfect scenario, but it's the best and only option at this point," said Collin.

"If something happened to you, I couldn't live with myself," said Lukas.

"If something happened to our country because Penh got that laptop, I couldn't live with myself. So let's put a plan together."

Reluctantly, Lukas agreed and signed off with the promise to call back with a plan.

Collin closed his eyes and tried to picture himself diving a hundred feet down in the dark to the wreck, encountering Stinky's corpse once again, and rummaging for the lost computer. It seemed overwhelmingly hopeless. He sucked in a long breath through his teeth and tried to push away the fear and dread.

* * *

Puerto Lempira, Honduras
  June 16, 5:49 a.m. Caribbean Time

The slowing of the plane's engine roused Collin from a deep sleep and brought his conscious back from a dark place. The pilot, noticing his stirring, bumped Collin's shoulder with the back of his hand and pointed straight ahead toward an empty golden-sand beach nestled between two rocky outcroppings and bordered by dense green jungle. Collin strained to focus in the pale pinkish light of dawn. As he did, a tiny wooden hut appeared. Two men flanked the small building; one held binoculars in one hand and a cell phone to his ear in the other. The second man held a rifle to his shoulder with its long scope near one of the man's eyes, the end of the rifle following the path of the plane as it swooped in for a watery landing.

"Welcome to Puerto Lempira," said the pilot. "I hope, for your sake, your stay is short and pleasant."

Collin climbed out of the door and stood on the pontoon until the plane had completely stopped. When he hopped down, he landed on luxuriously soft sand in waist deep water. The man with the binoculars had moved to the edge of the water, still on the phone. Collin approached him cautiously, sensing the man's ill temper and feeling like an intruder.

"There's breakfast in there waiting for you and a shower in the back of the hut. Keep it short. There ain't a lot of hot water."

"Thanks," said Collin, still unsure just how welcome he was.

"If you're tired, there's a cot in the back bedroom. It's got a net around it. Be sure to zip it up if you don't want to be eaten alive by the bugs."

Collin looked for the man with the rifle, but he was nowhere to be found.

Inside the hut, he found a small round table with two mismatching, brightly painted, heavily chipped wooden chairs. A sturdy table ran the length of the wall under a window overlooking the beach and the cove. There were storage bins stacked underneath one side and a fat round propane tank on the other. In the middle, a black plastic pipe jutted down and stopped inches above a floor drain.

The propane tank connected to a two-burner, portable stove standing on the table. A large frying pan contained a substantial amount of scrambled eggs, mixed with some sort of red and green vegetables, cheese, and a brown meat that smelled like sausage. Two plates on the counter looked to contain the remains of the same egg concoction, so he assumed it to be safe to eat. Until he smelled the sausage, Collin hadn't stopped to consider how hungry he was. He found a plate and a fork and scooped the rest of the egg onto the plate.

So engrossed in the food was he that Collin didn't notice the man with the rifle enter the room until he placed a tall glass of orange juice next to Collin's plate. "Fresh squeezed it myself just this morning. Help yourself."

Thirst had also been pushed out of his mind until the orange juice appeared. "Thank you. I appreciate it. It's very kind of you guys to let me hole up here for a while."

"Don't get too comfortable. Our contact tells us you'll be back out of here as soon as that plane returns with fresh air tanks for you," said the man as he folded his large frame into the seat across from Collin.

"Yeah, that's my understanding," nodded Collin. He finished the last of his food and drained the orange juice. Looking at the glass, he said, "That's good stuff. Thanks again." Collin pushed back from the table and rose from his chair.

The man with the rifle watched him carefully. He stood and took a step toward Collin.

As he stood, Collin felt dizzy and swooned, but just managed to catch himself on the table, using both hands to steady his balance. "Whoa," he said as his eyes rolled back in his head.

That was the last thing he remembered.

Chapter Thirty

L ondon, England
June 16, 3:15 p.m. London Time

The news was not the good news Nic was hoping for, but it was not the bad news he had expected, either. An officer from the Colombian Coast Guard was on the phone and had just informed him that their dive team had arrived at the site of the wreck before six o'clock in the morning and had located the boat using sonar equipment as it was no longer visible. They searched the boat and the area surrounding it and were unable to locate the body of Collin Cook. Parts of the boat, which had broken into several sections, had sunk to a depth of over one hundred twenty feet. Debris was scattered all over the ocean floor and an Asian man's body was found trapped inside the cabin, but not the Caucasian's.

"It's no surprise that boat went down where it did. Those are very dangerous waters, especially in bad conditions," said the Coast Guard officer over the phone.

"Certainly you're not giving up, are you?" asked Nic with a rising tone in his voice.

"I don't see how your man could have lived through that. If he was in the cabin also, I don't think he could have survived."

"Trust me, he has survived worse. He's out there somewhere. We need to find him," said Nic, trying to impress upon the seemingly unconcerned Colombian officer the urgency of the situation.

"We have established a search grid based on the wind, tides, and current to search for the body. We will communicate the results upon the conclusion of our search," replied the officer.

Nic wasn't entirely pleased, but he knew he had to keep his tongue in check since he lacked the authority to order these men to obey him. He knew he had to use gentle persuasion, which was neither natural nor comfortable for him. "May I suggest you search the entire area under the assumption that our man may have survived? Like I said, he has a habit of living through the worst situations. You will need to hurry. This man is very crafty. We don't want him to get away."

"Yes, sir, I understand and will report our findings promptly, sir."

When the conversation ended, Nic stood and paced his cubicle. Times like these he wished he could be everywhere. He wished he could pilot a boat or a plane and search the entire area himself until he found the pesky and perplexing Collin Cook.

As he paced, wondering what to do next, he decided to report to his boss and his counterparts in the US. Maybe in the course of conversation, some brilliant idea might emerge that would somehow close the net around his prey. Dutifully, Nic passed the information first to Alastair Montgomery, his section chief, who once again seemed checked out, and next to Reggie Crabtree of the FBI. "He's gone, Reggie," Nic began. "There's no way the Colombians are going to find him. He's got what, a nine- or ten-hour head start?"

"What have you got to go on?" asked Reggie.

"Not much. The Colombians are going to search everywhere, including the islands. But that hardly matters now, does it?"

"Hardly matters?" said Reggie in a mocking tone. "How can you say that? He can't just disappear. It almost sounds to me like you're giving up, Nic."

"I assure you, Reggie, I'm not giving up. I'm merely frustrated by our inability to catch this guy. I'm frustrated that we don't know where he is, how he got there, or what he's going to do next. I'm frustrated that he could have gone anywhere in that time span if he's got that little rubber boat again and enough petrol."

"What are your options, Nic? Get the Colombians to widen the search grid?

Call in aerial support? Try to predict where he'll show up next, ready to apprehend him? I think we all know how well these tactics have worked out for us in the past."

"What do you think we ought to do, Agent Crabtree?" asked Nic sardonically.

"Wait."

"Wait? What are you on about? Wait where?" Nic's voice pitched higher with each incredulous query.

"Wait right where we are. He'll show up eventually. And when he does, he'll try to make contact—either with his family or his lady friend or the Captain of that boat that sank. Watch and listen to those people and you'll find Collin Cook. He has not gone long without making contact with one of them."

"What are you saying? Give up? After all this work, you want to just give up?" Nic's elevated pitch bordered on falsetto.

"Not at all. If he survived, we can assume he'll resurface at some point. Rather than wasting energy and resources on a futile search, we wait for him to show up again," said Reggie. "We know he's not a threat on his own, so we wait it out and let him draw Penh out of his hole. Then we nab them both."

"Your plan is to sit back and wait?"

"It's called surveillance, Nic. Standard police practice. It's not as exciting as the hunt, but a lot more effective in this type of situation. When he shows up or calls or emails or whatever he does, we'll move in. I don't see that we have too many other viable options, Nic. We can't chase him if we don't know where he is or where he's going, right?"

Nic thought for a moment. Clearly dejected, he agreed nonetheless. "It just feels better being proactive rather than reactive."

"Maybe so," said Reggie. "But this is our best option right now. We have everything in place. If he's alive and well, we'll know about it and we can be proactive then."

* * *

Puerto Lempira, Honduras
June 16, 6:04 p.m. Caribbean Time

Collin awoke with a start, throwing his body over the edge of the cot and landing in a crouched position, like a panther ready to pounce. Water dripped down his face and onto his shirt. One hand gripped the side of the cot, the other ready to strike at the first thing that moved.

"Geez," said the man who had held the rifle. "Remind me not to stand too close next time I wake you up."

Collin apologized. "I was having a pretty intense dream, that's all."

The dream hung in the air above him, ragged and tattered. It wasn't real, but it was. It had substance and meaning, but it was too ethereal to grasp, especially with the shock from the cold water. The remnants of the dream stayed with him, casting its own shadow across the room in the fading twilight, leaving Collin feeling dark and hollow.

"Time to bug out, man. Your plane's back and your number's up," the rifle man said with a gesture toward the cove where the pontoon plane was taxiing on the water's surface toward the beach.

Collin looked around for something to gather up but realized he had come ashore with nothing except the clothes he was wearing. He unzipped the mosquito net that encased the cot and stepped past the rifle man, crossed the room with the makeshift kitchen and eating area. A plate of tacos sat untouched.

"All yours, man," said the rifle man.

Collin grabbed the paper plate and stepped out onto the sand.

The pilot saw him and waved him over. Collin gestured a thank you and good-bye to the two men who remained at the hut and climbed into the plane. The engine never stopped running. As soon as Collin sat down, the pilot was revving up again, preparing for takeoff.

Without a word, the pilot signaled for him to put on the headset. "Listen up, friend. We're heading straight back to the site of your wrecked boat, OK? Probably take us about five hours to get there, so we'll go over the plan on the way," said the pilot.

Collin nodded and bit into his first taco.

Lukas's voice came through the headset. "Yes, let's go over everything, step by step."

"OK," said Collin as politely as he could while he chewed, still trying to bring his brain out of the foggy dream. Images of Penh's smug, arrogant countenance; Stinky's ghost-like, horrified face; and puddles of blood lurked in the shadowy corners of his subconscious.

"I should ask how you slept, my friend," said Lukas, who tried to suppress a chuckle.

Collin cocked his head and winced. "Fine, I guess. Just having a little trouble waking up. Why are you laughing?"

"Yes, I was afraid of that," said Lukas. "I'm not laughing, really. I have to admit that I had the two agents at the hut slip a little sleep aid in your orange juice to make sure you got the rest you need. I figured all the excitement of late may make it hard for you to fall asleep."

"That explains why I was so dizzy and why I can't seem to kick my brain fully into gear." Collin rubbed his stubbly face and blinked hard. "I feel like I should be pissed, but I'm too numb for it to register."

"Yeah, sorry about that, my friend. It was for your own good. Now, your pilot has been busy today getting everything ready for your mission tonight."

"That's right," said the pilot. "I'm not a diver, but I've learned a lot about it today. The guys who helped me come highly recommended by the Agency, so you can trust them."

"OK. Sounds good. Thanks," said Collin, trying to be as positive as possible.

"You've got two air tanks in the back," the pilot explained. "Both filled with nitrox—thirty-two percent oxygen mix instead of the normal twenty-one percent. Helps you dive deeper and stay longer without the need for long decompression stops on your way back up. It really helps to shorten your ascent time, which I thought would be important."

Collin, who was still trying to shake the shadows of his dark dream, strained to focus on the pilot's words. Decompression stops in scuba diving were calculated based on the maximum depth and time spent at that depth. They were necessary to allow the body to release nitrogen accumulated in the cells by the pressure underwater. Failure to stop could lead to the bends, a potentially serious condition that could cause air embolisms in the joints, blood vessels, lungs, or brain. Mild cases, he remembered learning, caused discomfort. Severe cases caused death. He didn't remember all the details, but knew he had to avoid it since there was no recompression chamber handy.

"OK. How do I program that into the dive computer?"

"Already done," said the pilot. "Had the professionals in Cancun take care of all the details for you."

"I guess that makes me feel better." Collin leaned back and blew out a breath. "How deep are we talking?"

Lukas answered and said, "It's hard to say exactly, but probably over a hundred feet."

Collin swallowed hard, remembering that he had never gone past seventy-five feet. He'd never needed to. All the interesting stuff, including the fish and lobster he hunted, generally could be found between thirty and sixty feet deep.

"I've also programmed the exact coordinates Billy Bob gave me for the location of the laptop you're going after into your underwater GPS, which is attached to your BC on the right hand side," the pilot said, patting his rib cage on his own right, indicating the location of the GPS. "You'll need to get in and out as quickly as possible. At depths of over one hundred feet, you probably have a max of about seven minutes before you should start coming up. If you're down there even five minutes, it's probably best to do decompression stops at sixty, thirty, and maybe even fifteen feet for at least two minutes each, just to be safe."

"Collin," Lukas broke in, "it makes me extremely nervous knowing you are doing this alone. Believe me, if I could, I would either have our dive team doing this retrieval, or I would make sure you had a certified partner."

"I understand the dangers. But we've got to do what we've got to do. Like you said, there's a lot riding on this."

Chapter Thirty-One

W*estern Caribbean Sea, 2 miles north-northwest of Providencia Island*
June 16, 11:06 p.m. Caribbean Time

Flying low and fast, Collin and the pilot approached the site of the shipwreck shortly after eleven p.m. The pilot pointed out the Island of Providencia on his radar, ahead about two and a half miles. Knowing his dangerous mission would be underway in just moments, Collin's stomach began to tighten, and his throat went dry. He drained a water bottle before landing to keep himself occupied, hoping to chase away the desert in his mouth.

Not many things scared Collin, but the idea of plunging one hundred feet into the darkness alone worried him. Having no experience wreck diving, other than yesterday's emergency dive, only fueled the anxiety. Knowing that there were things he didn't know that he probably should know about this sort of technical dive raised his blood pressure. He closed his eyes and took deep breaths.

The pilot slapped his shoulder and pointed at the water below them. The rocky islet where the *Admiral* had foundered appeared suddenly on Collin's right, just below them. The pilot circled the area in a low, tight turn. Seeing nothing unusual on the water, the pilot finished the loop and landed, like before, a hundred feet from where Collin had originally emerged from the *Admiral*.

"You OK, man? You don't look so hot?" he asked as he studied Collin's face.

"No choice, right? I volunteered for this; I have to be OK," he said. After a thoughtful pause, he added, "Don't worry. Once I get in the water, I'll be fine."

As Collin geared up, the pilot worked to secure the plane with anchors.

Along with the two air tanks marked with bright fluorescent stripes, Collin found two more items in the back seat of the plane. One was a "shorty"—a three-millimeter-thick wetsuit with short sleeves and legs that came to his mid-thigh. The other item was a fishing spear. Shaped like a trident fastened to the end of a long yellow pole, it had a rubber loop on the opposite end where the handle was. Collin passed his hand through the loop and held the pole about halfway along its length, stretching the rubber strap to its max. Then he released and let it fly. The spear shot out in front of him, poking into the water six or eight feet beyond his position before the elastic leash snapped it back to his hand.

The pilot poked his head through the door and caught Collin's eye. "Thought that might come in handy, just in case you meet up with something you'd like to spear."

Having noticed that Collin left his fins behind on the last dive, the pilot had purchased a new pair, which fit Collin better than the previous pair.

Forcing back the growing dread, Collin suited up and checked all of his gear. It was a bit awkward balancing on the pontoon as he prepared, but he made it work. With the dive light dangling from one wrist and the spear from the other, Collin crouched down and eased himself into the water. Butterflies let loose in his stomach, but he pulled the mask down over his eyes, put the regulator in his mouth, and deflated his BC, known as a buoyancy compensator, to allow himself to sink below the surface before his nerves had time to get any more agitated.

Using the underwater GPS, Collin swam toward the wreckage below the surface, plugging his nose and blowing out to relieve the pressure on his ears while descending. As he moved through the water, his confidence gradually replaced the dread. Despite his rising confidence, he still felt very much alone and exposed.

* * *

The pilot watched as first Collin disappeared and then as his trail of bubbles was no longer visible. He double checked his anchoring system. Satisfied that the plane was secure, he wrestled a long black case out of the rear cargo hold and placed it on the back seat. He then removed a small inflatable raft and unfolded it. The third item in the hold was a compact plastic container. This and the raft he carried to the front seat. He opened the plastic container by unclicking the plastic locking mechanism on either end of the lid and pulled out a long black cord, which he plugged into the plane's DC socket. Flicking on the power button produced a high-pitched whining sound. The air pump and raft weren't used often, but they would sure make his life easier tonight.

Once the raft was fully inflated, the pilot rummaged through the cargo hold for the two halves of the plastic oar, which he fitted together and laid across the raft while he jockeyed the big black case into a balanced position on the pontoon, leaning it against the struts. He kept a hand on the case and a hand on the oar as he carefully sat in the raft. With his weight evenly centered, the pilot lifted the case and placed it lengthwise in the raft between his knees so that it hung over the bow of the little boat.

With the oar, he paddled his way ten or twelve yards to the rocky islet and found a large flat rock on which to unload the case, then the oar, then himself. He pulled the raft out of the water and used its string to tie it to a smaller rock. He then moved to a high flat boulder near the crest of the tiny island of rocks, opened the case, and began assembling a high-powered sniper rifle, complete with laser-sighted scope and silencer.

No sooner had the pilot set up and started scanning the horizon through the scope, than a forty-foot fishing yacht approached from the southeast, most likely coming from Providencia, or perhaps San Andres, farther south. The boat plowed northward through the same channel his passenger had swum into and began to slow to a stop. He heard the power cut to the engines and voices chattering, but they were too distant to understand. Through the scope he could see one man driving, one man on look out, and two men

238

wearing dive gear sitting atop the gunwale at the back of the boat. The pilot fixed the first diver in the crosshairs and was just about to pull the trigger when both he and the other diver launched themselves backward into the water.

From the looks of things, the two men left on board the boat were locals, probably fishermen hired to take paying customers out for a night dive. Shooting them would accomplish nothing, so he checked his watch, glad he had provided his passenger that spear and hoping Collin would not shy away from using it.

$$* * *$$

As Collin continued to descend, his head, eyes, and ears began to ache with the mounting pressure. He checked his depth gauge: it showed him at ninety feet, deeper than he had ever been, and still no sign of the boat's cabin. The water was much cooler at this depth, making him glad for the wet suit.

One hundred feet, no cabin in sight. Visibility was reduced to ten feet in the murky water. A few seconds later, the white hull of the *Admiral Risty* appeared and before he could slow his descent, his fins collided with the upturned starboard side, striking it at about amidships. He landed on his knees with a thud, collected himself quickly, and checked his watch. He pushed the timer button and told himself five minutes was plenty of time. His depth gauge showed one hundred eighteen feet.

When he reached the wreck, Collin shone his light all around. He was shocked at the damage the boat had sustained. He didn't have time to dwell on it, though. Instead, he focused on the GPS and the little blinking dot that indicated the exact location of the laptop. It was straight below him.

Collin worked his way to the hatch and carefully squeezed through the doorway. The GPS indicated the computer was behind him. Thinking through the layout of the cabin, Collin realized that across from the bathroom, there was another closet and a large storage drawer beneath it. Luckily, there were no obstructions and Collin was able to open the closet and the drawer with relative ease. The bag he was searching for lay wedged at the back of the large drawer. This bag was similar in size and color to the gym bag he had pulled out the night before.

This bag, like the Captain's sea bag, was tough and rubbery and sealed against the water. Maneuvering carefully so as to not damage the bag or the computer inside, Collin freed it from its hiding place. Running his hands along the edges, he could tell by the weight, size, and heft that it was his laptop. Collin played his light into several other cabinets and drawers just to ensure that he didn't miss anything important.

Checking his watch, only three and a half minutes had elapsed. As Collin moved to the doorway, he noticed a subtle change in the cabin—a flicker piercing the darkness above him. He switched off his light and peered out the opening. What he saw paralyzed him and stole his breath: the beams of two flashlights panning side to side, signaling two divers coming for what he had.

Chapter Thirty-Two

Western Caribbean Sea, 2 miles north-northwest of Providencia Island

June 16, 11:20 p.m. Caribbean Time

Collin checked the time on his dive computer for the hundredth time, it seemed. What was taking these guys so long to get here? If Penh was able to track the laptop the way Lukas was, certainly he must have given them the same coordinates. They should be swimming straight toward him. Not being able to see or hear them spooked Collin and made him worry that they were aware of his presence.

Collin waited in the thick blackness, motionless, wondering. His hand, held inches from his face, was invisible to him. The stillness and silence were eerie and disconcerting. He tried to control his breathing and keep his head under the overhanging bulkhead to catch and dissipate his bubbles. The waiting was killing him. What if they had seen his light or noticed movement? What if they were preparing a surprise attack? He played every scenario through in his head, which tested his patience as he waited for the two divers to enter the confined space of the cabin.

Finally, a banging on the hull, not far from the doorway announced the arrival of the two marauders who had come to steal Collin's laptop. The thought angered him. The gall of Penh to send these guys to take what was not theirs. Thinking about the intentions of these two guys who were helping a scumbag like Penh fulfill his malicious aims brought a wave of heated fury to the surface, steeling Collin for what he would do next.

Collin pressed himself into the space between the steps and the passage to the bathroom as best he could and while his heart thumped and his pulse hammered in his ears, he tried to keep his bubbles from alerting the intruders to his presence. He also forced his hands to not shake.

The first diver struggled to fit through the doorway with all of his dive gear on. Collin struggled to be patient and wait for him to get all the way into the cabin and for the second diver to start squeezing through.

After he entered the space, the first diver swept his light in an arc around the cabin. Collin could hear the second diver's tank clattering against the bulkhead above him and knew he was trying to enter through the narrow doorway. As the first diver turned toward the rear of the boat, Collin flicked his high-powered dive light on full beam and pointed it right at the man's face. At the same time, he rushed forward, knife in hand, and cut the man's air hose. The man began to flap and flail. Collin turned in one motion toward the man stuck in the doorway and let the spear fly at center mass. Luckily, both divers wore thin three-millimeter wetsuits like his. The thrust of the spear with its three razor-sharp prongs was enough to pierce the wetsuit and lodge into the man's body, producing a pinkish plume of blood. The second diver released a torrent of bubbles as he thrashed about trying to pull the spear out of his chest.

Collin whipped around to check on the first diver and found that he had recovered sufficiently to find his octopus, the secondary air hose and breathing regulator. With one smooth swipe, Collin cut that hose and the man's exposed arm as he moved toward him.

Collin pulled the second man through the doorway into the cabin with a firm tug on his arm. The second man was thrust into the body of the first man, the end of the spear making contact first, pushing it deeper into the flesh. Collin grabbed the rubbery black bag with his laptop and pinned it against his ribs using his arm. He scurried through the tight opening as quickly as he could while the two men continued to struggle for survival. Pumping his legs and pulling with his free arm, Collin headed for the safety of the surface. That's when he remembered two commandments of scuba that were drilled into his head during training: first, never ascend faster than your bubbles;

and second, safety stops on the way up.

Collin checked his depth gauge and saw that he was already at seventy feet. He began to push backward to halt his progress and pressed the air release button on his buoyancy compensator to let out air and thus reduce its upward pull. At sixty-two feet, he halted and focused on counting to one hundred slowly. He turned off the light so as to not reveal his location. He pulled the strap over his shoulder to free up both hands. At the same time, he looked below him to see if there was any sign of pursuit. The dive computer was counting down while he was counting up. When he reached one hundred, the computer still showed thirty-three. Seeing splinters of light from below, he chose to ignore the computer and continue his ascent.

At thirty feet, he repeated the process for a safety stop, but since the lights from below were growing closer, it was all he could do to count to one hundred. He watched the timer on the dive computer. The lights were growing larger and brighter. Collin wondered what motivated them. He was nearly paralyzed as he watched them, trying to determine his next step. Without the spear, Collin was armed with nothing more than the Captain's dive knife. Add to that the fact that he had the laptop hanging from his shoulder, which would further hamper his already diminished ability to attack. When he looked back at his dive computer, the counter had reached zero. Before he continued upward, Collin noticed the lights weren't stopping. Maybe the bends would do his dirty work for him. He didn't bother to stop at ten feet. The higher he rose, the faster his ascent, though he tried to slow down by releasing air from his BC. When he breached the surface, he had no idea which way to go. He used the compass to orient himself and began swimming toward the rocky islet where the plane was anchored.

Collin kicked and paddled as fast as he could, sensing his enemies would soon surface. He had no plan of attack, no plan of defense. Just swim like crazy to the plane. That was all he could think about—all he could do, really.

Seconds later, he heard splashes and voices behind him. The two had surfaced. Collin slowed to a stop to reduce his profile. One of the voices didn't sound too strong. In fact, it was choked with pain. The other voice called out something he couldn't understand. Then a powerful engine roared to life in the distance and started coming closer. Fearing he would be seen, Collin started to swim again, this time doing the breaststroke to maintain silence as best he could.

The engine noise slowed, and Collin heard more voices, much closer this time. Then the engine cut to idle. His curiosity got the best of him. He turned toward the sound of the boat and watched in rapt fascination as the two men on board, with the help of the uninjured diver, hauled the guy with the spear into the boat. There was a flurry of activity and lots of yelling. There was stress and horror in the voices. The throaty purr of the engine came back full volume and the boat started moving again. At first, it moved toward the lights on the island in the distance. Then his heart dropped when he saw fingers pointing in his direction amid more yelling.

Collin checked in all directions and realized that the boat must have moved into a position where the people on board had been able to spot the plane, which was otherwise hidden behind the rocky islet. His presence underwater had alerted the divers, who likely wanted to return the favor.

The boat banked sharply in his direction and a powerful search light popped on, scanning to locate him. It found him as he fumbled to get his regulator in his mouth and deflate his vest so he would drop below the surface. Before he could manage any of that, he heard glass break and saw the diver standing in the front of the boat crumple to the deck. Before he was fully submerged, two more shots hit the side of the boat as it leaned hard into an about-face turn. Collin continued to descend, figuring it was safest to be under the water.

When he reached the wall of rock that rose at a steady angle to the surface, he moved north and west along that wall until he saw anchor lines. Looking up, Collin followed the ropes to where they were connected to the plane's pontoons. He rose to the surface as the pilot, standing on one of the pontoons, began hauling up the anchors.

"Get in. Let's go. We oughta getta move-on now," he said matter-of-factly.

Collin obeyed and within two minutes they were airborne again.

244

* * *

CHAPTER THIRTY-TWO

Puerto Lempira, Honduras
 June 17, 4:50 a.m. Caribbean Time

Collin stayed awake the whole flight back to the hut. It was still dark when they landed in the cove, yet the rifle man and the binocular man were in their familiar guarded positions near the hut.

Collin had spent much of the time talking with Lukas, learning all he could about his mother's condition and how she had weathered the kidnapping and what her prognosis was for the cancer treatments. Lukas told him everything he knew, which was really everything Rob had passed on to Lukas, knowing Collin would need this information.

He asked about Emily. Lukas paused. "She's hurting, Collin, but she's going to be all right in the end. She's a tough gal, and smart. She'll be OK. Your whole family is looking after her."

This knowledge, especially since it came from the ever-reliable Lukas Mueller, brought much needed comfort and solace to Collin's soul. Lukas was never one to speak until and unless he had the facts and the belief in what he spoke.

"Rob says she'll be staying a while at your parents' home, in fact. Your sister and brother are there, too, so she'll have lots of support. She needs that right now, you know."

Collin thanked Lukas for the information and asked him to thank Rob for being there. He lamented killing Stinky and injuring one of the two divers, as well. Lukas talked him out of his remorse by reminding Collin of what they had done to him, Tog, his mother, and Emily.

"Remember, Collin, sometimes it's requisite that one man die so many others can live," Lukas said. "These men were themselves killers, guns for hire working for a proclaimed enemy of the United States and Western civilization. You've done your country a great service."

"I wish I felt what you were saying," said Collin.

"You will tomorrow," said Lukas. "If not, the next day or someday very soon."

The call ended and Collin was left to ponder these thoughts in tormented silence for the rest of the return trip.

By the time he reached Puerto Lempira, Collin felt like the walking dead.

The two men who inhabited the hut simply nodded at Collin as he trudged up the sandy beach. Something about them was different, like they could read him from far away. Likely, they knew what he had done and perhaps that qualified him for admittance to their fraternity. Maybe Lukas had told them, not that it mattered. Collin had only one thought on his mind as he treaded up the beach through the soft, thick sand.

"Got any more of that orange juice?"

Before You Go

Thank you for reading "Off Course." I hope you have enjoyed reading this portion of Collin Cook's adventure as much as I enjoyed writing it. As a writer, I appreciate the opportunity to tell a story and would like to share it with the world. Stories are compelling because of the plot, the action, and the characters, not because of gratuitous or salacious scenes or vulgar language. A good story shouldn't need to rely on such lurid content. My goal is to provide you with good, clean fiction that you wouldn't mind letting your kids read. To that end, I humbly request your input. Please leave a review on Amazon and share your opinion with other readers. It helps them to know whether this is a book they might enjoy, and it helps authors such as myself to find an audience who enjoys the kind of stories we tell.

For an exclusive look into the history between Collin and Emily, here's a link to a free copy of Off Limits.

Turn the page for a preview of Off Guard, the third and final episode of Collin Cook's adventure.

Thanks again and happy reading.

Off Kilter – Collin Cook's saga begins

Off Course - Collin Cook's saga gets rough

Off Guard – The breathtaking conclusion of Collin Cook's saga

Off Chance (novella) – Friction between Penh and Lukas leads Lukas to the NSA

Off Limits (novella) – Collin and Emily's high school years

Off Track (novella) – Captain Sewell's remarkable journey

Other books by Glen Robins:

Chosen Path- A novel dealing with the very real threat of North Korean terror attacks

Born Into Espionage (Fall 2021)

For a preview of the next phase of Collin's saga, continue to the next page for excerpts from "Off Guard," the exciting conclusion of Collin Cook's journey.

Preview of Off Guard

Off Guard

Chapter One

Puerto Lempira, Honduras
  June 17, 4:50 a.m., Honduras Time

Collin trudged up the beach, away from the plane, through the soft, pale sand in the grayish pre-dawn light. Each step requiring more effort than the last as his feet sank into little craters of his own making. The effort to lift his knees and drag his weight forward was slowly depleting what little energy he had left. It had been a long, sleepless night, capping off a week full of long and sleepless nights. Things had not gone the way he had planned.

Given his lack of sleep over the past three days and the energy he had expended to save his own life and safeguard the security of the country, it was no wonder Collin struggled to traverse the hundred and fifty feet up the sloping shore to the tiny hut where he hoped the magical, sleep-inducing orange juice sat chilling in the refrigerator.

Collin's whole body hurt. Penh's men had seen to that. His face was bruised from the multiple beatings they had inflicted on it. After repeatedly being punched and kicked, his ribs and mid-section ached as well. All the swimming and diving over the past twenty-four hours to save himself and retrieve his laptop from the bottom of the ocean had given his arms, legs, and lungs a fantastic, though exhausting, workout.

Yes, he wanted some food and some sleep, in that order.

His batteries were indeed running low and he needed to rest. Despite his weary body, Collin's mind was keyed up over recently transpired events. Sleep didn't come, not without help. The murder of one and possibly a second person weighed heavily on his soul. He looked ahead at the simple hut, a wedge of pale yellow light spilling through its doorway, and adjusted his course to be sure not to waste a single step. When he reached the half-open bamboo door, he stumbled into the tiny beach house on the Caribbean coast of Honduras, looking for the orange juice, the magical orange juice laced with a powerful sleep aid—he didn't even know what it was—that had helped him just the day before to get the best sleep he had gotten since his wife and children died in that thunderous wreck on Interstate 80, coming down the mountain from Lake Tahoe, eleven and a half months ago.

Yes, Collin Cook was ready for food and sleep. He was pretty sure he deserved it.

With his laptop onboard the plane, safely enveloped in the rubbery water-tight sea bag, Collin felt he had accomplished his mission for the day. He had scuba-dived deeper than he had ever dived before to rescue it. He had fought off another pair of Penh's hired thugs who had also dived to the wreckage of the *Admiral Risty*, spearing one of them in the chest. He had had to swim through the plume of that man's blood to exit the boat, a harrowing experience for anyone.

His next mission, which he was ready to embark on immediately, would be a day-long siesta.

Lukas Mueller, Collin's friend since middle school and a deep cover, high-ranking NSA officer, had reminded him during the long plane ride back from the site of the wreck that if he wanted to live, Collin had to stay at least one step ahead of Penh.

All of Lukas's talk of coming up with a plan and executing it flawlessly rattled around Collin's weary brain. He knew what hung in the balance, or at least he had an idea. Lukas had been light on the details, giving Collin only what information he needed to take the next step. There was more going on in Lukas's complex and finely-tuned brain than he shared with his simple, civilian friend. But Collin was OK with that. He wanted to live and he wanted to protect his family and country. Those were his two primary motivations for getting this involved in something that he really shouldn't be involved in.

Lukas told him lives were at stake, that national security could be breached. Collin's involvement in this whole mess, those accidental and unfortunate, hadn't ended yet. There would be no safety for him or anyone associated with him until Penh was put away for good.

But all that could wait a couple hours, couldn't it? Collin thought.

Four days ago when he boarded the *Admiral Risty*, the idea was to sail away with his newest group of friends, the friends who had twice helped him dodge and elude those who were chasing him, namely, Interpol, the FBI and the nefarious cyber-terrorist Pho Nam Penh. The crew of the *Admiral Risty* were practically like family now. Captain Sewell, with his calm and shrewd demeanor and his sage counsel, reminded Collin of his dad and had, in many ways, become like another father figure to him. Collin had planned to spend several weeks or maybe even months cruising through the Caribbean with the crew while he figured out what to do next. No one would find him in the Caribbean. It's an easy place to hide.

Collin thought he had out-waited all his would-be captors, that all of Penh's men, and the law enforcement types on Grand Cayman had given up, figuring him to be dead. The FBI had even posted it on their website. He should have been dead, by all measures of reason and logic.

Hurricane Abigail should have killed him. Everyone knew that. Everyone except Pho Nam Penh and Collin's faithful parents. And his parents only knew he was alive because of his two best friends in the world, Lukas and Rob.

It was a miracle he wasn't dead, which made it apparent in his mind that there was something he was supposed to do. Something important enough for him to survive against all odds.

Now, after what Penh and his goons had put him through over the past several days, he only *wished* he was dead. It'd be easier. The only problem was that Collin might be the only person that could stop Penh. Collin was the burr under Penh's saddle. The itch that couldn't be scratched. The enigma that haunted Penh and upset his otherwise perfect plans to crash the world's economy for his own benefit and change the power structure in the Western Hemisphere. And Penh needed him alive to retrieve the $30 Million Collin had hidden and that Penh still thought was his.

Exhausted and hollow, Collin wanted to eat, take a big swig of the magic orange juice, and not worry about such weighty matters until he awoke.

The two agents of whatever ilk or agency that were stationed at the hut in Puerto Lempira saluted Collin, as it were, with slight head tilts as he approached them from the plane. Collin sensed new respect. Although they didn't exactly herald his arrival with fanfare or a ticker tape parade, both the guy with the sniper rifle and the guy with the binoculars treated him differently than they had twenty-four hours ago.

After Collin entered the hut, the one with the binoculars followed him in and grabbed an armful of dirty dishes that were stacked on the rustic wooden table. "Make yourself at home," he said as he rounded the table and headed for the makeshift kitchen. The dishes clattered as he lowered them into the sink and turned on the water. "Want anything to eat? I haven't fixed a real breakfast yet, but if you want some cereal, go ahead."

"I'm fine with that," Collin answered. "Anything, really. I'm starving." Collin poked through the assortment of boxed cereal on a shelf near the refrigerator. All American cereals, probably brought down by the pilot from an American grocery store on his last supply run. He chose Wheaties with a banana, then searched for a bowl and spoon. Collin noticed for the first time how the lighting inside created an atmosphere reminiscent of Christmas. He hadn't noticed it before, but the main illumination was a string of small, low-watt bare bulbs hanging on hooks in a serpentine pattern along the slats of the ceiling.

"Heard your mission was a success," said the man with the binoculars. Neither of the men at the hut had introduced themselves. Collin doubted they ever would, figuring the less he knew, the better.

"I guess so," answered Collin, unsure what to say.

"I don't know who you're with, but we're all on the same team, trying to protect the Homeland. So you doing your job makes it easier for me to do mine."

Collin paused, bowl and cereal in his one hand, a jug of milk in the other. He cocked his head and stared at the other man for a moment. He hadn't spent much time thinking about the macro significance what he was doing. He never considered his role to be anything beyond just trying to keep himself and those he loved alive. But Collin had volunteered for the risky, deep sea dive to save the laptop because Lukas had explained that there were pieces of code on it that, if discovered by Penh, could allow Penh into the NSA's computer network. That could create problems untold into perpetuity. Collin felt a swell in his chest as he realized what he had done would help keep his country safe. "I suppose," he said, then turned toward the table. Pondering his next words, he finally added, "But with me, things are complicated. Always have been, probably always will be."

"I hear you," said the other man. "Seems to be a recurring theme in this line of work."

As Collin sat to eat, his phone rang from the pocket of his cargo shorts. It was Lukas. Had to be, since he was the only one who knew this number.

"You're at the hut, right?" said Lukas with his efficient, Germanic precision.

"Yeah, just got here."

"Good. I need you to hook up that laptop. The guys will show you the secure port to plug it into."

"The laptop? Now? You're kidding me, right?"

"No, why?" asked Lukas. Lukas' tone conveyed the all-business frame of mind he was in.

"It's all the way down at the plane," sighed Collin, doing his best to imitate a teenager. "I don't know if I have the strength to walk all the way down there and back."

Lukas picked up on Collin's sarcasm, then pushed past it. "Yeah, yeah, you big baby. Get it and plug it into the network so I can see what kind of mischief Penh might've done."

Collin was already on his way, knowing Lukas was right. The sand seemed even thicker and his legs heavier as he tramped his way to plane. The pilot, who was checking the engine, looked at him curiously. Collin pulled the back door open and cradled the sea bag in his arms like a baby and summoned his strength for the grueling trek back up the sandy slope.

Binocular man helped Collin hook the laptop up to a server in a small room in the back of the hut. There Collin listened intently while Lukas muttered to himself, then gave Collin instructions, through the phone over the clicking of computer keys. The clicking stopped and Lukas groaned. "Don't get comfortable, my friend. We've got to move," he said.

"What are you talking about?" asked Collin, still dreaming of food and slumber.

"He's installed a tracker."

"So, he knows where I am right now?" A cold knot formed in Collin's stomach. "I guess a long nap is out of the question." Stress tended to bring the sarcasm to the surface.

"Yeah. Afraid so," Lukas said. The keys were tapping in a furious rhythm in the background. "You being there could compromise the safe house. With only two assets on location, there's not enough fire power to protect you if Penh sends in a team to find you."

"Can't you do something to throw them off long enough to get your own team in here or something?" Collin asked, still hopeful of a good nap.

"If I try to scramble the signal, it will only raise eyebrows and cause them to be more cautious. That could reverse much of our progress."

"Figures," sighed Collin as his head dropped. "He wants everything he can get and he's obviously dug deep enough into that computer to know there's something more than a guy like me would ever have on it."

"Right," said Lukas. "And if we make changes to it at this point, he'll know someone with more experience that you've got is tampering with it. Again, my concern is that he'll be wary and start covering his tracks. Our best hope is to try to catch him off guard if we can."

"Look, I'm not trying to run away from him at this point, my friend. This thing won't end until he gets what he wants or gets thrown in prison."

"Or is dead," added Lukas. "I wouldn't mind seeing him dead, truth be told."

"Right, you sinister bastard," chuckled Collin. "You don't mind as long as someone else does the dirty work."

"I didn't say that," Lukas protested. "I'd be happy to pull the trigger."

"What are you saying there, my friend?"

Lukas paused, sucking in a breath. "There's history between me and him. Bad blood, you know. I've seen what he's capable of. That's why I've kept him on my radar all these years. At some point, a ruthless juggernaut like him was going to rear his ugly head and I vowed I'd be there to cut it off if I possibly could."

"Dude," Collin said, careful not to use Lukas's name out loud, as he'd been instructed, "I'm getting the chills right now. You're sounding pretty scary."

"Yeah, I know. But that bastard killed a friend of mine out of revenge . . ." Lukas's voice trailed off as if the memory had clamped his throat shut. "Then he tried to frame me for it."

"Why didn't he go to jail then?"

"No one could prove it. It looked like an alcohol-fueled overdose, but we're talking about a mature, studious MIT grad student with the career-track she'd always wanted buttoned down, not some sorority-rushing freshman. She was not the party type."

"Sounds like she was more than a friend."

"She was. We had plans . . ." Lukas's voice trailed off.

"Then how do you know it was Penh?"

"I just know. Things like that don't stay secret forever, but everyone who knew him knew he'd find a way to shut them up for good if they ever confronted him."

Collin waited, expecting Lukas to continue. When he didn't, he prompted his friend. "So, how did it end?"

"We all graduated two weeks later and went our separate ways. That's when I accepted the offer from the NSA, even though I could have made much more money somewhere else. With their resources, I knew I could track him and perhaps prevent him from doing what he's about to do now, carrying out his threat to cripple the West and punish them for their greed and abuse."

"So, you knew about his plans since graduate school?" asked Collin.

"Yeah. I probably had more interaction with him than any other classmate.

For some reason, I befriended him and he trusted me. He opened up to me and my friend Theresa. When she threatened to expose him to the authorities, he killed her. Made it look innocuous. But I knew her well, knew she'd never drink like that."

"Do you think he knew that you suspected him?"

"Maybe, maybe not. I played dumb, but also steered clear of him."

"And Penh knows you work for the NSA?"

Lukas snorted. "No. Because it was all very clandestine, the offer I signed and accepted came from what appeared to be a legitimate IT company in Manhattan. That's what I told everyone and that's what was posted on the school's website. Now, disconnect the laptop and get going. When you get to Mexico, I'll have a security detail set up to guard you and the computer. We'll run a ruse to lead Penh into our trap. That way you'll be safe and so will the national security network."

Collin slapped the top of his knees. "Sounds like a plan, but can I eat first?" said Collin, as he began to shut down the computer.

Lukas didn't respond immediately. Only the sound of the keys tapping at a furious pace could be heard. "If you can get it done before the pilot finishes refueling."

Collin stood and walked to the kitchen, where he could see the beach through a large, plate glass window. The sun rose early at the lower latitudes of Honduras, especially so close to the summer equinox. In the purplish rays of the new day, the pilot was wrestling two large red cans, one with a yellow spout sticking out of it, down to where the plane sat anchored on the beach. "Where am I going?"

"Mexico City. Your itinerary after you get there is a bit sketchy, but we're quite certain Penh's plans revolve around Mexico City. It's coming together in pieces, but all the intel we have points there."

"That's very unusual, don't you think? Why Mexico City?"

"This whole thing is unusual, Collin," sighed Lukas. "We've been monitoring various known hackers from around the world for months. Many of them think they are invisible and, therefore, presume they can travel without detection. But, they are known to us and we've been watching them with great interest, as you can imagine. And, it appears they are all converging on Mexico City this week. There has also been a fair amount of money moving into the country from some of Penh's many shell companies to various foundations and interests in Mexico, all have a common denominator."

Collin expected him to continue, but he didn't. "What's the common denominator?"

"A certain Mexican senator."

Collin snorted and shook his head as he began to wolf down his cereal, shoveling in two or three bites each time Lukas spoke, then chewing furiously before he began to talk again. "If he's got a tracker on the laptop and he sees me going to Mexico City, won't that tip him off that we're on to him?"

"Not necessarily. Think about it. Mexico City is huge. Easy to hide. A hub of transportation and commerce," said Lukas. "It's a logical place for you to catch a flight back home to the States. Plus, we've got assets in the area, ready to move on this. They can provide you with security."

"Won't my presence cause problems for the assets there?"

"Not necessarily. Penh will track you but will be more focused on the rest of his plan. Our other men can remain undercover and do like they always do."

"Will I be able to talk to my family and let them know I'm alright?"

"Maybe. We'll see."

Off Guard Chapter Two

Kuala Lumpur, Malaysia
  June 17, 7:12 p.m. Malaysia Time; 5:12 a.m. Honduras Time

Pho Nam Penh fumed at the far end of the rickety table in the smoke-filled room. He sat leaning back, legs crossed, cigarette between his fingers. The seven men huddled around computer screens remained silent. The only sounds in the darkened room were the beeps and clicks from an array of computer equipment and the whirring of fans blowing thick, muggy air around in a vain attempt to cool the men and the machines. That and the breathing of Pho Nam Penh as he inhaled and exhaled through his nose, trying to tamp down the rage that filled him.

Collin Cook was the source of Penh's frustration and anger. He had once again vanished into the night, eluding Penh's hired help and the authorities Penh had manipulated into aiding in the hunt. Cook was not among the survivors of the shipwreck found by the Colombian Coast Guard. That was bad news, but it was old news at this point. The really bad news was that the divers Penh had hired and sent to the wreck came back empty-handed and injured. Cook had thrust a fishing spear into the diaphragm of one Penh's hired divers, cut the oxygen tube of the other, and escaped with the computer. Penh needed that laptop to retrieve the money Cook kept hidden from him. $30 million dollars. Although he had pilfered plenty of cash from other sources, those sources were no longer available due to the heightened security after his recent high-profile heist. Every bank and financial institution had beefed up their systems, moving the "low hanging fruit" out of reach for the time being. The $30 million Cook stole was now needed more than ever to placate the high-priced hackers on the payroll.

Penh had spent a fortune amassing the team and bribing authorities as he spun a web of deceit and intrigue aimed at bringing the United States to its knees. Funds were now running short. But that was only part of the story, a part no one else would ever know. The real issue now revolved around maintaining his profile as a leader. These men and the others in his organization needed to know beyond a doubt Penh's supremacy. It was unacceptable to be made a fool by the likes of a common man like Collin Cook. Cook had defied him repeatedly and his men knew it. To regain the respect of those men, Collin Cook had to be made an example. He had to suffer in the most extreme way to pay for the gross indignations he had caused Pho Nam Penh and the potential set-backs to the cause. It was the only way to reestablish the proper order of things.

One man among the group of expert computer hackers, the same man that stood before him days before and announced that he had a positive I.D. on Cook in the Cayman Islands, stood and cleared his throat and bowed to Penh before he dared speak. Penh acknowledged him with a grunt and a nod of his head.

"Sir, I am sorry to share this news with you, but our diver, the one injured by the spear, died shortly after he arrived at the hospital." The man bowed again and took his seat.

"He died bravely," Penh muttered. His eyes were fixed straight ahead. He didn't move for several moments. "He honored the cause with his courage."

The man stood again, bowed, and responded. "Yes, sir, he did."

Another long pause ensued while Penh stared at the dark curtains on the opposite side of the room. "What about the other one? The one that was shot."

"He is expected to make a full recovery, sir."

Penh breathed in audibly, held it, then spoke slowly. "He, too, has honored the cause with his courage, but he, too, has failed." Penh stood abruptly, sending his chair crashing into the bare concrete floor behind him. "How? How does this commoner evade us?"

No one said anything. Each man looked intently at the screen in front of him until the same spokesman arose and cleared his throat and bowed again in deference to their leader. "Sir, if I may, it appears there was a sea plane in the area of the wreckage. The shots that were fired at the boat that carried our brave divers came from the vicinity of that plane. It also appears that Mr. Cook boarded that plane and that it departed to the north moments after the shots were fired."

Penh cocked his head and squinted his eyes. "So, Mr. Cook is indeed receiving assistance from some external source. But who?"

The spokesman for the group sat quickly and began to peck at the keys of his computer. He looked up at Penh, who was pacing at the far end of the room, and added, "I have something here."

Penh grunted and lifted his head.

"It's a signal coming from Mr. Cook's computer. It appears he is on the move."

Penh stepped quickly to the man's side. The man pointed at a pulsating blip on the screen in southeastern Honduras.

"Very well. Send a message to our team in Mexico City informing them that I will move up my arrival date. Now that we know Cook is, we can execute on schedule. Let's bring the moth to the flame and scorch him." Penh turned on his heels and stormed out the door. His footsteps could be heard as they pounded along concrete hallway outside and down the metal stairs.

All seven men let out a collective sigh as it were and the tension in the room dissipated with Penh's departure. Nervous glances were exchanged. The foreman surveyed the other six men with a steely glare, then sat down. The tapping and clicking of keyboards and mice resumed, timidly at first, then more vigorously as the spokesman reminded them of the task ahead of them and the amount of work they needed to do to accomplish it.

* * *

London, England
  June 17, 1:28 p.m. London Time; 5:28 a.m. Pacific Time

Dejection wasn't quite the right word. Nor was irritation. No. The best way to describe Nic Lancaster's mood alternated between utter frustration and absolute humiliation. Or maybe futility. Every time he thought about Collin Cook, one of those emotions took control. Collin Cook, the everyday American who was supposed to be so easy to find and track and apprehend had proven to be anything but. It should have been an easy assignment. Nic, the brightest and hardest working young detective in Interpol London's Cyber Crime Task Force, felt he was destined for the fast track. All he needed was to break one big case and his lane on the fast track would be assured. His name in headlines and front page photos would surely follow.

Finding this Collin Cook fellow appeared on the surface to be just the kind of case he was looking for. Cook was supposed to lead Nic to the "big fish," Pho Nam Penh, the cyber-terrorist responsible for shutting down the Royal Bank of Scotland for a full day back in April and pilfering millions of dollars from dozens of international banks over the past several months. He and his group were the primary suspects in these and several other embarrassing attacks, but they were, for all intents and purposes, invisible. At least until a photo surfaced online showing Penh sitting with Cook in a London pub. That's when Nic got his big break, the assignment that would propel his career into the next realm.

This Collin Cook was nothing more than a former electrical supply salesman from California who had experienced a great tragedy and was wandering around Europe apparently trying to find himself. The photos that came to light on the Internet showed otherwise. Cook, perhaps because he had become disaffected with life, had turned to crime. His new cozy relationship with Penh, as evidenced by the London photos as well as a second set of photos released a few days later showing Cook meeting with Penh and his top lieutenants in the Bahamas in early April, made him a suspected accomplice in a rash of high-stakes online larceny. Common man turned criminal. It was sad, but not completely unique.

None of that was Nic's concern, however. Bringing Cook and Penh to justice was all that mattered to Junior Detective Nic Lancaster. That and his moment in the spotlight, hauling in such an elusive criminal as Pho Nam Penh.

Since receiving this potentially break-through assignment, however, Nic had had to awkwardly explain how each confirmed sighting of Cook had resulted in a dead-end. Cook had managed to not only evade him, but embarrass him at every turn. First, Cook was a no-show on the raid of a Caribbean sailboat eye witnesses swore they had seen him board the day before. Second, Cook had somehow slipped through the net Nic and Interpol had dropped over the Executive Suites Hotel in Panama City, Panama. Planted trained agents, feigning hotel staff while working another case, had reported that Cook was staying there and was in his room, but Cook managed to slip away and disappear. When Cook reappeared two weeks later at the JW Marriott in Lima, Peru, Nic spared no resources. He went all-in, sending a Peruvian commando squad into room 2321, the one triple confirmed to be Collin Cook's room. At four o'clock in the morning, the room was empty and Nic Lancaster faced the worst torment of his young career for that maneuver.

But that wasn't the end. Cook managed to sneak out of Peru and into Argentina; and from Argentina to Canada; and from Canada he was somehow able to cross the border into the United States. He showed up in Chicago, where he outran, out-maneuvered, and outsmarted a group of FBI agents sent to detain him at the Chicago Convention Center. Should have been easy, but this amateur evaded eight trained agents and wasn't seen or heard from until Nic's counterparts, FBI Agents Reggie Crabtree and Spinner McCoy, tracked him to Key West, Florida. From the marina there, Collin drove a small dinghy headlong into the mounting Hurricane Abigail and was presumed dead. No one survives a Category 2 hurricane in a twelve-foot rubber dinghy with only a 15-horsepower engine. No one, that is, except the enigmatic Collin Cook.

Two weeks had passed since Cook's supposed demise. Nic had been given several other, lesser assignments in the meantime. He viewed these menial tasks as a punishment, but realized he had to work his way back into the good graces of his bosses. Most of those menial tasks were completed successfully, as they were essentially grunt-work assignments that required little brain power and zero elite-level talent. But Nic had managed, by working late hours and weekends, to keep track of the Cook case because, as he learned,

Crabtree and McCoy had not given up on it. And if they weren't giving up, neither was he, except for when he had to deny his involvement to his boss.

Nic was asked just two days ago for his help. This put him in a difficult spot in light of recent inquiries and his vehement disavowals to his superiors. But, to his surprise, his boss, the unpredictable Alastair Montgomery, had not only agreed to help, but had used his impressive social and professional network to get the Colombian Coast Guard involved in the search for the sailboat Cook was alleged to be on.

Once again, all signs pointed to Cook being dead. The sailboat went down and several survivors were found floating in the water nearby. The Captain and crew all vowed to the fact that Cook had been killed and his body disposed of two days before in the middle of the Caribbean.

Nic was ready to wash his hands of the Cook case after his chums from the academy begged him to let it go. It had done enough damage to his ambitions, they said. It was time to lick his wounds and move on. Time to rebuild. His career may not take the meteoric rise he had hoped for, but it was still salvageable. Their urgings almost worked, at least when he was awake. The problem was the dreams he kept having. Perhaps they were daydreams, conjured up as a way to inspire greatness within himself. Maybe it wasn't real, but the sweet sniffs of the essence of victory they provided was a powerful motivator.

Nic was still working on a sandwich and a bag of crisps at his desk when a call came in from a San Francisco number. He knew it was Crabtree's mobile. He knew he didn't want to answer it. But, he also knew he should. Professional courtesy and all.

"This thing is *not* over yet, Lancaster," came the low, fatigued voice of Reggie Crabtree.

"Why did I know you would say something like that?" Nic crunched on a crisp and ground it between his teeth loudly to exaggerate his nonchalance.

"Because, deep inside, you want the chance to prove that you were right and to get this guy," said Crabtree, who Nic knew had not slept much the past few nights as they all frantically worked to figure out how Cook disappeared again. The two of them had been in frequent contact since the Cook case hit Nic's desk. Crabtree and McCoy, his FBI counterparts, had worked on this case as hard as he had and were closer to it in some ways than he was. They had more invested, emotionally speaking. "There's no hiding that, Nic. You're too good a detective to let this case sully your record. You don't want this thing hanging around your neck for the rest of your life. Not when the collar is so close at hand. You need redemption and I think I have a way for you to get it."

"What are you on about now, Reggie?" asked Nic, his voice rising an octave with that uncomfortable stress that comes when determination and disbelief occupy the same brain at the same time. "We have four eyewitness accounts stating that Cook was killed and dumped overboard."

"We have four very similar stories from four of Cook's friends who have aided and abetted him at least twice before. They're in this thing with him somehow and will say whatever needs to be said to protect him and possibly themselves."

"What about the Asian guys? Didn't they say something similar?"

"They said he was dead, sunk with the ship. But they are considered unreliable sources, especially since only one body, their leader's, was found on the boat."

"Then what information are you going on?" asked Nic, leaning back in his chair and staring at the ceiling. He wiped the sour cream and onion powder from his fingertips onto his slacks.

"Two divers were brought into a hospital on the island of Providencia about an hour ago," explained Crabtree. "One died shortly after arrival. Killed by a fishing spear to the diaphragm. The other had a gunshot wound to his shoulder. The surviving diver and the other two people on their boat told authorities that the man who speared the other diver swam toward an airplane and that the airplane flew away to the north."

"So . . ."

"So, the guy was white, not Asian. He had long brown hair."

"Once again, I don't see the relevance," stammered Nic, trying desperately to sound disinterested.

Reggie exhaled in mock frustration. He must have sensed Nic was getting excited, but was trying to control his display of emotions as best he could. Reggie played along with Nic's charade, for now. "You know what I'm trying to say, Nic. You sense it in your gut the same way I do. We're detectives and detectives know when something ain't right. This whole situation smells. It smells like Collin Cook to me. He's up to something and he has someone helping him. We need you to help us figure out who it is. Then maybe we can find him and get some useful information about our pal Pho Nam Penh before he strikes again."

Nic involuntarily let out a little chortle. He was hooked again. The pump inside him that filled his veins with ambition and energy kicked into gear once more. "I don't know why I should believe anything you say anymore, Reggie. What have you got in mind?"

www.ingramcontent.com/pod-product-compliance
Lightning Source LLC
Chambersburg PA
CBHW051420170626
46809CB00006B/2248